A
STORM
OF
SHADOWS
AND PEARLS

ALSO BY MARION BLACKWOOD

Marion Blackwood has written lots of books across multiple series, and new books are constantly added to her catalogue. To see the most recently updated list of books, please visit: www.marionblackwood.com

CONTENT WARNINGS

The Oncoming Storm series contains quite a lot of violence and morally questionable actions. If you have specific triggers, you can find the full list of content warnings at: www.marionblackwood.com/content-warnings

A STORM OF
SHADOWS AND PEARLS

THE ONCOMING STORM: BOOK TWO

MARION BLACKWOOD

First edition

ISBN 978-91-985645-7-0 (hardcover)
ISBN 978-91-985645-3-2 (paperback)
ISBN 978-91-986386-1-5 (ebook)

Editing by Julia Gibbs
Book cover design by ebooklaunch.com

www.marionblackwood.com

*For my parents, who have been instrumental
in shaping me into the person I am today*

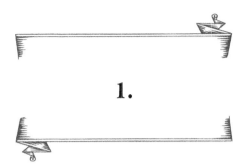

1.

I was casing a jewelry store when the ships arrived. The soft spring wind caressed my face as I lounged on the sun-warmed roof tiles, studying the owners going about their business. Then I heard them. The bells. They were constructed centuries ago and were meant to warn Keutunan of coming invaders. None had ever come. Still, they rang them every year during the Midsummer festival to make sure the big, metal contraptions still worked. There was only one problem. Today was not Midsummer.

A sudden flash of danger mixed with disbelief washed over me as I sprang up and whipped my head towards the distant harbor. Straining my neck, I scanned the blue ribbon of water visible across the rooftops.

"Well, I'll be damned," I whispered and dropped the hand I'd used to shield my eyes from the sun. "I've gotta see this."

In a burst of speed I took off along the Thieves' Highway, heading towards the Harbor District. Running at breakneck pace, I soon cleared the wide gap between the two buildings separating the Merchants' Quarter from my destination. I almost scared a nesting seagull to death as I came crashing down on the other side but I used a tuck and roll technique to smoothen the landing so I figured he'd live. A panicked squawk and the sound of frantically flapping wings followed me as I raced for the next roof. Before long, the flat, wide structure that was my target became visible and with one last leap, I landed on the roof of a wooden pavilion. In addition to its being used by many fishermen to store boats during the off season, it also provided a great view of the waterfront.

I let out a low whistle. "That's not something you see every day."

On the horizon, three tall ships were fast approaching. They were the biggest ships I'd ever seen. Granted, I hadn't seen all that many boats in my life but they made Keutunan's fishing vessels look like dinghies. Crouching on top of the roof, I watched them draw closer. On the streets below me, the commotion was increasing with every minute. Frightened mothers pushed their unwitting children back up the street, fishermen cleared their gear off the pier, and Silver Cloaks came scrambling in from every side street.

The three ships had come to a halt further out in the bay. Squinting against the sun, I tried to make out the details of the colorful flag swaying in the breeze atop one of the masts. It looked like an animal with two swords crossed behind it but it wasn't any animal I'd ever seen. The beast was rearing and it made me think of a dog or a bear but with more hair around its neck. Strange. Then again, flags weren't exactly my area of expertise. I'd only ever seen the dark blue one with entwined silver-colored thorns flying over the walls of the Silver Keep.

"Make way for the king's soldiers! Make way!" someone yelled further up the street.

Heavy footfalls and rustling armor echoed between the houses as squads of Silver Cloaks came pouring in. I switched from looking at the armed men forming ranks below to studying the activities of the ships. They were lowering something made of wood over the side of the ship.

I let out a surprised chuckle. "Well, would you look at that? They have boats... on their boats."

While they continued lowering their wooden rowboats, another party arrived at the docks and positioned themselves in front of the armed soldiers. I recognized the man in the colorful clothes. It was Lord Raymond, a high-ranking member of the Council of Lords. The other men, clothed in sand-colored robes and nervously shuffling their feet beside him, could only be members of the Scribes' Guild. Out in the bay, the three small boats made steady progress towards the shore.

"Be ready for anything!" the captain called in a deep, steady voice below me.

Seriously? Be ready for anything? I rolled my eyes. If they'd been planning to attack they'd probably have brought more than the fifteen people sitting in those tiny boats. Still, better ready than dead, I suppose. In the months since the appearance, or rather the *reappearance*, of the elves, the people of Keutunan had become a bit more accustomed to the idea that there were other people besides themselves out there. However, I didn't think a lot of them had believed that we would actually find any, and they sure as hell hadn't been expecting others to find *us*.

The entire harbor seemed to be holding its breath as the newcomers docked and then one by one climbed onto the pier. They wore loose-fitting clothes of bright hues in several layers and at their hips swung curved swords. Interesting. Once they had all disembarked, they formed an orderly procession and advanced towards solid ground. The swords stayed in their waistbands. A smooth voice broke the silence and carried the sound of a rhythmic language to my ears. And everyone else's ears too, for that matter. A nervous ripple spread through the soldiers as they glanced around waiting for orders. The man with the short-trimmed beard standing at the head of the strangers furrowed his brows. He tried again.

This time a harsh-sounding language flew across the harbor. It sounded more like a battle cry than a greeting, which made some of the Silver Cloaks raise their weapons in alarm. Hands found sword hilts among the group of newcomers as well before the bearded man threw out his hand, motioning for them to stop. He heaved an exasperated sigh and tried again.

"We are not here to instigate armed conflict," he said in his smooth voice.

A murmur went through the gathered crowd. The scribes glanced to Lord Raymond, who managed to look both shocked and relieved at the same time.

"I am glad to hear that," he said with a short nod.

The bearded leader of the small group jerked back in surprise. "You speak the tongue of the elves. That is a surprise."

Lord Raymond opened his mouth to respond but then closed it again. The leader of the newcomers waved a hand as if to say that it wasn't important.

"I am General Marcellus, one of the mighty rulers of our great nation Pernula," he said.

Wait. *One* of the rulers? That didn't make any sense. How could a kingdom have more than one ruler? However, General Marcellus paid no mind to my internal confusion and instead continued his introduction.

"We are overjoyed to have found your splendid civilization and would like to discuss the possibility of a partnership between our great lands. Do I have the good fortune of addressing a leader of your fine city?"

"No," Lord Raymond stated. "I am merely an advisor to King Edward Silverthorn, ruler of Keutunan. The king has asked me to welcome you on his behalf and, if you would be so inclined, to escort you to meet him at the royal palace. I feel it is best if you continue this discussion directly with His Majesty."

General Marcellus broke into a smile, showing off brilliant white teeth. "That sounds like a wonderful idea. Please lead the way."

Lord Raymond nodded and then snapped some orders to the captain of the Silver Cloaks. The king's guards spread out in formation to escort General Marcellus and his people to the Silver Keep. After Lord Raymond gave the signal to move out, the whole procession started advancing towards the palace. I did as well.

Yeah, I know. It was technically none of my business what rulers of cities were discussing but let's face it, I like snooping about. And more than that, I like knowing what's going on so that I can plot and scheme accordingly. Call it professional curiosity. I grinned as I stalked along the rooftops, following the odd mix of people below. There was no way I was missing this.

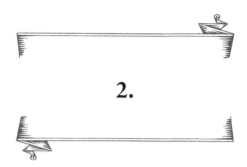

2.

Sunlight streamed through the tall windows of King Edward's throne room, making the huge chandelier below me cast dancing shadows on the opposite wall. I tiptoed across the beams until I reached my favorite eavesdropping spot.

"–certainly is an interesting proposition," King Edward said. "However, it begs the question, what would you want in exchange for sharing your knowledge with our builders and scribes?"

It had taken me a bit longer to sneak in than it had taken them to simply walk through the front door, so I had missed the first parts of this conversation. Based on the king's response, I figured that the partnership General Marcellus had talked about down by the docks included sharing knowledge. Probably how to build tall ships. That would certainly be of great value to Keutunan.

"I could give you an answer about trading or resources, but in truth," Marcellus said and spread his hands, "that would only be a pretext, and since I believe that strong partnerships are best forged in complete honesty, I will be truthful with you. We need allies. The war on the continent draws ever closer and we fear that it will not be many years until it has reached our great nation of Pernula. However, if we have allies, we might be seen as too difficult a target and be spared the wrath of war."

King Edward drummed his fingers against the armrest of his obsidian throne. "I see," he said. "I thank you for your honesty. This appears to be a conversation better suited for a designated meeting. With comfortable chairs and tasty food," the king added with a smile. "You must be exhausted after your long journey. I shall have the servants prepare rooms for you. I apologize, how many did you say you were again?"

"That would be most kind, King Edward," the general said. "Most of our people can stay aboard our ships. There is plenty of room. If it is not too much trouble, the fifteen of us that you have met today would be very grateful to have a room here in your beautiful city."

The young, black-haired king nodded slowly. "We shall meet again this evening then, and discuss this matter further."

"I look forward to it."

Smartly dressed servants in black and white appeared from the side doors to escort the Pernulans to their rooms. I stayed perched on the beam, watching them file out. Well, this had taken an interesting turn. If they actually made good on that promise and shared their engineering knowledge, it would definitely lead to economic renewal. I grinned. Which would mean more money to steal. I was also excited about the possibility of taking a round trip on one of those tall ships, just to see what was on the other side of the wild sea.

The news about the war, however, was both intriguing and troubling at the same time. If there was a war going on, it had to mean that there were lots of other civilizations over there on what General Marcellus had called *the continent*. That was interesting. But being dragged into someone else's war didn't sound all that appealing. War is bad for business. No, it was always best to stay out of other people's problems. I had learned that the hard way when I was young and a lesson like that tends to stick with you. Painful memories of Rain slipped out through the cracks around my heart. I shoved them back in and shook my head.

Since I concluded that it wasn't my decision to make, regardless of my very strong feelings about not getting involved, I figured that it was time for me to leave as well. After all, I had a jewelry store to rob.

THE SCENT OF LEMON balm followed me as I ran my fingers through the plant's fresh green leaves. Putting a hand on the sun-warmed bricks, I jumped the short fence and left the lush rooftop garden filled with herbs behind. I had come quite some way from hating everything green and leaf-covered.

These last months, Liam and I had spent a lot of time adventuring. During the fall and winter, we had visited Tkeideru several times and also explored the forest. The forest exploration was carried out in the safe company of Haela and Haemir, I might add. Come on, I'm not *that* much of a woodsman, I would've gotten lost two hours in. It had been nice, though. We'd seen a lot of beautiful sights, but unfortunately no other civilizations. Or dragons, for that matter.

Early spring had been spent visiting the different villages up and down the coast. Not much to see, really. Or steal. Now we were halfway to summer, as the lemon balm I just stroked could attest to, and I was back to my usual shenanigans.

"I'd better get down here," I muttered to myself and started climbing down the side of the building.

Most of my surveillance had taken place up on the roof of Cartier's jewelry store but I figured that I needed to do some close-range scouting of the front as well. I dropped down on a side street a couple of crossings up the road and shook my muscles loose until I had adopted a carefree posture. After a deep exhale, I stepped out of the shadows and onto the busy street. I drifted along with the tide of people on New Street, the crowd carrying me ever closer to my target. It seemed like an ordinary day. Men and women strolled up and down, someone was mending a broken wheel on a covered wagon, and the chatter of people and creaking of leather were in the air.

A flare of danger rushed up my spine. I scanned the area with urgent sweeps. Nothing seemed out of the ordinary but I couldn't shake the feeling that something was off. Even though I was only a few paces from the jewelry store's front door, I decided to abort my mission. I hadn't survived this long by not trusting my gut. Gently detaching myself from the stream of people, I started weaving a circular path to discreetly return the way I had come.

"Her! Get her!" a man's voice rang out.

The sound of heavy thuds followed it. When I whipped my head around, I saw a horde of armed men pour out of the covered wagon. *Shit.* I took off sprinting.

"Thief! Stop her!" the voice from before boomed across the street.

Shoving unprepared citizens out of the way, I scrambled to escape. Thundering footsteps followed me. At the next crossroad, I took a sharp right and then immediately veered left, intending to make them lose sight of me. It didn't work. My pursuers were gaining ground.

"Get out of my way! Stop the thief!" they roared behind me.

Heart hammering in my chest, I ducked behind the next corner. I needed to get off the street. There were no easily scalable walls in sight so I tried to map out the area in my head to plan in which direction I should be running. Clanking metal and slapping feet followed me into a wide square. Distressed vendors cried out in surprise as I darted between their stalls towards the easternmost exit. Casting a brief glance behind, I saw my pursuers flood through the market stands like a tidal wave. A bang rang out as I crashed right into a wooden pushcart that an unwitting salesman had rolled right in front of me while my attention had been occupied elsewhere.

"Damn!" I bellowed and drove my fist into the inconvenient obstacle. "Move!"

The cart stayed firmly in my way as the vendor stared at me wide-eyed. With a frustrated groan, I pushed past him and sprinted towards the exit. That surprise roadblock had made me lose precious seconds and the armed men were practically snapping at my heels now. This wasn't going to work. I needed to think. The blackout powder.

While continuing my headlong rush, I dug around inside one of my new belt pouches until I found a small glass vial. Now I only needed a location. There. A little ahead, the street branched off into three smaller roads with plenty of windows and balconies dotting the walls. Straining my legs, I picked up speed and increased the distance between myself and my hunters. This had better work. Or that apothecary and I were going to have some serious problems.

Right as I reached the three-way fork in the road, I threw the small bottle behind me. The sound of shattering glass filled the street as it hit the stones. A whoosh followed it. It sounded like something huge caught fire but it was actually a chemical reaction that produced a big, black cloud. Under the cover of artificial darkness, I scaled the wall of the middle building until I could draw myself up and roll over the edge. My chest heaved. On the streets below, men coughed and shouted.

"You, take that street! And you, check that way. We'll take this one."

"Don't let her get away!"

Feet slapped against stone again but soon the sound of running footsteps grew fainter. I closed my eyes and sent a quick prayer to Nemanan, God of Thieves. Damn. That had been close. Analyzing the situation, I concluded that the owners must've seen me when I took off in such a hurry towards the docks. Or someone else had seen me and tipped them off. My desire to see the ships and the newcomers had trumped my precaution concerning stealth. Shaking my head, I reminded myself not to make that mistake again.

When my breathing had returned to normal, I sat up and peered down the side of the building. The black cloud dissipated, leaving only broken glass on the ground. It had worked as promised. That apothecary had just earned himself a new regular.

"Alright, time to head back," I said and pushed to my feet.

Now that my jewelry store stakeout was a bust, there was no point in staying out here in the daylight. Better to head back to the Thieves' Guild and sleep. I began trotting across the rooftops. Tomorrow would be better.

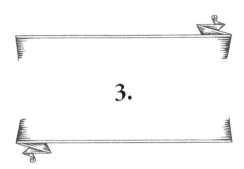

3.

Tomorrow started off better. While prowling the Merchants' Quarter in the small hours of the next day, I surmised that a few hours of sleep, a chat with Bones, and some breakfast with Liam at the Mad Archer had done me well. News about the Pernulans had spread like wildfire and there was probably not a living soul in the entire city who didn't know about them by now. I had not only shared what I knew with my friends in the guild, but also with our three Guild Masters. They'd spread the word that it was business as usual in the Underworld, but had told me to stay alert. Stay alert? As if I wasn't always alert.

Two figures dropped down behind me. I yanked out the two hunting knives strapped to the small of my back and jerked around to face them. Their blood red cloaks rustled as they settled from the fall. I blew out a noisy breath as I heard a third figure land behind my now turned back.

"Man, seriously?" I said while turning back around to the lone figure. The tension left my body and I waved the knives exasperatedly in his direction. "Again with the ambushing!"

The black-eyed Master Assassin smirked. "Care to reconsider that 'never again' comment?"

Bastard. Last time I'd seen Shade had been at Edward's coronation. He had no doubt been busy running his guild and helping the new king consolidate power in the months since, and I had spent more time outside Keutunan than inside its walls, so we hadn't seen each other since that day. In the events leading up to the treaty with the elves and our assassination of King Adrian, Shade had managed to ambush me twice and during that last meeting I'd told him that it would never happen again. Apparently, I'd been wrong.

I let out an indignant huff. "So did you actually want something or are you just here to show off?"

"The king wants to see us," he said with a short jerk of his head. "Come on."

I opened my mouth to question why in Nemanan's name the king would want to see me of all people but Shade was already striding away. A tall figure dressed all in black making his way through the shadows. Before he could disappear entirely in the darkness, I stabbed my hunting knives back in their holsters and jogged to catch up. The remaining two assassins followed behind. I tried not to dwell on the fact that they were probably there in case I had decided to refuse.

"How have you been, Storm?" the Assassins' Guild Master asked me once I caught up.

I had to bite my tongue to keep from laughing out loud. *How have you been?* As if we were two ordinary neighbors who hadn't seen each other for a while and not two shady underworlders with an incredibly complicated relationship that involved as much blackmail and ambushing as it did trust and alliance-forming.

"Oh, you know, plotting and scheming," I said with a light shrug. "You?"

He glanced at me from the corner of his eye. "Same," he said, a smile tugging at the corner of his lips.

"So, what does King Edward want with me?" I asked as we drew closer to the Silver Keep.

Shade was silent for a while. "Wait and see," was all he finally said.

Fine, keep your secrets. I shook my head. Assassins. As the gigantic fortress that was the Silver Keep rose before us, the red-cloaked assassins scattered and vanished into the night. The side door that Shade led us to was normally guarded, which I knew because... uhm... reasons, you know. The guards must've been sent away or paid off because when he held open the door, it only revealed a deserted corridor. We followed the silver-speckled passage in silence until we reached the heavy wooden doors of what had been King Adrian's study. I assumed his son had kept up the tradition.

"There had better not be a trap waiting for me in there," I said, only half-joking, and stabbed a finger in the direction of the room.

"If there is, it's too late. You're already screwed," Shade answered with an unreadable mask on his face.

I narrowed my eyes at him. *It would probably be bad if I punched him in the face. Shame.*

"After you," the black-haired assassin said and pushed open the door.

He was right; if it was a trap, it was already too late. I blew out an annoyed breath and stalked inside. The room looked much like it had when King Adrian had been running the show.

Bookcases overflowing with books covered the walls and a big wooden desk occupied the floor. The young king looked up from a scroll he'd been reading and when his black eyes met mine, his face broke into a smile.

"The Oncoming Storm, good to see you," he said.

"And you, Your Majesty," I said with a polite nod. I didn't go as far as bowing because, well, I don't bow to upperworlders. But King Edward had only ever been kind to me, and he had even saved me once, so he had earned my respect and deserved politeness.

"I'm told you already know about the situation with the Pernulans since you apparently dropped in on my first meeting with them," King Edward said and lifted his eyebrows at me.

I glanced sharply at Shade, who smirked at me. Damn. "I... uh..." I began.

Edward waved a hand in front of his face. "It doesn't matter." He shook his head as an amused expression settled on his face. "At least you've stopped stealing from the keep."

This conversation had taken a rather unexpected turn. I opened my mouth to answer but couldn't think of anything suitable to say.

The black-haired king moved on. "Anyway, that's not why I called you here today. It's about the Pernulans. They have made some very interesting propositions which, if honored, would prove very beneficial to Keutunan. However, we all know better than to trust people carelessly. We don't know what their intentions are yet, so it's best to proceed with caution and continue to gather information."

I already knew where this conversation was headed and I didn't like it.

"Shade knows a lot of what's going on in the Underworld, of course," Edward continued. "But he and his guild also have to cover the Upperworld–"

"Don't trust your lords?" I cut in.

King Edward continued as if I hadn't interrupted. "–which means that with all these new Pernulans running around, they'll be spread thin. An extra pair of eyes, and one that can see into places the Assassins' Guild can't, would be very helpful."

"No," I said.

"No?" The king looked taken aback.

Heaving a deep sigh, I elaborated. "No. Do not drag me into your mess again! I didn't want to be involved in matters of state before and I sure as hell don't want to be now. So leave me out of your political problems."

"Drag you into it?" Shade said with an incredulous note in his voice. "If I remember correctly, you managed to land yourself in that last mess all by yourself."

I crossed my arms over my chest. Well, he wasn't wrong. Technically, it wasn't Edward's fault that his father had blackmailed me into getting involved in the power struggle last year. My own actions had managed to draw the late king's attention, leading to the blackmail and the involuntary involvement in the business of kings and queens.

"How did the Pernulans even find us?" I said instead, trying to deflect the question.

There was a slight pause before King Edward replied. "We don't know. And besides, it doesn't really matter."

I frowned at him. "What do you mean *it doesn't really matter*? Isn't it super important to know how a foreign civilization found us? And why now?"

"The king said to drop it," Shade said and leveled a hard stare at me. "It doesn't matter how they found us, they're already here so our priority is finding out what their game is."

Loosening my frown, I gave him a light shrug. I guess he did have a point. "Alright, fair enough. But the answer is still no. I don't want to get involved in any more political problems."

"I don't understand." King Edward tilted his head slightly to the right. "You chose to take an active part in the elven business last year. Why not now?"

"That was different!" I huffed. "Last year I was trying to prevent people I had come to care about from dying a slow but certain death. Now you just want to involve me in politics, which I know nothing about, by the way."

Shade studied me with unreadable eyes. "I could always make you."

I opened my mouth to say something snarky in reply but then closed it again as I realized that I didn't know if he was joking or not. I never really could tell with him. Considering everything that had gone down between us last year, I wouldn't put it past him to threaten me with black-marking Liam just to get me to do what he wanted. He knew that there was no way I'd let him put a kill order on my best friend. I stared at him. The Master Assassin lifted an eyebrow at me.

"Shade," Edward sighed before turning to me. "It's alright. But could you just keep your eyes open?"

"Fine," I conceded. "If I see a shitstorm coming, I'll let you know. But then I'm taking cover. Deal?"

The young king nodded. "Deal."

As Shade guided me out of the keep, I gave myself an internal headshake. Tomorrow would be better? What a joke. If I ever say that again, remind me to slap myself. I had almost gotten dragged into another dangerous political game. Last time, Liam had gotten kidnapped and gods know what else they'd done to him, then he'd almost died, and then Elaran had had to sacrifice years of his life to save him. No, I was done getting involved in other people's problems.

"This is where we part ways," Shade said once we were outside the walls of the Silver Keep. He started out but then stopped and turned back around again. "Oh, and, Storm?" he said, locking eyes with me. "This conversation stays between us." He took off down the street.

"Threats," I muttered to his retreating back. "Every bloody time."

The cool night wind loosened strands of dark brown hair as it ruffled my braid. I watched the Assassins' Guild Master disappear into the night. We would meet again. Of that I was sure.

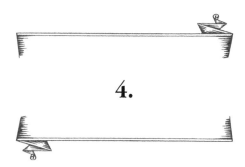

4.

Laughter and cheerful voices filled the warm room. From our vantage point by the back wall, we could barely see the roaring fire behind the mass of tables filled with food, ale, and happy patrons but we could feel its warmth.

"Wonder if they know they're drinking in a thief bar," Bones chuckled and nodded to the group of Pernulans clustered together in the middle of the room.

I blew out an amused breath. "Probably not."

In the week since the ships arrived, some Pernulans had started trickling in from the boats. The few who had braved the waves to come and explore our strange city usually kept to themselves but at times they would venture into the various taverns around town.

"Would it be a bad idea to pickpocket them?" My mouth drew into a wide grin. "Just to say welcome, you know?"

"Yes." Liam shook his head at me with a sigh. "Besides, you know how Barrel and Hilda feel about stealing in their tavern."

"Fine," I conceded.

Bones let out a rumbling laugh. "Always making trouble, you two."

"Us *two*?" Liam said in mock outrage. "*She* makes trouble. I just try to duck the flying bullets and slashing swords that follow it."

Deep laughter filled the room again. "Fair enough. Right, Storm?" Bones said and nudged an elbow in my ribs.

"Right," I said drily. "Well, while you finish discussing my mess-making skills, I'm gonna go get some more ale." I gave Liam a playful shove to the back of the head as I walked past and started weaving my way through the throng. That rhythmic language I had first heard at the docks followed me as I passed the Pernulans' table. They were staring into their ale mugs, looking very unimpressed. If they thought the ale was bad at the Mad Archer, they were in for a nasty surprise at basically every other tavern. The drinks here were among the best in the city.

"Hey, Barrel!" I called as I got to the bar.

He was studying something in his hand but looked up when he heard my voice. "Storm," he said, "look at this." He walked over and held out his massive hand, palm up.

Leaning forward on the wooden counter, I peered at the small, white ball. "Is that a... pearl?" I said with furrowed brows.

"Yeah."

"Where did you get that from?"

"Those... uhm..." Barrel began and nodded towards the newcomers.

"Pernulans," I supplied.

"Yeah, those Pernulans used it to pay for the food and drink."

"Huh." I stared at the strangers in brightly-colored clothes for a moment before turning back to the burly tavern-keeper. "No offense, Barrel, the food and drink here is good but it ain't worth that much."

Barrel gave a slow nod. "They're also using it to rent some rooms upstairs but yeah, I know."

After a quick scan around us, I folded his fingers over the precious object. "Don't let anyone know you have it. You know you and Hilda are protected by the guild, so no one in the Underworld will touch you. But there are people in the Bowels who'd kill for something like this."

Running the Thieves' Guild's unofficial tavern and treating all its guild members with kindness had earned Barrel and his wife protection long ago. We had put out word in the whole Underworld that they were off limits but the rogues who'd been kicked out of their Underworld guilds and lived in the slums of the Bowels didn't follow any rules or answer to anyone. They killed as they pleased. And trust me, for something as rare and valuable as a pearl, they certainly would.

"Will do," Barrel said and stuffed the shiny sphere in his pocket. He shook off the somber mood that had settled and cracked a smile. "Ale?"

"Yeah. Three, please."

When I got back to our table, Liam and Bones teased me a bit more about getting stuck in one mess or another. I didn't mind. After all, they were right; I did seem to have a certain penchant for trouble. They could make as much fun of me as they wanted, I still enjoyed spending time with them. And that was saying something about our friendship. Normally, I throw knives at people who make jokes at my expense.

"Alright, I should be heading back," Bones announced when we were about halfway through the mug. "Gotta get some sleep before my next shift."

"Bottoms up?" Liam said with a mischievous smile.

Our robust gate-keeper chuckled. "Bottoms up."

"Go."

We all chugged the rest of our ale as fast as we could and then one by one banged our empty mugs on the sturdy wooden table. After lifting a brief hand to Barrel at the bar, we stepped out of the cozy tavern and onto the cold stones outside. I took a deep breath, inhaling the crisp air, before running a hand over the ten throwing knives lined up behind my shoulders. The night was still young. I smiled. Plenty of time for some trouble-making.

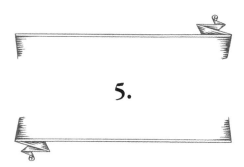

5.

"What's wrong?" I asked, glancing at Liam from the corner of my eye.

"Nothing."

After we'd said goodbye to Bones, Liam and I had drifted aimlessly through the city. I'd suggested several fun nighttime activities, including breaking into the Silver Keep to snoop, but he had only shrugged. Eventually, we'd found ourselves down by the docks.

I studied his normally cheerful face. Ever since we'd gotten back from our trip, Liam had been acting strangely, but I couldn't quite put my finger on what it was. He just seemed off and his mood swings were as sudden as they were frequent.

"You're lying," I stated. I know I probably should've been gentler, but being blunt is sort of my thing.

He didn't even try to deny it. His eyes had a faraway look in them as he stared out across the dark blue sea. While we watched, three rowboats full of Pernulans slowly made their way towards the small, hidden dock at the far end of the harbor.

"Yeah," my friend finally admitted.

"So, what is it?"

He hung his head and watched his legs dangle over the side of the pier, brown curls falling into his eyes. "Life."

"That's a very broad topic. Wanna narrow it down?" I joked, and bumped his shoulder with mine.

"What's the point?" Liam said.

"Of narrowing it down?"

My friend jerked his head up and stared at me, eyes full of frustration. "Of life! What am I supposed to be doing?" He threw his hands up. "Why am I even alive?"

"What do you mean?" I asked, perplexed, because to me the answer was obvious.

"I mean there has to be a reason! But I don't know what that reason is." Liam's dark blue eyes flooded with sadness, and something else, but I couldn't quite place the emotion. "Elaran gave up years of his life for me. He will *die* earlier than he was supposed to. Because of me."

Understanding dawned on me like a red sun. Guilt. His eyes were filled with guilt. I should've realized it straight away; my eyes had looked exactly like that after Rain died. Putting a hand on his arm, I tried to think of something uplifting to say but I came up blank.

"Is this what's been bothering you all these weeks?" I asked. For some reason, I couldn't meet his eyes, so instead I occupied myself with pulling small splinters from the wooden crate next to me.

"Yeah. Actually, more than a few weeks. Ever since that day when I found out, it's been eating at me. Slowly at first but now..." He heaved a deep sigh. "I don't know."

"He saved you because you're a kind person. Not like, well, the rest of us..." I let out a humorless laugh before turning to look straight at my best friend. "If anyone deserves to be saved, it's you."

Liam chuckled and gave my upper arm a soft push. "I don't think you're so bad."

I snorted. "Yeah, thanks."

"But seriously," he said and flopped down on the pier, legs still kicking over the side, "what am I doing with my life?"

A startled seagull squawked somewhere behind us. I lifted my shoulders in reply to his rhetorical question.

He turned his head towards me on the wooden boards. "No. What *am I* doing with my life?"

Oh. So that hadn't been a rhetorical question. Man, I needed to work on my conversation skills.

"Well, you're–"

A shot rang out. Before the sound had finished reverberating through the night, a bullet exploded into the crate next to my head, sending chips of wood flying across the pier. I ducked and threw my hands up to protect my head. Liam let out a small scream shortly before a second bang tore through the mist. Scrambling to get away, I flung myself across the gap separating my body from the relative safety of the crate. A bullet whizzed past in the air, right in the spot my head had occupied only seconds before.

"Liam!" I shouted and reached around the side of the box. "Stay down!"

He twisted around and pushed forward using his knees and elbows until he reached my outstretched hand. Another bullet grazed Liam's hair. In a rush of panic-induced adrenaline, I thrust out both arms and heaved him to safety. He landed on top of me just as a fourth bullet flew past the crate and disappeared into the sea.

"Are you hit?" I demanded while disentangling our limbs.

He shook his head and hunkered down next to me while I shoved a hand into one of my belt pouches and fished out a transparent orb. Without even pausing to pray that it would work, I lobbed the glass ball over the barrier in the direction of the attackers. A deafening explosion roared across the harbor.

"What in Nemanan's name was that?" Liam exclaimed.

"Fuck if I know. I got it from that apothecary."

That blast would at least stop our assailants from advancing for a couple of minutes. Pressing my back to the wooden wall of the box, I tried to get my breathing under control. Shit. This was bad. Two more shots echoed across the harbor, followed by two sharp thuds as the bullets buried themselves in the side of our makeshift barricade. I whipped my head from side to side, trying to find an escape route.

There was another stack of crates further down but we'd never make it there without being hit. At least not both of us. We could jump into one of the boats tied up behind us, but that wouldn't really help either because we wouldn't be able to get away in it fast enough. The box vibrated as two more shots connected with our hiding place. Crap. These felt different. The tremors hadn't been that strong before which could only mean one thing. The shooters were moving closer.

"Gods damn it!" I cursed. "Where are those bloody Silver Cloaks when you need them!"

Liam stared at me with desperate eyes as two more projectiles shook our temporary shelter. Damn. This box wasn't going stay intact forever. It was only a matter of time before a bullet tore through the wood. I looked at Liam. Every hit was more forceful than the last, proving that our attackers were advancing steadily. I needed to get him out.

"Alright, listen up, we don't have much time," I whispered in his ear. "I'm gonna draw then off while you disappear."

Liam opened his mouth to protest but I held up my hand.

"Do *not* argue with me right now," I hissed. "Just do this. Please. For me. I can't think when I have to worry about you getting shot! So please, just do what I tell you."

He looked a bit hurt, but better insulted than dead. "Fine," he said.

"I'm gonna make a run for that stack of crates," I said and pointed to the left. "While they're focused on me, you'll get into the water. Lower yourself slowly and as quietly as you can so they won't hear what you're doing. Same when you're actually in the water, swim as quietly as you can. Go under the pier until you hit the shore at the far end and then get straight to the guild."

"Yeah, got it. But what are you going to do after you reach those crates?"

I blew out a frustrated breath. "I don't know! But I'll figure it out once I get there."

Wooden splinters flew across our faces as a bullet blasted through the side of the container. My hand found a small bottle in my belt pouch.

"Now!" I hissed to Liam and threw the vial to the left.

The glass broke and black smoke filled the air with a whoosh. Flying to my feet, I sprang forward and sprinted right into the dark cloud. A bullet followed me but missed by a finger's length as the haze swallowed me. Another shot echoed across the dock, speeding past me under the cover of darkness. There was only one problem. My temporary smokescreen wasn't large enough to stretch all the way to the next wooden shield. When I reached the end of the dark mist, I pushed off the ground and dove towards cover.

Searing pain shot up my side as I disappeared from view and rolled behind the tower of crates. I pressed a hand to my ribs. It came back red. Fuck. One of the bullets must've hit me in the side. It didn't appear to be life-threatening but I was still bleeding. I had to make a quick exit.

"We know you're here," a voice called. "Come out, come out, wherever you are."

The black cloud had dissipated which meant that I could see the crates we'd previously taken cover behind. By leaning back slightly, I could just barely make out the spaces we'd occupied. They were empty. I breathed a deep sigh of relief. Liam had made it out.

"The Oncoming Storm," the voice continued, "what a joke. More like the Trembling Leaf."

The darkness inside my soul boiled in anger but I forced it down. I needed a clear head. Throwing one of my knives was out of the question because they'd put a bullet in my head as soon as I popped up to throw it. With nimble fingers, I inventoried the contents of my two new belt pouches. Two vials of blackout power. One exploding orb. Blood ran down the side of my abdomen. *Think*. They had seen both tricks before so the element of surprise was gone. As soon as they saw the black smoke they'd fire into it because they knew I'd use it as cover. *Wait*. A grin spread across my face. They already knew.

I pulled out all three objects and carefully placed them on the boards. This would require precise timing. Sucking in a deep breath, I closed my eyes and sent a quick prayer to Cadentia, Goddess of Luck. When I opened them again, I grabbed both bottles of blackout powder and threw them simultaneously in opposite directions. Once I heard them crash down on either side of the crates, I snatched up the exploding orb. Two shots rang out and whipped past in the dark fog to the left. I hurled the glass ball in the direction the bullets had come from and even before it hit the ground, I rolled over the side of the pier. The earsplitting roar of the fire masked my fall as I tumbled headlong into the dark water and disappeared from view.

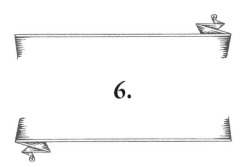

6.

The cold water swallowed me as I sank below the surface. Kicking my legs, I swam forward so that I'd be under the pier before I raced back towards the land of breathable air. I broke the surface gently and limited myself to small, soft breaths in order to avoid detection.

"You alright?" the voice from before asked somewhere above me.

"Alright?" another man's voice bellowed. "My whole bloody cloak's on fire!"

"Better your cloak than your pants," the first man muttered. "Did you see where she went?"

"No, I was busy ducking the fucking fire she threw in our faces!"

I continued moving quietly through the water. The shore wasn't that far off. If I could make it there undetected, I'd be fine. Pain shot up my side with every slow stroke but I bit my tongue and kept pushing forward.

"We can't lose her," the first man said. "He'll have our heads if we screw this up!"

Their voices were getting fainter. Right now, I didn't have the brain capacity to consider who the 'he' they were talking about could be. One arm and then the next. One kick and then another one. The end of the broad pier appeared in the distance. I took a bracing breath and climbed onto the shore. Red water dripped from my clothes as I slunk towards the nearest side street. With one hand pressed to my ribs, I jogged up the road. Blood leaked between my fingers. I needed to get off the streets as fast as possible.

Most underworlders don't bother with secondary locations because they can live in their guild's headquarters. I've never been keen on the idea of putting all my eggs in the same basket. When shit hits the fan, I want options. I thanked my distrusting self from my current bleeding self as I started moving in the direction of my Harbor District safe house.

THE OLD WOODEN DOOR groaned as I leaned against it, pushing it open. Stale air and dust-covered furniture met me when I stepped across the threshold and into the small room. After kicking the door shut, I collapsed into the nearest chair. Damn. This night had turned into a shitshow. I winced as I lifted my shirt and studied the wound underneath. The bullet had caught me in the side while I'd twisted during the dive. Red blood leaked from the gash but it could've been worse. It needed stitching, though. I was pretty sure I'd stashed a sewing kit somewhere in here. The chair wobbled behind me as I heaved myself up and moved towards the set of drawers.

A soft creak drifted from the staircase outside the door. My whole body tensed up. Shit. I barely had time to twist behind the door before it crashed open. Two pairs of boots stampeded across the threshold. I had wanted to slam the door shut before the second man got through but I hadn't been quick enough. Both of them were in the room. I had to act fast.

Moving swiftly, I snuck up behind the last one while drawing one of my hunting knives. Shining metal flashed through the air as I drew the blade across his unsuspecting throat. A wet gurgling filled the room, followed moments later by a crash. The ruckus the dying man's gun had caused when it clattered to the floor made the other invader whirl around. His eyes widened in shock when he saw his dying partner clutch his throat but the surprise drained rapidly, leaving only rage. He lifted his hand and fired.

As the bullet exploded out of the pistol I realized that I was standing way too close to leap out of the way. Instead, I grabbed the back of his partner's shirt and slipped behind his body. I only hoped the bullet would get stuck somewhere in there so that it wouldn't pass through him and hit me too.

The body jerked back as the shot connected. Whether it had passed through him or not was unclear but it hadn't hit me at least. Good. However, I was having trouble staying upright while holding the weight of the dead man so I shoved his limp body towards his partner. The remaining man stumbled as the weight of his now dead friend pushed him back. I flung one of my throwing knives at him but he ducked it while twisting out from the falling corpse. My knife buried itself in the wall behind him.

Now that he'd wasted his shot on his friend, the man didn't have time to reload his pistol, so he hurled it at my head instead, intending to knock me unconscious. I side-stepped it just in time but while I'd been busy dodging the flying firearm, my attacker had ripped the vibrating blade from the wall. Twirling back around, I just had time to see him rush me.

With fear filling my chest, I threw another knife but I didn't have time to aim so it sailed past him uselessly. Releasing a roar, he slashed at me. I brought up my forearm to shield my face and let out a short cry as the cold blade sliced my skin. While my attention was focused on blocking his knife attack, he landed a hard kick on my hip, sending me stumbling backwards. I tried to regain my balance but stepped on something round, and slipped. The floor raced up to meet my body as I fell while my attacker launched himself towards me. Air rushed out of my lungs. I desperately tried to refill them and get my hands up to protect myself before his heavy body landed on top of me. I only half-succeeded.

A knife flew towards my face but I managed to catch the wrist attached to it before it skewered my eye. My other arm was stuck on the wrong side of his arms. He used both hands to push the knife closer and he was gaining ground with each second. I threw my free hand out in search of something, anything, that would help. My fingers found the round object I'd slipped on earlier. *Yes*. Fumbling, I tried to get my hand in the right position around the metal contraption. The knife moved closer at an alarming speed. It'd have to be now.

I released my grip on his wrist right as I jerked my head to the side. With the sudden loss of resistance, my assailant drove the knife right into the wooden floorboards next to my head. While he was busy recovering, I swung the object now firmly placed in my right hand and shoved it into his chest. I pulled the trigger.

Utter disbelief spread across the man's face as his dead partner's unused pistol blew a hole in his ribcage. His body control gave out and he crashed down on top of me. Blood oozed from the wound, creating a spreading pool on my chest. Using every bit of strength left, I pushed up his shoulders and rolled him off me before I let my arms fall back to the floor again. My chest heaved. *Fuck.*

Only my heavy breathing sounded as I lay on the dusty wooden boards now littered with weapons and dead men. The metallic smell of blood filled the room. I knew I couldn't stay here. No help was coming. I was still bleeding, and after this battle, even more now than before. If I blacked out here, I'd most likely die. Heaving a deep sigh, I pushed myself into a sitting position. The room swayed before me. After retrieving both my missing throwing knives, I stumbled into the hallway and started carefully making my way down the stairs. My hands left red smudges on the railing.

A thin mist of saltwater met me as soon as I stepped outside. Taking a couple of steadying breaths, I pressed a hand to my bleeding side and began my labored walk towards the Thieves' Guild. Muted dripping followed my every step. Blood, water, or both – I wasn't sure. Running footsteps sounded up the street just as I crossed into the Merchants' Quarter. I scrambled into a side street as fast as my banged up body would allow and drew myself up against the wall. Black spots swam across my vision. Before long, a squad of Silver Cloaks ran past without noticing the bleeding figure in the shadows.

"Now you're coming," I muttered after they'd disappeared. "They peppered us with bullets and I set off two bloody detonations, and now you're coming."

Shaking my head wearily, I started out again. My heart pounded in my chest and I swore I could hear the blood rushing through my body and out of the wounds. At long last, the gray stone building that was the Thieves' Guild rose before me. I stumbled the last few steps down and rammed into the metal door. With no strength left, I simply slid down the door frame. I was having trouble making out the details of the frame on the other side. Lifting my hand to knock was more than I could manage so instead, I banged my knee against the metal.

"When... the green..." I mumbled as the hatch in the door slid open but I couldn't bring myself to finish the sentence.

The door was shoved open. I hadn't been prepared, and even if I had been, I didn't have enough strength left to catch myself so I just tipped to the side and landed on the ground. Voices talked around me but they sounded so far away. The last thing I remembered before passing out was a pair of strong arms lifting me up and carrying me down into the safety of Thieves' Guild.

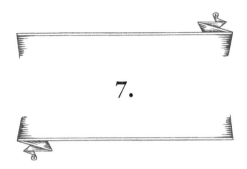

7.

"How do you feel?"

"How do I feel?" I snapped. "I feel like I'm going to kill someone if I have to spend another second in this bloody room."

Liam shook his head at me. "Be nice. He's only doing his job."

"*You* try being cooped up in the same room for weeks and see how cheerful you'd be," I muttered.

Doctor Vestus sighed and began packing up his tools. "I know that for someone of your... profession, being on bed rest for weeks is not ideal. However, they have done you well. Your wounds have healed nicely and you should have no trouble moving about by now. They'll leave scars, though."

Yeah. Just a few more to add to my rather vast collection. I studied the gangly doctor. He rolled up a long bandage in a neat ball and tied it off with a knot. I knew that I was being unfairly grumpy. He had done a remarkable job getting me healthy again and he hadn't asked once where I'd gotten those very conspicuous wounds. And he'd put up with my snarky comments. That alone should've earned him a medal. There was a reason he was my first choice when I needed medical attention.

"That's alright," I said. "Thanks, Doc. For everything."

"Mm-hmm," he commented and buttoned his brown coat. "I wouldn't normally agree to being brought blindfolded to a patient... and especially not to one who possesses as many knives as you." He glanced at the various blades scattered throughout my small room. "But for the amount of money you're paying me..."

I snorted. *Nice transition there, Doc.* With a couple of quick strides, I closed the distance to my desk and pulled out the topmost drawer. Some leather pouches of various sizes occupied the space within. I picked one of the biggest ones and dropped it into Doctor Vestus' open palm. A brief smile spread across his thin lips as he weighed it in his hand before stuffing it into one of his deep pockets. With a short cough, he straightened and picked up his brown bag from my bed.

"You cut it awfully close this time," he said. "Don't let it happen again."

I rolled my eyes at his retreating back. "Yeah, great advice, I'll try not to get shot and stabbed so much next time," I called after him as he disappeared through the door.

"I'll see him back to his house," Liam said with one foot out the door. "Are you going to go see the elves?"

"Yeah. Elaran's gonna throw a fit if I miss this check-in."

"Tell them hi for me," Liam said before waving goodbye and following Doctor Vestus into the hallway. "Oh, and try not to get yourself killed this time!" his voice echoed back to me, followed by a hearty laugh.

I grimaced at the empty doorway. "Very funny."

My side felt a bit stiff, but not horribly so. After stretching a little to soften it up, I put on most of my knives and then pulled my dark gray cloak around me. It was only afternoon so I had to wear it in order to hide all my weapons. With one last look over my shoulder, I stepped through the door.

"Oh!" Guild Master Caleb exclaimed.

"Guild Master," I said, alarmed when I realized that I'd accidentally walked straight into him. "I apologize, I wasn't looking where I was going."

Great. I hadn't even taken one step outside my room and I was already in trouble.

Master Caleb straightened his rumpled clothes and cracked a smile. "It's fine. I'm glad to see you up and about."

Caleb was by far the kindest of our three Guild Masters, so if I had to pick one to run straight into, I'd at least picked the right one.

"Do you want to come in?" I asked and motioned towards the rest of my room.

He waved a hand dismissively. "No, no need. I can see that you're on your way out and this will only take a moment. I've heard back from all the other Guild Masters. None of them know anything. Whatever this attack on you was, it didn't come from anyone in the Underworld."

Or so they said. I frowned. He was probably right, though. I mean, I was in no short supply of enemies throughout the city but I couldn't think of anyone who hated me enough to risk starting a guild war. That was against the Underworld's most sacred rule: respect the guilds.

"However, I can't speak for the inhabitants of the Bowels, of course," Guild Master Caleb continued. "Or these new... what are they called?"

"Pernulans," I filled in.

"Right. Yes, I can't account for them." His brown eyes turned pensive. "There seem to be more of them now. Have you noticed?"

"No, Guild Master," I replied with a small cough. "I've been in bed."

He shook his head as if to clear it of cobwebs. "Right, of course. Well, I should be going. I just wanted to update you on the situation."

"Thank you, Guild Master. I appreciate that."

He nodded. "Be on your guard."

"I will."

The brown-haired Master of the Thieves' Guild turned on his heel and strode back the way he had come. I filed the information I'd received in the scheming part of my brain and followed him. I needed to talk to Elaran. But first, I had to make a pit stop in the Merchants' Quarter. Joy filled my stomach like warm food. Finally, I would get to rejoin the world of the living. Pulling my cloak tighter around my shoulders, I jogged up the stairs. I grinned as the metal door appeared at the top. The Oncoming Storm was back in business.

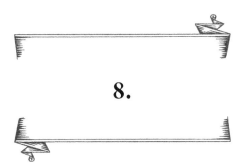

8.

"What are you doing here? You can't be here!"

"That's not very polite, Haber," I said and casually shifted my cloak so that some of the blades under it became visible.

After leaving the Thieves' Guild, I had strolled through the Merchants' Quarter. I knew I had to meet Elaran and the twins soon but there was one person I needed to see first. It was a certain brilliant man who had only recently opened a shop at the edge of this district.

"You can't be here," the bespectacled apothecary reiterated while rushing to the window. He threw hurried glances in both directions of the street. "Please leave."

"What's gotten into you?" I frowned at him as he pulled the curtains across the windows and flipped the sign on the door from 'open' to 'closed'. "I'm here to tell you that I've tried the exploding orbs now too. They worked as well as the blackout powder. I wanna buy more. Of both, actually."

Apothecary Haber skirted past me and took up position behind his counter. "I can't sell to you. Please leave."

I drew a hunting knife from behind my back and slammed it into the wooden countertop. "Alright," I pressed out between clenched teeth, "my very limited patience ran dry weeks ago and

I have yet to refill my supply, so you're gonna tell me what in Nemanan's name is wrong with you, right now, or I'm gonna start carving something up."

Haber shrank back against the wall and swallowed. "I can't sell to you."

"You said."

"No, no. I mean, I can't sell to *you*." The terrified apothecary glanced from side to side and lowered his voice. "They came here. A couple of weeks ago. Told me I could never sell any of my, my... new inventions to you again."

"*They* said? Who are they?" I asked. When Haber didn't reply, I raised an eyebrow at him. "And what do you think *I'll* do if you refuse to sell to me?"

He looked at me with pleading eyes. "Please. Don't you think I would give you what you want if I could? You were one of my first customers. And you're one of my best-paying ones."

"So why don't you?"

"They're threatening my family," he whispered.

How mundane. It seemed like that was the standard threat most people made to get others to cooperate. Couldn't they be a bit more creative? And yet, it worked. Every time.

I gave him an exasperated stare. "I could threaten your family too."

Haber's mouth dropped open. He worked it up and down several times but no sound made it past his lips. At last he swallowed, closed it, and continued watching me. I drummed my fingers on the counter. The seconds stretched on but the apothecary kept silent. Cocking my head, I studied him.

"Huh," I said at last. "But you still won't sell to me because..." I paused and wrinkled my eyebrows. "Because you're more afraid of them than you are of me. Who *are* these people?"

"Please," he begged. "I can't say."

"What would happened if these mysterious extortionists would suddenly, say, turn up dead?" I asked and spread my hands.

"Your next order would be on the house," Apothecary Haber announced with sudden force.

I gave a short nod while raising my eyebrows in surprise. "I see. Until next time, then."

The brilliant chemist nodded back. After checking the streets, I opened the door and slunk out of his now darkened shop. Outside, I struck up a brisk pace and moved towards West Gate.

Evening was fast approaching and the city was teeming with people trying to finish today's tasks. The smell of fish wafted up from the docks and mingled with the salty sea air. Last minute shoppers, playing children, and workers heading to the nearest tavern bustled past me oblivious to my brooding.

Someone had forced Haber to stop selling to me and I'd bet my whole fortune that it was the same person who'd ordered the attack by the pier. The shooters had said 'he' so it was a man, of that I was sure. As I've mentioned before, I'm not exactly short on enemies. However, most of those are other underworlders, and Guild Master Caleb had said that it wasn't anyone from our world. That only left the rogues in the Bowels, the upperworlders, and of course the Pernulans. As far as I knew, I didn't have that many enemies among those groups. Well, except for all those lords and ladies whose mansions I'd robbed over the years. I let out a small chuckle. But none of them would've known that it was me who'd stolen from them. At least, I didn't think so. As West Gate appeared in the distance, I shook off my musings. One problem at a time. First, I'd have to deal with an annoyed Elaran.

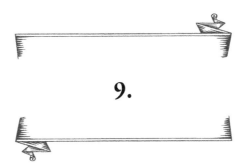

9.

"I was beginning to think you weren't going to show," the auburn-haired elf commented as I walked through the door of the small cabin.

"Oh give me a break, Elaran," I replied. "I almost died a few weeks ago so you're lucky I'm here at all."

We were in the same cabin that Queen Faye and King Edward, then *Prince* Edward, had met in months ago to discuss a partnership. And an assassination. Both had worked out well. Eventually.

"You almost died?" Haela asked, shock filling her voice.

"Yeah," I said. "I got shot. And then I fell off a pier. And then knifed, and there at the end I almost got skewered too."

The black-haired elven twins, Haela and Haemir, stared at me with mirrored looks of astonishment. Elaran continued leaning against the wall with his arms crossed over his chest. His yellow eyes showed no signs of surprise whatsoever.

"What did you do to piss them off?" the grumpy ranger asked.

"What did *I* do?" I said and threw my arms out.

"Yeah. Knowing you, you sure did something."

Haela giggled at that. I shook my head. Elves.

"Oh shut up," I muttered to Elaran. "You're not exactly winning any popularity contests either."

"Yeah, I am."

"Guys," Haemir interrupted. "Focus, please?"

"Fine."

The twins were already seated in two of the chairs by the table so I pulled out another one and dropped into it. After a moment's pause, and a deep sigh, Elaran did the same. Silence settled inside the cabin while only the occasional bird chirped outside the window.

The eternal grump that was Elaran crossed his arms over his chest again. "So, what news?"

"Is it true another civilization has arrived?" Haela cut in before I could reply.

The auburn-haired archer blew out an exasperated breath and threw up his hands. Haela grinned sheepishly.

"Well, is it?" she pressed. "We've seen the ships from the coast."

"Yeah," I said and nodded, "yeah, it is. They arrived shortly after our last check-in and they've become a pretty normal sight in town by now. You could come see for yourselves?"

"You know it's not that simple," Haemir said and shifted his eyes to stare at the rustling leaves outside the window.

I gave him a sad smile. "Yeah, I know."

People were slowly coming to terms with the news that elves actually existed, and more importantly, that they were not the evil villains that history books had made them out to be. However, the elves of Tkeideru didn't visit our city yet because there was still too much prejudice. Centuries of mistrust weren't something that could be cured in a day.

"So, come on, what are they like?" Haela said and leaned forward on the table, excitement burning in her eyes.

"Oh, uhm..." I began because I'm not exactly an expert on people. "They're okay, I guess?" I finished with an uncertain shrug.

The excited twin leveled a very unimpressed stare at me. What? I'd spent most of the time since they arrived locked up in my room, trying not to die. How was I supposed to know what the newcomers were like? However, I could tell from her facial expression that Haela wasn't going to let this go so I racked my brain for observations I'd made during today's trip around the city.

"I guess they're pretty nice," I said. "When they first arrived, they mostly kept to themselves but now they're everywhere in town. Like, I saw them drinking with upperworlders and stuff."

"How very informative," Elaran said before adding under his breath, "as usual."

I scowled at him but he ignored it and instead started firing off rapid questions. "What do they want? Why are they here? Where did they come from?" He lifted his eyebrows. "Do you know?"

"Well..." I began as a broad grin settled on my face. "I sorta eavesdropped on their first meeting with King Edward, so yeah, I do know."

Haela grinned back at me while Elaran managed the impressive feat of rolling his eyes and shaking his head at the same time.

"So?" he prompted.

After flashing him a teasing smile, I shared what I knew about the Pernulans, the war they'd mentioned on the continent, their need for allies, and what they had offered in return.

"Huh," Elaran commented once I'd finished. "Did your king take the deal?"

Furrowing my brows, I thought back to my walk across the city. Since I had declined Shade and Edward's proposition to spy, I didn't have a direct line of communication to what happened in the Silver Keep.

"I think so," I said at last. "When I passed the Artisan District on my way here I think I saw our carpenters and builders and others working *together* with the Pernulans."

"Interesting," Elaran said and ran a hand over the tight braid on the side of his head.

The elves fell silent as they pondered the information I had shared. Not seeing a reason to rush them, I turned to gaze out the window. The sun was setting, painting the landscape in red and gold.

"What about this attack on you?" Elaran said after a while, interrupting the comfortable silence that had settled. "Anything we need to be concerned about?"

Why, yes, thank you. Because someone trying to kill me was only important if it meant trouble for him as well. I blew a strand of hair out of my face. Classic Elaran.

"I don't think so," I said. "I mean, I still don't know who's targeting me but, no, I don't think so."

"They tried to shoot you?" Haemir asked.

"Yep." Tapping my chin, I thought back. "Well, I think the first time was when they were hiding in a wagon outside a shop I was gonna..." I flashed a short grin. "Never mind. Anyway, they knew I'd be there so they were lying in wait. The second time they sorta just found me and started shooting. And stabbing. But the most troubling part is that they're blackmailing one of my suppliers so he won't sell to me."

Elaran drew back a little and furrowed his brows. "How is that the most troubling part?"

"Because that means they're messing with my business." I shrugged. "And I take that more personally."

"More than someone trying to kill you?"

"Yeah. Obviously."

Elaran opened his mouth but then closed it again. He shook his head. "You're very strange."

"I've never claimed otherwise."

Haela chuckled at that while Haemir just looked thoughtful. "When did this start?" he asked.

Tracing circles on the table with my finger, I considered his question. "A few weeks ago, I suppose." A sudden thought made me look up. "Actually, now that I think about it, it was the same day the Pernulans arrived."

"You think they might be connected?" Elaran asked.

"I don't know," I said. "What would they gain from it?"

The room of elves offered a collective shrug in reply. It was indeed an odd coincidence but I couldn't come up with any logical reason for it. Conversation shifted from attempted murder to more mundane matters. My elven friends updated me on news from Tkeideru and passed along greetings from Faye and the others. When the darkness outside announced the sun's complete disappearance, we made our way out of the cabin.

"Tell Faye and Keya and... well, alright, tell all of them I said hey," I said to the elves as we were about to part ways.

"Will do," Haela replied and fired off a mock salute before turning around to follow her brother and Elaran into the forest. "Oh and, Storm?" she called over her shoulder as she trotted away. "Try not to get shot next time!"

I threw up my hands. "Why does everyone keep saying that? As if I got myself shot on purpose!"

Idiots. After one last huff, I turned around as well and started jogging back towards Keutunan. I would, though. I would try not to get myself shot next time.

NIGHT HAD DRAWN ITS blanket over the city and the occupants of the Marble Ring had taken cover indoors to escape the thick waves of fog that had rolled in from the sea. Candlelight flickered in the windows of the mansion across the street. I studied it. The house was one of the bigger ones and my surveillance tonight had revealed that security was tight.

"Nah, not worth the trouble," I whispered. "Right?"

"You're the thief, you tell me," a voice from the shadows replied.

Shade materialized out of the darkness. He moved closer and took a seat on the edge of the roof. I stayed perched on the tiles beside him.

"I hear you almost got yourself killed," the Master Assassin said.

"Got *myself* killed?" I blew out a noisy breath. "Man, I feel like I've had this exact conversation three times today already. They were trying very hard, you know."

"So I hear."

Turning my head slightly, I glanced at him through narrowed eyes. "It wasn't you, was it?"

"Why would I try to kill you?" Shade said, not taking his eyes off the street below.

I tipped my head from side to side. "Well, you never know."

He let out a pleasant chuckle. "Besides, if it had been me trying to kill you, you wouldn't be sitting here today."

"Right," I said and returned the chuckle. "Keep telling yourself that."

Silence settled as we both no doubt considered how a full-blown showdown between the two of us would actually play out. I was pretty sure I didn't want to find out.

"Do you think the Pernulans are involved?" Shade asked after a while.

"Elaran said the same thing."

"Smart man. Well, do you?"

Pinching my lip, I considered that same question again. As I said before, I figured that it could just be a coincidence. But then again, I am too paranoid and pessimistic to put much faith in chance. If it was them, I had to know. It was probably worth investigating at least.

"Don't know yet," I said. "But I think I'll look into it."

"Hmm," Shade commented. He turned to peer at me, cocking his head slightly to the right. "You know, if you're going to sneak aboard one of their ships, tonight is a great night for it."

He was right. The thick fog would provide excellent cover if I wanted to approach their ships undetected. It was too good an opportunity to pass up.

"Yeah, I think I will," I said and gave myself a short nod.

Even though I hadn't nodded at him, Shade replicated the gesture. "Will you tell me what you find out?"

"What's in it for me?"

The Assassins' Guild Master snorted and shook his head. "How about this: I'll help you out with something in the future. When you need it."

I tapped my chin, weighing my options, before reaching a decision. "I can work with that."

"Good." He stood up. "I have to get back. Good luck."

"Yeah, thanks."

"Oh, and–" he began.

"I swear," I cut off, "if you tell me not to get myself shot this time, I'm gonna throw a knife at you!"

Shade lifted his eyebrows in surprise and stared at me for a moment. Then his mouth drew into a lopsided smile and a mischievous sparkle spread through his black eyes. "Careful now. Remember what happened last time you tried to threaten me?"

"Yeah, that went horribly, thank you for reminding me," I grumbled.

He just laughed his rippling laugh. "Goodbye, the Oncoming Storm."

After watching his lean muscular body disappear into the shadows again, I shook my head. Bastard. He had given me a great idea, though. Snooping around on their boat might bring some clarity. I stood up, checked all of my knives, and gave my body a good stretch before taking off down the Thieves' Highway. It was time to get some answers.

10.

Waves lapped against the side of the rowboat as I pulled on the oars. The lights burning on the tall ships cut through the mist and guided my path. I knew I couldn't search all three of them so I'd settled for the middle one because that was the one from which General Marcellus had disembarked. Throwing a quick glance over my shoulder, I saw that I was almost there. No alarm had been raised. Yet. I stroked the water gently with the oars. The mist might hide me from view but it also carried sound very well.

Thankfully, I managed to reach the side of the ship without being detected. A gust of wind ripped through my clothes, making me shiver. Stashing my cloak in one of the fishing boats by the shore had been a necessity because it would've made climbing harder. However, I still missed its warmth. After sending a prayer to Nemanan, God of Thieves, I grabbed the closest rung and started climbing the ladder.

My heart fluttered with nervous excitement. I had never been aboard a boat this big so I didn't know what to expect on the other side of the railing. As I approached the top of the ladder, I slowed down. No sound came from above. Before continuing further, I took a deep breath of salty sea air to steady my nerves. It didn't work. Pushing aside my apprehension, I climbed the last stretch and edged my head over the top.

With eyes shifting from side to side, I scanned the deck. It looked empty but I stayed watching on the ladder for a while longer anyway. The minutes stretched on. After deciding that I was as certain as I would ever be, I slunk up and raced to the big mast. My heart hammered in my chest. Hiding in the shadows, I waited. No alarm sounded. Good. I started sneaking across the deck.

Wood creaked as the ship shifted in the water. I flinched every time, thinking it was a Pernulan stalking me, but I made it all the way across and up the stairs to that raised part of the deck at the back without being spotted.

Murmured voices drifted up from a structure that looked like a tiny house sitting close to the staircase. I waited. The voices weren't moving. When I edged closer, I realized that the tiny house actually covered an opening in the boards. I stuck my head around the corner and peered down. The voices were much stronger now. They floated up the narrow stairway leading down into the ship.

"–sounds like an excellent idea," a man's deep voice said. "That way we can both get what we want."

"Indeed," another man answered.

"But what guarantees do we have that you will keep your end of the bargain once it's done?" the first voice continued.

"You don't trust us?"

"No, it's not that..." the deep-voiced man began. "But we're risking our necks here and we want to make sure that it will be worth it."

Suspicion flared up my spine. *What* would be worth it? This sounded like a conversation that was not meant to be overheard, and that piqued my interest even more. They were speaking a language I could understand, which meant that it must be a mixed company of Pernulans and people from my city. However, I didn't recognize any of the voices.

Having a clandestine night meeting on a ship far out in the harbor was high up on the sketchy scale, so depending on who took part in this meeting, this could either be a slight inconvenience or some serious trouble. If a shitstorm was coming, I needed to know so that I could steer clear of it. Based on that, I figured that finding out who the voices belonged to was a priority. After a quick prayer to Nemanan, I crept down the first few steps and into an empty room.

"It will be worth it," the second man said with confidence.

"If you keep your word, yes. Forgive me but the things we've discussed here tonight don't exactly inspire trust. What's to stop you from screwing us over too?"

It definitely sounded like some kind of deal was being struck, though I had obviously missed the part where they talked about what each side would bring to the table. I had to at least figure out who was involved. Taking soft, shallow breaths, I crouched and peeked through the slits in the staircase.

An open door at the end of the room revealed a great cabin where a burly man with a curved sword at his hip stood next to a small counter. He was pouring liquid of a dark amber color into a wide glass. Seated at a wooden table in front of him was a blond man with dark blue eyes. He looked to be about the same age as the burly man, so probably in his forties. I'd never seen either one of them before.

"I understand your concerns but there is nothing to fear. We are not looking for conflict. We just want peace and stability."

The blond man scratched the back of his neck. "That's good to hear but..." he began in his deep voice.

"How about this then? We will help you with your... other problem too. We cannot get involved too much of course, but we can–"

The sound of two other voices, speaking in a rhythmic language, interrupted the conversation. That in itself wouldn't normally have been cause for alarm. However, there was one problem. They came from outside. I didn't hesitate one second. In a burst of speed, I shot to my feet and ran for the exit. If they rounded the corner of the tiny structure before I made it out, I'd be trapped. I ran several scenarios in my head. They all ended badly. I had to make it. The distance up those steps felt much longer now than it had on the way down. Panic bloomed in my chest. The voices grew louder.

At last, I burst through the opening and out into the night. A cry of surprise rang out as I flew up on deck. From the corner of my eye, I saw two silhouettes flinch at the movement before I grabbed a hold of the tiny house, swung myself around, and sprinted back down on the other side. They shouted something. I didn't understand what they said but they sounded alarmed. Or, more accurately, like they were *sounding* an alarm. Shit.

Smattering feet echoed throughout the ship as I raced down the stairs to the deck I'd arrived on earlier. I was pretty sure the feet making noise weren't mine. They belonged to other people. Lots of other people. Men popped up from below the ship like crocuses in the snow. Their presence blocked off most of the escape routes. I skidded to a halt as two of them ran straight in my direction but they hadn't seen me yet, so I threw myself down behind a cluster of barrels stacked against the railing. Trying to force my breathing under control, I put a hand over my mouth. The men hurried past without noticing the armed thief hiding in the darkness.

After letting out a long, slow exhale, I scanned the area. There were people everywhere but fortunately for me, none in my immediate vicinity. I took aim on a couple of crates further down and dashed forward. The wall of another raised deck, the one at the front of the ship, broke my headlong rush as I rounded my new barricade. Shouts rose in the night. Someone had seen me. When I threw a quick glance out from my cover, I saw men pointing in my direction. Crap. Whipping my head from side to side, I tried to find a way out. Running feet closed in.

There. I pushed off from one of the crates and managed to grab the railing on the high deck behind me. Straining my muscles, I pulled myself up until I could reach the next plank on the railing. I kept at it until my feet found purchase on the upper deck and I could haul myself over the balustrade. A soft thud sounded as I fell and landed hard on the wooden boards on the other side. Pursuing footsteps and urgent voices followed me. I only had seconds before they'd come thundering up the stairs on the opposite side.

My darting glance searched desperately for someplace safe. There wasn't any. This deck was empty save for a mast at the front. Behind the railing, the ship's sharp prow cut through the mist. Cold dread spread through my body. I was trapped. My hunters had made it up the stairs. They shouted something and stabbed a finger in my direction. I was out of time. Only one thing left to do. Pushing off the floor, I sprinted forward and jumped the railing. I barely missed a step as I landed on the other side and continued my rush. I couldn't believe I was doing this. This was insane. Damn. With one last headshake at the folly of it all, I jumped off the prow and dove straight down into the cold, dark water.

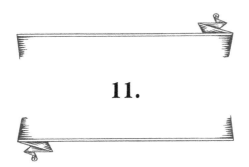

11.

The shock of the cold water jarred my soul. Fighting against the oppressive darkness, I kicked towards the surface. My clothes together with the various knives strapped to my body weighed me down. I gasped in the chilly night air as I finally broke the surface. Shouting voices echoed through the mist. This was bad. However, I didn't have even a second to contemplate that this might be the end of me. Just another thief drowned in the harbor. I had to keep moving.

As I swam around the side of the ship, I cast a glance over my shoulder. The rowboat I'd arrived in had drifted off, just as I'd suspected. I only had one option: swim towards the shore and hope I reached it before the deep claimed me. Water sloshed around my ears as I swam through the mist. Thankfully, at least the lights burning by the pier guided me in the right direction.

Drawing deep, ragged breaths, I tried to move as fast as I could without wearing myself out. A strong wave washed over my head, filling my mouth with salt water. It brought on a violent coughing fit which made me gasp for air. Staying afloat was getting harder with each arm stroke.

A strange burst of giddiness filled me and I had to stop myself from laughing out loud when I remembered my comment to Faye and the others from last summer. They'd asked me if I knew how to swim and I'd replied that it was a necessary skill when people were trying to drown you. And here I was again. Almost drowning. I thanked my past self for practicing how to swim fully clothed and armed. Though, I'd never swum this far before.

Strength was draining from my limbs as blood from a severed head. I knew I didn't have long before they gave up all together but the shore was so close now. I could make it. I had to make it. When I at last felt the shifting sand beneath my boots, I wept with relief.

Wading to the beach, I stumbled the last few steps and collapsed on the wet sand. Soft waves rolled over my ankles. I twisted onto my back and stayed there, chest heaving. Sand coated my cheek but I couldn't muster the strength to lift my hand and brush it off. I just lay there, sprawled on the sand, and listened to the lapping waves and the strained sound of my own breathing.

If I'd had even a smidgen of energy left, I would've slapped myself for doing something so ridiculous. I had almost died today. Again. I'd literally only been out of my room for one day after recovering from my last near-death experience before I ran headlong into danger again. And I was no closer to learning who was targeting me. I had to play this smarter.

Dark clouds blew across the moon and the night breeze combined with my drenched clothes chilled me to the bone. It was time to move.

I gathered whatever strength I'd regained and crawled to my feet. After taking a short detour to retrieve my cloak from the fishing boat, I started out towards the Thieves' Guild. The cloak was dry and helped my shivering a bit. While I walked, I took stock of my tools.

Since Haber had refused to sell to me, my new leather pouches had been mostly empty anyway but the lockpicks I'd kept there were gone with the waves. And my boot knife probably occupied a spot at the bottom of the harbor by now. It could be easily replaced, however, so I wasn't too saddened by its loss.

As I drew the cloak tighter around my shoulders, I thanked my well-made custom waistcoat for keeping most of the other knives in place during my water acrobatics. I'd have to show both the waistcoat and the knives some extra love, though. They'd survived two trips to the sea in only a few weeks' time. As the stone building that was the Thieves' Guild rose up before me, I added a mental note to spend additional time cleaning and oiling them. But first, I needed dry clothes.

"WHERE IN NEMANAN'S name have you been?" Liam demanded.

After exchanging passwords with Stone Wall, I'd tried to slip through the halls and into my room unnoticed. Needless to say, I'd been quite unsuccessful. Liam stood with his hands on his hips, blocking the hallway leading to my room.

"Why are you wet?" he continued, looking me up and down.

"I'm not that wet," I tried in a half-hearted attempt at humor. Muted dripping punctuated my words.

Liam looked unimpressed. "What did you do? Swim across the harbor?" he added with snort.

"Uhm..." was all I managed to reply.

Disbelief washed over my friend's face. "By all the gods! You *did* swim across the harbor, didn't you?" He threw his hands in the air and started pacing back and forth in front of me. "You are unbelievable. The doctor clears you and not a day later you... you do... this! Are you trying to get yourself killed?"

I scrunched my eyebrows. "No?"

"Was that a statement or a question?" Liam snapped.

"When the hell did you get so confrontational?" I countered before a wave of fatigue made me put a hand to the wall to keep from falling over. "Can we not do this right now? Or I might actually die of pneumonia," I said and pulled at my soaked shirt.

Liam's eyes softened. "Yeah, of course. Sorry." He glanced away. "I'm just worried about you, you know?"

"I know," I sighed. "Breakfast at the Mad Archer tomorrow? The sun's almost up and I really wanna clean and oil my stuff before I pass out."

"Yeah," Liam said and then surprised me by drawing me into a hug.

Feeling my best friend's arms around me filled me with a warmth that the brightest of fires couldn't have replicated. "You're getting wet," I mumbled into his shoulder.

"Don't care." He held on for a few more heartbeats before releasing me. When he did, a sunshine smile had settled on his lips. "See you tomorrow," he said and gave my shoulder a light push before retreating down the hallway to his own room.

"Yeah, see you tomorrow," I whispered.

As I closed the door to my room and stripped out of my wet clothes, I decided that maybe I should learn to follow others' advice. After all, people had been telling me all day not to get myself killed next time. Maybe I should listen. But then again, I don't really care what other people think; I do what I want anyway. I grinned as I slipped into warm, dry clothes. Yeah. There was no changing that. I would just have to see where my stubbornness took me next.

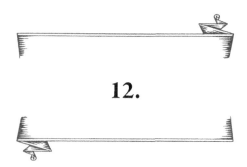

12.

The heavenly scent of warm food filled my nostrils as Hilda approached with two plates of fried fish and potatoes. My stomach growled in response.

"There we are," Hilda said and wiped her hands on her apron. "Straight out of the pan."

"Thank you," Liam and I said in unison.

"Oh you're very welcome, dear. Now, don't burn your tongue," she added before waddling back to the bar.

We dug in. It tasted as good as it had smelled so for a couple of minutes we simply occupied ourselves with stuffing our faces. Murmured afternoon conversations enveloped our pocket of silence. Most patrons there at the moment were members of the Thieves' Guild having breakfast.

"You know," I began and stabbed a piece of potato with my fork, "we never finished that conversation down by the docks."

Liam looked up in surprise but then offered a shrug. "We did have other things to worry about. And besides, it's not important."

"Yes, it is. I feel like we're always so focused on my problems."

"But that's just natural, because they're worse than mine. Someone is out to get you and you almost got killed."

"Well, yeah, but that happens a lot."

Liam stared at me. "My point exactly."

Damn. Okay, I knew right when I said it that 'people often try to kill me' hadn't been a particularly effective argument for my case. I was rapidly painting myself into a corner so, demonstrating my lack of social graces, I decided to force the conversation back on track.

"You almost died too, Liam. Of course that's gonna affect you."

He was about to argue but then slumped back in his chair. "Yeah. And Elaran sacrificed himself to save me. And what am I doing with my life?"

"A lot," I replied because this time I knew he hadn't meant it as a rhetorical question. "You're doing a lot with your life."

"Yeah? Like what? I steal stuff from people and then sell it to other people so I can continue stealing from people." Liam pushed away the plate in front of him. "What kind of life is that?"

I poked at a potato with my fork. "You're also with me."

His face softened. "I know." My friend gave me a sad smile. "But I feel like I should be doing more."

Uncomfortable feelings burrowed into my chest. I dropped my eyes and continued chasing the yellow ball around the wooden plate. "Are you unhappy? You know, with your life?" I said in a small voice.

"No!" Liam said and then scrunched up his face. "Yes? I don't know..."

Hurt stabbed at my chest like thousands of tiny needles. I thought we had a good life, but Liam wasn't happy. Dread constricted my throat. I didn't want him to feel that way but I also couldn't bear to lose him. My chest felt too crowded and I didn't know what to do about it. I was about to ask Liam what would make him happy but before I could, a brown-haired man passing our table tripped on an outstretched leg and stumbled right into me.

The darkness in my soul ripped to the surface, crackling like lightening around me as I shot to my feet with a hunting knife in each hand. "Watch where you're going," I snarled and glared at him with eyes that had turned as black as an oncoming thunderstorm.

At the sight of the madness dancing in my normally green eyes, the man stepped back and raised his hands. "Sorry. It was an accident, I... sorry." He continued stepping back until he walked straight into a bald man with bulging muscles.

"What's going on?" Bones said, looking from one to the next before his gaze settled on me. "Storm?"

Using all my self-control, I shook myself out of the trance and pushed the darkness back into the deep pits of my soul. I shoved the knives back in their holsters. "Nothing. We're good."

While I dropped back into my chair, Bones patted the man on the arm. "Don't worry about her," he said as the man withdrew, casting nervous glances over his shoulder all the way to the door.

Wrong. Do worry about me. Because if Bones hadn't shown up when he did, I don't know what would've happened. What I would've done.

Bones lowered himself into the chair next to me. "I've never asked you about... well, that," he said and motioned at me.

No. Very few people had. The ones who had seen it hadn't exactly dared stick around to ask questions. And even if they had, I wouldn't have had a lot of answers for them. Even I didn't entirely know what it was that I had let in the night I'd gotten Rain killed. I had wanted revenge and I had gotten it. But the darkness was here to stay, it would seem.

"Please don't," I said, rubbing my forehead.

Bones lifted his broad shoulders in a shrug. "Done."

If there was one thing I loved about our sturdy gatekeeper, it was *that*. He wasn't nosy; he never pressed the matter if he noticed that people were reluctant to share. I gave him a grateful smile.

"Have you had breakfast?" Liam asked.

"No, but Hilda said she'd bring it over in a minute," Bones replied before shifting his gaze back to me. "Are you any closer to finding out who's declared war on you?"

He might not be nosy, but there were very few things happening in the guild that he didn't know about. Bones never demanded that people tell him things, but everyone shared news with him anyway. Maybe it was because of that.

"No, unfortunately not," I said. "Been trying to figure it out, though."

"She's been trying very hard too," Liam cut in and grinned at me. "Last night she even took a swim in the harbor."

I grimaced at my friend. "Very funny."

Bones, ignoring my comment, furrowed his brows and turned to peer at me. "Yeah, Stoney said you came back all soaked yesterday. Someone try to drown you, or what?"

"No..." I began and then tipped my head from side to side. "Well, in a way, I suppose. I kinda snuck aboard the Pernulans' ship."

"You what?"

"Yeah. I was thinking maybe they were responsible, but..."

"So they're not?" the gatekeeper asked.

I shrugged. "Not sure yet. But some kind of deal was going down between one of them and someone from our city. Didn't recognize them, though."

Bones stroked his chin. "Huh."

"Let's say it's not the Pernulans," Liam said. "Who would make the most sense?"

"The Guild Masters told me it's no one from our world," I said, "so I'm thinking either someone from the Upperworld or the Bowels."

A clattering of pots drifted from the kitchen and a few seconds later, Hilda appeared in the door behind the counter. She weaved her way through the mass of tables, steam rising from the plate in her hand.

"Here you go, dear," she said and put the stack of fried fish and potatoes in front of Bones.

Bones drew a deep breath, inhaling the fragrant aroma. "Thank you, Hilda."

She smiled and patted him on the shoulder before retreating to the bar. The hungry gatekeeper started shoveling fish into his mouth. I chuckled and shook my head.

"So, I'm thinking," Bones began and gulped down the food. "The rogues in the Bowels aren't organized enough for something like this, right?"

I sucked my teeth and considered his statement for a moment. "Right."

"So maybe check out the upperworlders? You've got a lot of enemies there, right?"

Liam snorted. "You bet she does."

I leveled a mock glare at him before turning back to Bones. "Yeah, I suppose I do. Can't think of anyone in particular, though. But I think I'll sneak into the Silver Keep and spy a little. They've got some kinda meeting tonight, don't they?"

"Yeah, the Council of Lords," Bones confirmed.

A wide grin spread across my face. "Perfect." I cast a glance out the window. "I have to get going."

"Why?" Liam asked. "That meeting doesn't start for another couple of hours."

"I've gotta talk to Shade."

Bones raised his eyebrows at me. "Why would you want to do that?"

"Because if I tell him what happened on that boat, he'll owe me." My mouth drew into a smirk. "And I like having people owe me."

"Bet you do," Bones said with a chuckle while Liam rolled his eyes from across the table. "Just... be cautious. Around him. You don't become Master of the Assassins' Guild by being kind and considerate."

I nodded. "Yeah, I know. I feel like every time I meet him he's either ambushing me, blackmailing me, or threatening me."

And there I was again, saying stuff that really wasn't helping my case. Idiot. My two friends stared at me.

I held up my hand before they could start protesting the sanity of my actions. "Yes, yes, I know. I'll be on my guard. Promise." Putting my hands on the sturdy wooden table, I pushed up from the chair. "I'll probably be out most of the night, so I'll see you guys tomorrow, yeah?"

"Alright," Liam said. "Be careful."

"Always am," I said and strode towards the door.

"No you're not!" my best friend called after me.

I flashed him a mischievous grin before slipping out the door. This was a solid plan. First, I'd meet the deadly Guild Master who threatened me almost every time he met me and then I'd break into the Silver Keep and spy on a highly secret meeting of the most powerful lords in Keutunan. Yep. A solid plan, indeed.

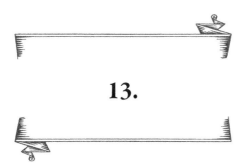

13.

A sharp sword pressed against my throat and lifted up my chin.

"Not here to fight," I said and spread my arms wide to show that my hands were empty.

Almost every time I'd met Shade, it had been on his terms. He'd tracked me down and materialized out of nowhere. And then, he'd disappeared just as suddenly again. I had no idea how to do that to him, so instead I focused on the locations I'd found him in at one time or another. Three stood out as the most likely: the Assassins' Guild headquarter, the Black Hand tavern, and the Silver Keep. I'd started with the Black Hand and gotten lucky. Well, if you could call standing alone in a room full of assassins, with a sword at your throat, lucky.

"If it isn't the bloody Oncoming Storm," the man with the sword said. "Again."

He had curly black hair and a fierce look in his eyes. I recognized him from last time I'd showed up unannounced in the Assassins' Guild's exclusive tavern. I'd dropped down from the ceiling then. That had been fun. And ridiculously dangerous.

"Hey, at least I walked in through the front door this time," I said with a nonchalant shrug.

The fierce-eyed man answered by pushing the sword higher up under my chin, forcing me up on my toes. Alright, yeah, that had been a bad move. I really needed to work on my social skills.

"Curly, ask her what she wants," a tall man with dark brown hair tied back in a bun called from a table to my right.

The man with the sword, Curly, locked eyes with me. "What do you want?"

"I'm here to see Shade," I said. In hindsight, I realize that I probably should've led with that. "I've got information for him."

"And what makes you think he's interested in this information?"

I smacked my lips. "He's the one who told me to bring it to him."

"That right?" Curly said and looked me up and down with hungry eyes.

Shit. Why had I ever thought that just striding through the door and into one of the most dangerous places in the entire city would be a good idea? This could turn into some serious trouble unless I figured out something smart to say. But what? The muscles in my calves protested from standing on my toes. *Think*.

"Let her through," a voice called with authority from the back of the room.

In a swift stroke, the sword disappeared from under my chin. I sank down on my soles again and ran a hand over my throat. It didn't come back red. Good. Before starting out, I shot a venomous glance at Curly. He stared back but made no move to stop me.

As I passed the tables of assassins, their eyes followed me. I felt more like a sacrificial lamb being led through rows of starving wolves than a person walking across a tavern.

Once I'd finally made it to the other side of the room, I saw my target and the owner of the authoritative voice. Shade. He was lounging in a wooden corner sofa that was covered with dark red cushions. A short fence of the same dark wood enclosed the couch and the table with chairs in front.

"Blades on the table," the Master Assassin said and pointed to a small side table just outside the cornered-off area.

I lifted my eyebrows at him.

"All of them," he ordered.

After an annoyed eye roll, I complied. Knife after knife hit the wood until a rather impressive pile had formed in the middle of the side table. I pinched my lip, weighing my options, but then shrugged and removed my last knife as well. The one hidden between my breasts. Shade had watched the whole process with impassive eyes.

I spread my arms in an exasperated gesture. "Satisfied?"

He nodded and twitched two fingers, beckoning me closer. Arrogant bastard. He kicked out the chair from under the table in front of him. It scraped against the floor before wobbling to a halt. "Sit."

That chair was the worst placed seat in the whole tavern. Anyone occupying it would have to sit with their back completely unprotected and a whole room of assassins behind. Damn. If that wasn't the smartest fucking power play I'd seen this decade I don't know what was. I hated being forced to sit in it with every fiber of my being but man, I couldn't help being impressed.

After lowering myself into the chair with great reluctance, I arched an eyebrow at him. "You really think I'd try to kill you?"

Shade's mouth drew into a lopsided smile. "You never know."

"Uh-huh," I muttered at the obvious use of my own words from earlier.

Now that the assassins were confident that I'd have no chance of attacking their precious Guild Master, they broke the dead silence that had settled. Murmured conversations and the clanking of plates, cups, and utensils resumed behind my back.

"You sat here watching? The whole time?" I said. "While I was over there by the door with a sword at my throat trying to convince your people that *you* had told me to come?"

The black-clad assassin smirked at me. "Yep."

Bastard. I narrowed my eyes at him and swore to myself that I'd balance the power scales between us one day. How in Nemanan's name I'd manage that, I didn't know. That was a problem for another day.

"Well," I said and shifted uncomfortably in the exposed chair, "do you want the information or not?"

"Yeah, what've you got?"

"There was some kinda secret meeting going on. A Pernulan and someone from our city were having a one-on-one down in the ship."

"I see," Shade said. "Did you recognize them?"

I gave an apologetic shrug. "No. So it wasn't one of the Pernulans I saw in the Silver Keep, because *them* I would recognize."

"What about the man from Keutunan? Upperworlder? Underworlder? What did he look like?"

Furrowing my brows, I tried to remember all the tiny details from my spy trip. "Upperworlder. He looked like an upperworlder. And talked like one too. He was maybe forty-ish, blond hair, blue eyes."

The assassin in front of me heaved an exasperated sigh. "Do you know how many blond men in their forties there are in this city?" I opened my mouth to answer but he cut me off by holding up his hand. "Don't answer that. I'll tell you. A lot. Didn't he have any distinguishing features?"

"No," I answered honestly. "He looked like your garden-variety upperworlder."

"Hmm. What about the meeting? What did they talk about?"

A clatter rang out behind us. The sound of scraping furniture followed it. I turned to see an assassin slam his plate and utensil back on the table while the rest of his companions laughed around him.

"It sounded like they were making a deal," I said after turning back around. "The blond man is gonna help the Pernulan screw someone over and then he's gonna get something valuable for it." Pursing my lips, I considered what else I'd heard. "Oh, and the Pernulan said he's doing it because he doesn't want conflict, he wants peace and stability."

"Huh," Shade commented. For a moment, his eyes took on a faraway look as he considered the information I'd provided. "Anything else?"

I shook my head. "No."

"Alright," he said, studying me with that soul-penetrating gaze of his. "Next time you need help, I'll help you out."

After giving him a brief nod, I pushed to my feet. I couldn't wait to get out of that chair and the awfully exposed position it put me in. Outside the short fence, I stopped to strap on all my blades again. The pile on the table grew smaller until only the ten throwing knives were left.

"You know," I said as I lined them up behind my shoulders, "if I really wanted to throw a knife at you, I could do it from across the room."

A sharp thud rang out and made me jerk in surprise. Glancing down, I saw a short knife protrude from the wooden fence. It was located roughly a finger's length from my left kneecap.

The Master Assassin put his hand back on the table and offered me a quick rise and fall of his eyebrows as an amused come-try-it look settled on his face. "Bet you could."

Throwing a knife back at him would be a bad idea. It would be an extremely bad idea. But man, I wanted to. I really, really wanted to. With great effort, I pushed the urge down and instead executed a theatrical bow.

"A pleasure doing business." Turning around, I began striding towards the door. "I'll be in touch about that favor," I called over my shoulder loudly enough for the whole room to overhear.

I may not have been able to throw a knife at him but I wanted his guild members to know that their leader owed me a favor. That small victory saved me from feeling completely outmaneuvered after this power showdown.

The tavern fell silent as I moved through the tables again. I could feel their eyes burning holes in my back but thanks to my rather impressive self-control, I managed to reach the front door without turning to look behind.

As the cool evening air enveloped me outside, I let out a small chuckle. Before leaving the Mad Archer, Liam had told me to be careful. I was pretty sure that the stunt I'd just pulled was the exact definition of *not* being careful. Oh well. You've got to risk a lot to win a lot. And now the Master of the Assassins' Guild owed me a favor. That was one dangerous thing down. Next up was breaking into the royal palace to spy on a meeting of the Council of Lords. I grinned as I took off towards the Silver Keep. This should be fun.

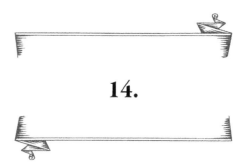

14.

I lobbed a pebble through the narrow opening in the doors. It hit the floor on the other side of the room with a slight clatter. When the occupants of the room turned as one to look for the source of the sound, I slipped in through the double doors and dove behind the nearest couch.

"Huh. Strange," a man's voice commented.

"Yes, yes, very strange," an annoyed voice said. "Now, Lord Fahr, will you answer my question? What are we doing here so early?"

Moving as silently as I could, I crept to the edge of the pink sofa and peeked out. The owner of the annoyed voice, a thin man in immaculate clothes, tapped his foot against the marble floor. Three more men, all equally impatient-looking, clustered behind him. I recognized all five men in the room because, as members of the Council of Lords, they belonged to the elite of Keutunan's nobility.

The man in front of them ran his hands through his well-oiled blond hair and broke into smile. "I have noticed that we are of similar opinion concerning–"

"Careful what you speak aloud, Lord Fahr," the thin man interrupted with a nervous glance at the door.

"Of course," the blond lord said with a slow nod. "Let's just say that we're of similar minds, then. I have asked the four of you here today because there is an opportunity for men like us." He started digging around in his satchel. After a brief search he pulled out four small pouches and dropped them into the hands of the others.

The thin man pulled at the strings of the velvet bag and peered inside. His eyebrows shot up. "And what would be required of us in exchange?"

"Nothing yet, Lord Feger. But when the time comes, you might be asked to sign a document or two, or open a door..." Lord Fahr showed off his brilliant white teeth again. "Or you might simply be asked to do nothing."

"I see," Lord Feger said and straightened his already spotless clothes. The three lords behind him glanced at each other. "And the rest of the Council?"

"Don't need to be troubled with this. After all, their minds are not as developed as ours." Lord Fahr met the eyes of each man. "We don't need an answer tonight. Just, consider it and let me know what you decide."

The four nervous lords slipped the soft pouches into their clothes and nodded. Lord Fahr nodded back just as soft footfalls sounded in the corridor outside. All five members of this rather curious exchange broke from the group and scattered across the room. When the double doors were finally pulled open, the suspicious group was trying its best to look busy.

"You're here early," Lord Raymond stated and swept his gaze across the room.

"Better early than late, wouldn't you say, Lord Raymond?" the man with the brilliant smile said.

Lord Raymond stroked his moustache. "I suppose."

I drew back behind the sofa. This had been a rather odd meeting. These lords were obviously up to something but it was impossible to know on whose behalf they schemed. It wouldn't surprise me if Shade was somehow involved in this. He was always manipulating people into doing things for him and I never really could tell what his end game was. While I pondered what had transpired in this antechamber, six more members of the Council of Lords arrived and took up positions throughout the room. I had to readjust my eavesdropping spot several times to avoid detection.

"Gentlemen, you are all here," an authoritative voice announced by the entrance. "Excellent. Shall we?"

King Edward strode across the room. The twelve council members quickly fell in behind him as they moved towards the other set of doors at the back. I stayed hidden behind the mountain of pink cushions until the last man had disappeared through the doors and pulled them closed behind his back. After waiting for the scraping of chairs to quiet down on the other side, I tiptoed across the room. With my ear pressed to the crack in the door, I settled in to listen.

"–all seated, let's begin," the king's voice said. "How goes the building, Lord Renfred?"

"Very well, Your Majesty," Lord Renfred answered. "The Pernulans have been very helpful and our builders are skilled. They only need to be shown once what to do and then they can replicate it. As long as they get a steady stream of supplies, the Builders' Guild estimates that they can have a tall ship ready by the end of summer."

By the end of summer? Excitement sparkled through my chest at the thought of taking a trip across the sea and back as early as this year. I pressed my ear harder against the door.

"Excellent. What about the scribes, Lord Raymond?" King Edward continued.

"The Scribes' Guild is making progress as well, Your Majesty. They are copying the designs that the Pernulans have provided and since they are now living together in the same building they are also learning Pernish. If the Pernulans continue to be as generous as they have been up until now, then our scribes should learn to understand and speak their language in no time."

"Good, good."

Silence fell in the chamber on the other side of the doors. I shifted position to prevent my muscles from growing stiff.

"Your Majesty?" a quiet voice asked inside the council chamber. I couldn't tell for certain if the voice belonged to one of the men who had received one of those velvet pouches before the meeting.

"Yes?"

"About this war on the continent, some of us are concerned..."

Someone coughed noisily inside the room. There was a slight pause.

"About what?" King Edward said when the previous speaker didn't resume his comment. "Speak your mind."

"Well," the quiet voice hesitated before continuing, "there are some of us who are... concerned that we are making a mistake getting involved with these Pernulans."

"Why is that?"

"They appear out of nowhere and ask us to choose a side in a war we know nothing about. How did they even find us? And why now?"

"How and why they found us is irrelevant," the king announced with force. "The important part is that they are here now. Do you doubt their intentions? Have they done anything to suggest that they cannot be trusted?"

There was a moment's pause. A chair creaked on the other side of the doors. "No, Your Majesty," the quiet voice said at last. "But is it really too late to ask them to leave? We fear that Keutunan would not survive getting caught in a war."

"Ask them to leave!" The king's voice was accompanied by the sound of a fist hitting a wooden table. "Why would we ask them to leave? Their presence here has sped up Keutunan's technological advancement by decades! Promising an alliance for a war that is taking place on *another continent*, and that may not even happen at all, is a small price to pay in the great scheme of things."

"Of course, Your Majesty. You know best."

The young king was right. The arrival of the Pernulans had been a blessing as far as technological development was concerned. However, I understood the man with the quiet voice too. Being dragged into someone else's war could easily be catastrophic for Keutunan. Maybe these voices of dissent were what the blond man had been trying to prevent? Those velvet bags might've been bribes to keep voices opposing the alliance with the Pernulans quiet. Or the exact opposite. They might have been an incentive to stir up trouble concerning this alliance. My mind kept wandering as the king and his Council of Lords moved on to other topics. Grain reports, a shortage of perch, and overpopulation in certain areas of town were less interesting so I only half-listened to those reports.

"Gentlemen," King Edward's voice rang out and broke my churning thoughts, "let us end today's meeting here."

Shit. I scrambled away from the door and dove behind my pink, fluffy cover again. The scraping of chairs was soon followed by creaking wood as someone pushed the council chamber doors open. Scattered conversations rose and fell as the king and the twelve members of the Council of Lords filed out and disappeared down the corridor. Behind the couch in the antechamber, only a disappointed thief remained. I hadn't found out anything useful about who might be targeting me. All they had talked about was matters of state and none of that seemed connected to my current precarious situation. Damn. Well, it had been worth a shot. After checking for stragglers, I popped up from my hiding place and snuck out the door.

Marking this down as a bust, I decided to head straight to my exit point. While weaving through the residential part of the Silver Keep, my ears pricked up the sound of a familiar voice. Me being, well, me, I couldn't help myself. I snuck up to the door and settled in to, for the second time tonight, eavesdrop on a conversation that was not meant for my ears.

"–what to do," King Edward said. "I feel like something's wrong, but I don't know what."

Only a woman's soft singing drifted out from the room.

The young king heaved an audible sigh. "I can't help but think that I should've listened to you and never gone down there. If this turns out badly, it'll be all my fault."

"The vault!" a woman's voice exclaimed. "No, no, don't go into the vault!"

"It's already too late, Mom," Edward said. He sounded sad. "I've already done it. You know that, remember?"

"No, no," the king's mother, Charlotte, said. "They always said, don't go into the vault. It will only call forth death and destruction! Don't go in!"

King Edward let out another miserable sigh. "Okay, Mom, I won't. I promise. Let me go get your medicine."

I detached myself from the door and sprinted down the hall. Just as I rounded the corner, the wooden door I'd listened behind creaked open.

"This has to work," King Edward said as he emerged from the room and started down the hallway in the opposite direction. "Please gods, this has to work."

Curious. I wondered what was inside that vault. Queen Mother Charlotte had acted as if the end of the world waited instead. However, everyone knew that she was a few bristles short of a broom. Apparently she'd lost her marbles when her eldest son had been kidnapped and his body had been returned burnt to a crisp. I suspect anyone would. Looking at the dead body of your child must be horrible in itself and seeing it burnt beyond recognition would make most parents go insane. Regardless, it sounded like King Edward had already gone inside and done whatever it was that his mother feared. Interesting.

I filed that piece of news in the scheming part of my brain and started out again. The night was still young and I had another place I needed to hit before the sun rose on the horizon. As I darted across the moonlit palace grounds, I prayed to Nemanan that my next stop would shed some light on who was targeting me. I really needed answers.

15.

The cool night air refreshed my lungs as I walked across the Marble Ring. Since my destination was located in the Merchants' Quarter, I didn't feel the need to use the Thieves' Highway. At this time of night, these parts of town were mostly deserted so the risk of running into lords and ladies wandering the darkness was slight.

"If I had known that Lord Raymond had a sister who was this beautiful, I would have asked him to introduce me long ago," a man's smooth voice said.

And I'd jinxed it. Why did I always have to jinx things? I jumped the nearest marble fence and landed in the flowerbed beneath. The damp soil under my cheek smelled of earth and grass.

"Oh, I bet you say that to all the ladies," a woman's voice said.

"Of course not, my dear," the man with the smooth voice replied. "There is only you."

The lady giggled. It came from right above me. "Tell me about the women in your country," she said.

"There are many women in my country," the man said. The sound had moved from right on the other side of the fence to a short distance further down. "But none of them are as beautiful and elegant as you."

Rippling laughter drifted from down the street. "Oh you're so sweet!"

Really? Beautiful and elegant were the compliments she desired most? I snickered down there in the dirt of the previously manicured flowerbed. If someone had told me I was beautiful and elegant, I would've laughed too. Though not for the same reason as the lady in the bright dress rounding the corner at the far end of the street. I brushed the soil and blades of grass off my perfectly average-looking face. After doing the same with my clothes, I shook my head and started down the street again. Some women could be so weird.

Once I reached Dead Men's Square at the edge of the Marble Ring and the Merchants' Quarter, I regretting not having used the Thieves' Highway. This place always gave me the creeps.

The ominously named square housed the main portion of Keutunan's holding cells, as well as the Hang Master's residence. But worst of all were the large, wooden structures in the middle of the four-sided space. The gallows. This was the part of town where people came to die. Or rather, to be killed. Ice cold shivers spidered up my spine.

I crept forward along the edge of the square, as close to the Hang Master's residence as I could get. Hugging the walls of the long building made me feel safer than walking across the open plaza even though I had to duck under each window.

Light spilled out from an opening ahead. I slowed down but kept moving forward until I reached one of the massive pillars on either side of the building's front door. Pressing my back against the cool stone, I strained my ears to make out any sound. Whispered voices drifted to my hiding place.

"No trial is necessary. No one needs to know."

"Hmm."

I peeked out from behind the pillar. Two men were standing in the light spilling out from the door. The first one I recognized instantly. There was probably not an underworlder in the city who wouldn't have known that face, for it haunted all our nightmares. The Hang Master. He was standing in the doorway with his arms crossed over his chest, facing another man who had his back to me. Since his face was turned away from me, I couldn't make out who it was.

"After the capture, don't send any reports," the unidentified man continued. "We'll handle everything. You just prepare the hanging."

The Hang Master looked skeptical at first but then nodded. His visitor brought a closed fist forward. After the executioner had put his palm under it, the mysterious man opened his hand and let a handful of objects rain down. The round balls caught the light as they fell. Pearls.

I drew back against the stone column as the unknown man started to turn around. His footsteps produced soft thuds as they retreated into Dead Men's Square. The door to the Hang Master's residence slammed shut. I stayed behind the pillar, drawing shallow breaths.

My head was spinning. I had overheard so many conversations tonight and I knew that they were all important but I didn't know why. A yarn of linked threads danced at the edge of my mind. I had a feeling that everything I'd heard this night was somehow connected but I couldn't yet untangle the web and put them all together in the right order.

For now, I just filed all the information I'd received in the scheming part of my brain. Staying too long in Dead Men's Square would only summon evil forces. It was time to move.

AFTER MY UNEXPECTED encounter in the place where people go to die, I'd wasted no time getting to my destination. Rowdy laughter escaped as I opened the door to a brightly lit tavern. It was by no means an Underworld pub but the owners weren't exactly strangers to shady people either. That meant news from both worlds usually passed through here.

"John," I called once I got to the bar.

Well-dressed patrons at the tables next to me studied my assortment of knives with wary eyes.

The tavern keeper lumbered over and then stopped on the other side of the counter. He towered over me by at least a head and a half. "The Oncoming Storm," he grumbled. "Whatcha doin' here?"

"I want information," I said and dropped three silver coins on the wooden tabletop. After casting a brief glance over my shoulder, I slid them over to the man in front of me. A group of Pernulans eyed me curiously on the other side of the bar.

A meaty hand appeared on the counter and collected the coins. "'Bout what?"

"There was a shooting down by the docks some weeks ago. Couple of explosions too. You know anything about that?"

John ran a hand over his graying beard. "Yeah. Heard someone paid some shifty soldiers to shoot up the harbor." He fixed me with a perceptive stare. "Heard they turned up dead. Don't know nothing 'bout the explosives, though."

"Hmm," I said. "What about these soldiers? What do you mean, are they Silver Cloaks?"

"Nah, more soldiers than guards. Heard someone's been recruiting, getting soldiers to leave the king's forces and come join some private army." John gave me a broad shrug. "Don't know who, though."

I drummed my fingers on the counter. That could be problematic. People collecting disloyal soldiers and creating their own army sounded like it could be the beginning of a war. Whether that war was directed at me or not was still unclear. A jolt shook me from my musings.

"Sorry," said a Pernulan who had accidentally bumped my shoulder, and held up his hands.

I shot him a venomous stare in reply. He backed off and disappeared through the front door. The graying barkeep was still studying me.

"Do you know why someone's amassing troops?" I asked.

John was silent for a moment. I could almost see the wheels turning behind his eyes. "Nah," he said at last. "But when there's change, people get spooked. They want safety. I'd feel safe with an army at my back."

He had a point. There had been a lot of change for the people of Keutunan, and in a rather short time span. First King Adrian had died. Well, not *died* as much as been assassinated. By my friends. And me. People didn't really know that, though. They thought he'd died from an animal attack while in the woods. But anyway, there had been a change in leadership and that always came with a transition period. Then the good people of

Keutunan had also found out that elves exist and that we're now allies with them. And as if that wasn't enough, a brand new civilization had sailed right into our harbor.

Looking at it that way, I could actually understand why people would feel the need to stock up on weapons and men to wield them. I didn't mind. As long as they didn't point them in my direction, that is.

"Thanks," I said to John and slid another two pieces of silver across the counter.

He nodded and scooped them up as I turned to leave. I needed to head back to the guild and sleep on this. There was just too much information swirling around in my brain for me to make any sense of it. And everything always felt better after a good sleep.

After shutting the door to the Black Sheep tavern behind me, I started out towards the Thieves' Guild in a brisk pace. I only made it a dozen paces or so up the street before something caused the hair on the back of my neck to stand up. Not hesitating a second, I threw myself behind the nearest fence where the cluttered back porch of a cheese vendor's shop greeted me.

A crossbow bolt buried itself in the wooden fence. I threw a quick glance around the side and almost took a bolt through the eye for my trouble. That glimpse had helped, though. It had revealed three men standing on the other side of the barricade. Two with crossbows, one with swords. Another shot connected with the wood, making the planks vibrate.

Again? Seriously? How many times had I been ambushed by armed men these last few weeks? Rage was building inside me like an oncoming thunderstorm. I'd had enough of people attacking me every single time I set one foot outside the door. Why couldn't people just leave me alone? The darkness was ripping at my soul, begging me to let it out. Two more bolts struck the fence.

"Would you give it a rest with the fucking shooting and stabbing!" I bellowed across the street. "Can't a girl just enjoy a nice nighttime walk without people trying to kill her every bloody time!"

The sound of wood hitting stone followed by steel against scabbards echoed as the men dropped the crossbows and got ready for a sword fight. Snickering drifted through the fence. "Save your childish tantrums. It's time die now."

That was it. I gave in to the darkness. It roared up from the blackest pits of my soul and set my every nerve on fire. A thundering storm bled from my eyes as I let the black fog take over.

Muted screams filled my ears as I flew at my attackers. Steel glinted in the moonlight. Blades clashed and knives slashed as a fight for survival turned into a massacre. It was over almost before it had begun.

My chest heaved. The trance lifted and the storm receded from my eyes. I let the darkness slide back into my soul while I studied the scene around me. Three bodies lay sprawled across the street. Blood painted the stones red. I looked down at my body. The same red color covered my clothes and my hands. Heaving a deep sigh, I bent down to find a dry spot on the closest man's pants.

After wiping my hunting knives clean, I returned them to the small of my back. I didn't even remember pulling them out. A metallic smell slowly filled the area.

I shook my head. Weariness seeped into my bones. I wasn't sure how much more of this I could take. Constantly being under attack was exhausting, and letting the darkness out in full force always left me drained. After a quick scan of the area, I started out towards the guild again. I had to find out who was doing this.

"YOU'RE COVERED IN BLOOD. Again. Why are you covered in blood again?"

I had bumped into Liam on my way down the stairs. He'd also been returning from whatever nighttime activities he'd been up to since we last saw each other.

"It's not mine," I replied before furrowing my brows. "I think."

Liam rolled his eyes at me. "Why do I get the feeling that this is a conversation better suited for breakfast tomorrow?"

I gave him a tired smile. "Sure is."

He took a step towards me but then seemed to change his mind. Crinkling his nose, he pointed a finger at me, tracing circles in the air. "You're not getting a hug this time because blood doesn't wash off as easily as salt water."

The sheer absurdity of it all made me burst out laughing. Liam shook his head at me while a smile tugged at his lips.

"What would I ever do without you?" I said after I'd finished chuckling.

"I know, right?"

I gave him a playful shove to the back of the head before I started down the stairs again. "See you for breakfast!"

"See you!" he called after me.

Yeah, what would I ever do without him? I didn't even want to consider something as awful as that. As I rounded the last corner, I could feel my bed beckoning me. Sleep sounded good right now. Discussing tonight's events with Liam sounded even better. But first, I had to visit the land of dreams.

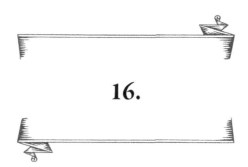

16.

"So, what do you think?" I asked and leaned forward on the table.

Liam stared at me with disbelief coloring his eyes. "About which part? Gods, woman, you did a month's worth of intel gathering in one night. Give me a minute to process."

For a moment, I simply watched my best friend as he tried to make sense of everything I'd just told him. The information had tumbled out of my mouth like a waterfall so he hadn't had a chance to ask questions after each recounted event. After a while, I left his mind to churn in peace and instead studied the scene around us.

Barrel was busy down by the bar, Hilda popped in and out of the kitchen, and the tavern's patrons ate and drank with content looks on their faces. Mirthful chatter drifted from every corner. The group of Pernulans who rented a room upstairs had left shortly after we arrived, so everyone here right now was a guild member. I smiled. Home.

"Okay, so here's what I'm thinking," Liam said at last. "The king did something in that vault that did something else–"

"Wow, don't do my head in with all these specifics," I interrupted with a mischievous smile.

Liam leveled an exasperated stare at me. "Someday all that sarcasm is going to get you in a lot of trouble."

I didn't feel the need to point out that it already had. Multiple times. Instead, I settled for a snort and a nod to concede that he was right.

"As I was saying," Liam began anew, "I'm thinking that King Edward did something risky in that vault and that the result of whatever it was is still not clear. And that thing may or may not have to do with the Pernulans in some way. The Council of Lords is probably divided in what they think about it so the king," he paused and scrunched up his face before nodding to himself, "the king, *or* Shade, is bribing some of them to back him up."

I tapped a finger on the sturdy wooden tabletop. "That... does sound reasonable. But Black Sheep John said someone's raising a private army. How does that fit in?"

Rowdy laughter rang out at the table beside us. A group of men slapped their friend's back and gave him encouraging nods.

"Storm?" Liam said, avoiding my question, and instead started tracing the rim of his mug. "How much do you trust Shade?"

"How much do I trust him?" I barked a laugh. "About as much as I'd trust a wolf in the forest."

"Okay, fair enough. Not trust then, but how sure are you that he's really on King Edward's side?"

My eyebrows shot up. I hadn't considered that. Whenever we'd talked about Edward, or he'd been in the room with us, Shade had always seemed protective of him. And loyal. But then again, he'd seemed loyal to the late King Adrian as well. All the way up until he'd slit his throat, that is. He was such a hard person to read.

"Sixty-five... and a half?" I said.

"Sixty-five percent?" Liam said. "Alright, that's pretty certain at least. It's just that he double-crossed the last king, so what's to stop him from doing that again if he thinks King Edward is doing stuff that's bad for the city?"

A valid point indeed. I took a sip of water from my mug. "I hear you. But what does that have to do with the private army? He's already got an entire guild of assassins at his disposal."

"I know, but hear me out," Liam said and gestured for me to slow down. "Shade thinks King Edward is taking the city in the wrong direction, maybe by allying with the Pernulans or maybe because of whatever happened in that vault, either way, he thinks Edward's going to mess up the city. So he bribes the Council of Lords to help him overthrow the king and he can't do it with just his assassins, he needs an army too, so he raises an army too!" he finished breathlessly and spread his hands with a triumphant expression on his face.

The table next to us pushed to their feet and started shuffling towards the door while I regarded my friend from under knit brows.

"Okay, say you're right, how's that connected to the shooting by the docks? And all the other attacks?" I pressed, firing off rapid questions. "Why would Shade want to kill me? And besides, he wouldn't need turned soldiers to kill me, he could just have me assassinated whenever he wanted."

I felt sick to my stomach voicing that last part out loud, but it was true. If he really wanted to, I had no doubt that the master of the death guild could have me killed without starting a guild war. Before the feeling of total helplessness could swallow me in its gaping jaws, I pushed the thought out of my mind.

"So, how does that fit in?" I asked my friend instead.

Liam put a hand to his forehead and then blew out a noisy breath. "I don't know! I don't know. That's the best I've got. You try thinking of something better."

Seeing as I didn't actually have anything better to offer, I just shrugged. Liam went back to tracing the rim of his mug. "What are you going to do now?" he asked.

"I have to figure out who's raising that army. Everything else is just politics that may or may not concern me, but whoever's behind that army is the one who's out to get me. I've got to focus on that." I looked out the window. The sun was setting, bathing the city in shades of red. "So, I'll probably be gone all night. Maybe tomorrow too."

"I get it."

I dropped my head into my hands and raked them through my hair. "I've gotta figure this out, Liam." After a deep sigh, I looked up again. "I have to."

"I know." He gave my arm a short squeeze. "You will."

After waving goodbye to Barrel and Hilda, we stepped out into the streets and faced the sunset.

"There's no point in me telling you to be careful, is there?" Liam said.

I gave him a light chuckle in reply.

"Yeah, didn't think so," he commented. "Just don't die, alright?"

"I have no plans on dying yet. See you sometime tomorrow, or at least, the day after that!" I called as I turned and trotted up the street.

"Remember, no dying!"

I just waved the back of my hand at him to signal that I'd heard him but after a few paces I felt bad and stopped to turn around. Liam was already gone. Staring back down the empty street, I shook my head. Yeah, thanks, Liam, I'd try to remember that.

A soft wind caressed my face while I remained rooted in the middle of the road. I wasn't sure where to go next. Maybe if I went snooping around the barracks? The soldiers might be discussing this outside recruitment with each other. Yeah. That was a sound plan. I started out again and took a right at the nearest side street.

A wall of steel met me. I stumbled back and whirled around to escape. The shrill sound of a whistle being blown followed me. Armed men materialized at an alarming rate on the opposite side too, and when I whipped my head from side to side, I saw them coming out of cross streets both ahead and behind me on the main street as well. The first wall of steel rushed me. *Shit*.

My escape route was blocked off in every direction but there was a bit more space on the main road than the side ones so I darted back towards it. The soldiers pouring out ahead were the ones furthest away so I ran in that direction, intending to get up on the roof before they could reach me. Blood pounded in my ears. I forced the dreadful panic away. *There*. I aimed for a broken crate and used it as a springboard to launch myself into the air. Clanking weapons closed in on me from every direction. My fingers found the edge of a windowpane and I heaved myself up.

Strong hands clamped around my ankle. I strained against the weight but in one forceful motion, they yanked me down. Defenseless against the sudden pull, I lost my grip on the window and fell headlong down the side of the building. Pain shot up my side as I landed on the broken crate and tumbled to the street. Heavy boots surrounded me like a dense forest. I whipped out my hunting knives and slashed at their ankle tendons. Agony-filled cries rang out as some of the soldiers dropped down beside me. I used the commotion to get to my feet.

A swarm of armed men crowded in around me with raised swords. This wouldn't end well. While crouching down in an attack position, I analyzed the situation and tried calling up the darkness. It didn't respond. Why hadn't it responded?

A fist took me in the side. I stumbled sideways and drew a desperate breath to refill my lungs but didn't quite manage before I had to duck a heavy wooden club. There was not a chance in hell that I'd manage to win a fight against all of these people. My best bet was to throw enough knives at them to create an opening through which to escape. Dodging a sword swung at my stomach, I stabbed the hunting knives back in their holsters and got ready to draw the ones perched above my shoulders.

I only managed to raise one hand before someone landed a kick to my lower back. Caught off guard, I toppled forward. A gloved fist slammed into my chin and sent me flying towards the street. Since I didn't have enough time to break the fall, my body crashed down hard on the stones. For a moment, I just lay there on my stomach, trying to gather my scattered wits again.

Steel against stone cut through the ringing in my ears as someone drove a sword into the street. The blade vibrated a finger's breadth from my neck. A second later, another sword rushed down on the other side. The two blades formed a cross over my neck, pinning my head to the ground.

"Cuff her," someone said.

They sounded very far away but I knew they were standing right above me. My ears continued to ring. Rough hands grabbed my arms and bent them behind my back but with my neck trapped between the two blades, there wasn't much I could do about it. Cold metal enveloped my wrists as the manacles slammed shut. This was bad.

The owners of the swords withdrew them right before I was hauled to my feet. In a desperate attempt to do something, anything, I threw my head forward and right into the nose of the man standing in front of me. It connected with a sickening crack. He let out a howl. Once I saw his eyes fill with pure rage, I immediately regretted my futile escape attempt. The furious soldier drove his hand straight into my solar plexus. At once, my breathing stopped working and waves of pain rolled over my body. His meaty fist drawing back was the last thing I saw before I disappeared into oblivion.

17.

My feet dragged behind me on the cobblestones. At first, I just watched the street move underneath me without understanding what in Nemanan's name was going on but as I slowly regained consciousness, I felt the hands encircling my arms. I wasn't flying. Someone was dragging my limp body along the road.

Lifting my head for too long was painful but I managed a quick glance at the surrounding area. I knew I'd seen this square before but trying to make my mind work was like trying to jog in mud. Slow and slippery. For the time being, I couldn't do much except let myself be dragged along while I drifted in and out of consciousness.

Agitated cries and metallic clanking filled my ears. I shook my head. My senses were returning to normal. When I lifted my gaze, I noticed that we were now indoors. Shock snapped my wits back in place. I finally realized where we were, and which square that had been. Dead Men's Square.

"No," I breathed. "No, no, no."

With panic-induced strength, I thrashed against the strong arms holding me. The men grunted as they adjusted their grip.

"In here," someone said behind me.

By digging my heels into the ground, I tried to stop our advance. It didn't work. I slipped forward on the damp stones as my captors hauled me to the open door of the nearest cell. Since the doorway was too narrow for three people to enter side by side, they simply heaved me through it. With my hands shackled behind my back, it was impossible to catch myself. I grunted as I landed hard on the floor but managed to struggle to my feet before the people who'd thrown me made it through the door.

They moved like soldiers but they weren't wearing the dark blue uniforms of the king's troops. A sword and a pistol hung at each man's hip. Their eyes took on a predatory glint as they looked me up and down. I backed up against the wall.

"Don't you dare touch me," I growled between clenched teeth.

A third man walked through the door. Just seeing his face made my chest constrict.

"Search her," the Hang Master said.

"No," I said and backed towards the corner. "I swear, if you put your hands on me..."

One of the rogue soldiers snickered. "You'll do what, exactly?"

He was right. They were about a head taller than me and twice as heavy. Even if they hadn't been, fighting with my hands behind my back would be impossible. If I only had a knife. A breath of clarity pushed to the front of my mind. I did. I did have a knife. Groping around behind my back, I found the handle of a hunting knife just as the men reached me. I whipped out the blade and twisted down and around, aiming to slice their hamstrings. The knife flew from my hand as the butt of a sword connected with my wrist. Metallic clanking filled the cell. Still on my knees, I was defenseless against the kick between my shoulder blades and once again found myself face down on the damp stones. A heavy boot pressed down on my neck.

"Try that again and I'll cut off a finger," one of the soldiers warned.

I swallowed against the weight. Shit. Before I could think of something smart to say, the boot disappeared. I only had time to feel the briefest moment of relief before I was hauled up and slammed face first into the wall. Pain shot up my cheek. While one of them kept a tight grip on the back of my neck, the other got busy stripping me of all my knives.

When he was done with the back of my body, his friend flipped me around and clamped a hand around my throat. He leered at me as he pressed me into the wall. I drew short, ragged breaths as I was stripped of my remaining blades and lockpicks. While he performed his intimate search, I tried to detach myself from my body as much as possible.

"Eighteen, huh?" the Hang Master said and cradled the box of knives the soldier had handed him. "These'll be a nice addition to my collection."

My heart sank. I had only brought eighteen knives this time so that meant they'd found them all.

"String her up," the master of the executioners said and jerked his head towards the middle of the room.

It was only then that I noticed the chains hanging from the sides of the cell. Panic bloomed in my chest. The soldier in front of me grinned and yanked me by my throat towards the center of the small room. Once we'd reached it, his partner unlocked the manacles on my wrists. Now that my hands were free, I desperately wanted to fight him, to fight them all, but the grip on my windpipe tightened until I was left struggling to breathe. My hands pulled uselessly on his fingers.

While the malicious solider in front of me had me immobile, the other one pried my hands from the fist that kept me from breathing and fastened metal shackles around my wrists. After one last squeeze, the first man grinned and released my throat.

I collapsed to my knees, desperately trying to suck air into my lungs. Chains rattled beside me. The three men watched me wheeze on the ground for a moment before the Hang Master broke the silence.

"Up," he said.

The soldiers pulled on each chain and I was hauled to my feet again. They only stopped when my restraints were taut. My feet still touched the ground, but just barely. I closed my eyes. This wouldn't end well. With my arms pinned like this, there was no way I'd be able to reach any lockpicks the soldiers might've missed. Why had they even dragged me here in the first place? Why hadn't they just killed me in the street like they'd tried to do before?

Two fingers appeared under my chin, lifting up my head. I opened my eyes to see the Hang Master's thin face in front of me. "The Oncoming Storm," he said and then spat on the stones beside my feet. "Your sins have finally caught up with you. It's going to be a pleasure hanging you."

My whole soul screamed. I didn't want to die. And not like this. Especially not like this. Being hanged in front of a cheering crowd had to be one of the worst ways to go. Why couldn't they just have killed me in the street? Or shot me right now? An idea pushed through my panic. I could make them.

I spit back in the Hang Master's face. "My sins? Ha! I bet you've done worse things than I've even thought about, you sick psycho!" Black spots swam across my vision when he backhanded me across the mouth. I offered him an arrogant, blood-soaked grin. "That all you got? A ten-year-old hits harder than that." I lifted my legs to kick him in the groin but he jumped back just in time.

A heavy punch connected with my side. It felt like being hit by a bat and it took all my self-control to pretend otherwise. I turned to the soldier who'd struck me and gave him as haughty a smirk as I could manage through the pain. "Harder than that too."

He drew back his fist again.

"Stop!" the Hang Master blurted out. He studied me with narrowed eyes. "Dying in a fight is too good for you. You deserve the humiliation of being hanged. And besides, I've been paid good money to make sure this hanging happens tomorrow morning." He mouth drew into a broad grin. "No fuss. No trial. No escape." The executioner jerked his head. "Let's go."

All three men withdrew, locking the door behind them. So much for my plan. At least it explained why they hadn't killed me on the spot. It was no longer enough to simply kill me, someone wanted to humiliate me. Sudden realization flashed through my brain. The bribe, the one that the Hang Master had taken the other night, it had been for *my* hanging.

My heart thumped in my chest. This couldn't be happening. I pulled at the chains keeping my arms stretched to my sides. They refused to budge. My breathing came out in short bursts as my pulse raced. I'd magicked my way out of impossible situations before, but nothing like this. I couldn't reach any of my tools, a guard patrolled outside the door, and I'd told Liam I'd be gone a while so no help was coming. I swallowed down the lump in my throat. It couldn't end like this. I had so much I still wanted to do. And what would happen to Liam if I died? Who would protect him?

I sent prayers to Nemanan, Cadentia, and even to Ghabhalnaz, the God of Death himself, asking them for help. No rescue came. Hot tears rolled down my cheeks but the moon outside paid no mind to my sadness. It only continued to illuminate the square outside. Dead Men's Square. Where people go to die. Where *I* would go to die.

18.

When morning came, the pain in my heart had subsided to a dull ache. All the fight had bled from me like the tears that had leaked from my eyes all night, so when the red sun rose, only bitter resignation remained. I didn't even try to fight the guards when they loosened the chains. As my passive eyes glided over their faces, I noticed that they weren't the same ones who'd brought me in. These were guards who belonged to the prison. Cold metal wrapped around my wrists once again as another pair of manacles was pushed shut.

"Don't try anything," the dark-haired one muttered and grabbed a hold of my upper arm.

I didn't bother responding. There was nothing to say. He led me through the narrow door of my cell, another guard following behind with a pistol pressed to my spine, and two more joining outside the bars. Excited murmuring rose from the crowd as we emerged into the brisk morning air. People pointed and whispered while I was escorted towards the large wooden structures in the middle of the square. The crowd parted before us. I watched their faces with unseeing eyes because I couldn't bring myself to care about anything anymore.

At least I'd finally get some rest. After today, I wouldn't have to worry about people trying to kill me every time I walked out the door. And I'd get to see Rain again. I smiled before a pang of sadness hit my chest. No, I wouldn't get to see Rain again. Because wherever she was, that wasn't where I'd be heading. My place in hell had been reserved from the day I let the darkness in. Shame. It would've been nice to see her. One last time.

Raising my head, I saw the gallows loom up in front of me. The detached melancholy snapped out of my head and my self-preservation screamed. I didn't want to die! With muscles on fire with renewed energy, I yanked my arm from the guard's grip. Surprise registered on his face as I slipped from his hand and dashed for the cover of the crowd. A shout rose and from the corner of my eye, I could see the guard in front of me twist around but I didn't stop. If I could just make it away from my escort, I'd be able to disappear in the throng.

The back of a closed fist connected with my stomach as the guard in front threw out his arm. I dropped like a stone. My whole chest hurt; it felt as though I'd run straight into an iron bar. Before I'd even had time to collect my wits and find my missing breath, they hauled me up and continued dragging me towards the podium. I tried to find purchase with my feet to stop their advance but it was futile. When we arrived at the stairs, they simply hoisted me higher and carried me up, feet dangling in the air. My heart beat so fast I was afraid it would rip from my chest. I didn't want to die. I didn't want to.

"Please," I whispered when they dumped me on the wooden dais. I hated how pitiful it sounded but I couldn't help it. "Please, I don't want to die."

The muscles in their jaws tightened but they said nothing as they led me to the trapdoor in the middle of the platform. My breathing came in fits and starts. This couldn't be happening. I had so many years ahead of me. Years filled with potential. And it would all end here. Today. My knees trembled. I whipped my head from side to side, hoping against hope that an escape would materialize out of the morning air. Something did materialize but it wasn't a way out. It was my death sentence. The Hang Master strode onto the podium.

"Good people of Keutunan!" he called out. "Lords and ladies and honest workers. Today we will bring justice to the many victims of this most awful criminal."

Who was he calling awful? His job was to kill people who only tried to make a living in a world that shunned them – and he called me horrible? I shook my head. It sure was easy to be righteous when you were born under the right circumstances.

"The Oncoming Storm," the Hang Master finished and swept a hand towards me. A buzz went through the crowd at the mention of my name. "She will die today and you will go home and feel safer than ever."

Eager faces looked up at me from the mass of people below. I wanted to scream at them. A lightning bolt struck. Why didn't I? If this was to be my end, I might as well make it an end worthy of remembrance.

"You are cursed!" I bellowed across the square. "From now until the end of your days, you will feel nothing but misery and despair. Your crops will rot, your cattle will fall sick, your parents will waste away, and your children will die."

The eagerness drained from their faces and was replaced by a mix of emotions. Confusion, uncertainty, and fear. Mostly fear. A grin tinted with madness flashed across my teeth.

"I call upon the darkness–" I continued.

"Shut her up!" the Hang Master screamed, interrupting my declaration.

"–and all the forces of evil in this world. You will never know peace and happiness. I will return from the deepest pits of hell and haunt you every–"

A strong hand clamped over my mouth. I tried to shake it off but the iron grip stayed firmly in place until another guard shoved a piece of cloth between my jaws. He yanked the knot tight behind my head. I tried to continue my stream of threats but only muffled grunts escaped.

"Kill her!" a man shouted from the audience.

"No, don't kill her! She'll unleash hell on us all!" someone else cried.

Ha! Served them right. Once I got down to hell, I'd try to make a deal with Ghabhalnaz to make good on my promises. A guard pushed the noose down around my neck. Yeah. I'd do everything in my power to come back and make their lives a living hell. With malice flashing in my eyes, I swept my gaze over the crowd. Lord Raymond's face stared up at me. Why in Nemanan's name was he there to watch my hanging?

"Good people!" the Hang Master called, breaking my fractured thoughts. "You have nothing to fear. This vile creature will soon be dead."

He moved towards the lever that operated the trap door. As my executioner put his hand on the wooden stick, I sent a prayer to Nemanan, thanking him for the exciting life I'd had and asking him for a clean death.

"Justice will be done," the Hang Master said with finality.

I took a deep breath through my nose. And then everything happened all at once.

A pistol was fired somewhere to my right. Lord Raymond jerked back in surprise and threw a quick look over his shoulder. He sprinted away while people around him cried out and whipped towards the sound, looking for the source.

Shot after shot rang out from every corner. Dark figures flashed through the throng accompanied by more blasts. People screamed and ducked and tried to scramble away as bullets flew straight up in the sky. I only had time to stare for a second at the chaos unfolding in front of me before I heard something heavy click. My stomach lurched as the trapdoor disappeared from underneath my feet and I fell towards the ground. This was it. I wanted to scream for all the years yet unlived. A short rope would take all that away right now and there was nothing I could do about it.

Metal glinted before me as a knife sailed towards my face and passed just over my head. I would soon be out of rope. But the cord never snapped taut. My body continued rushing towards the stones and I hit the ground hard. Victorious screaming from inside my heart about being alive drowned out my stunned brain's effort to make sense of it.

Soft hands released the knot and removed the cloth from my mouth before tipping me up on my knees. "You put on quite the show."

Twisting my head, I came face to face with a pair of black, glittering eyes. Shade. My mouth dropped open. And then I threw up. Repeatedly. I had meant to say something earnest, to express my profound gratitude, or to say anything, really. Anything other than the literal vomit that erupted from my mouth. But after coming that close to dying, I simply couldn't make my body obey me.

As I continued to empty the contents of my stomach on the gray stones, Shade picked the lock on my manacles. They fell from my wrists in a clatter of metal.

"Come on," he said and snatched at my shirt, "you don't have time to throw up right now."

He pulled me to my feet. All around us, people yelled and tried to escape the unknown shooters but between the mass of stampeding townsfolk, others were coming. Guards from the prison. The Master Assassin snapped his fingers in front of my face.

"Pull yourself together! I need you alert."

I wiped my mouth with the back of my hand and managed a nod.

"Follow me." He darted across the square.

Without a moment's hesitation, I followed. Adrenaline pumped through my veins, letting me dodge panicked citizens with ease. Someone shouted nearby and prison guards in their dark blue uniforms swarmed in around us. Shit.

Shade shoved a hand in his pocket. "Don't breathe it in." He threw a purple powder at the circle of guards around us.

A roar erupted as two men rushed forward. Shade ducked under the first man's arm and planted a boot in his side. The surprised guard toppled to the ground. While holding my breath, I sidestepped the second attacker and twirled around to kick him in hollow of the knee.

Air exploded out of my lungs as a helmet slammed into my stomach. I gasped as the owner of the helmeted head withdrew. A sandy substance lodged in my throat. The guard who'd rammed me wobbled to the side. Around us, the black-clad assassin dropped guard after guard. Or maybe they fell by themselves? They seemed unsteady on their feet. Now that I thought about it, I felt woozy as well. There was a strange prickling sensation in my limbs and the world around me swayed as I backed away from yet another falling guard. Black spots floated before my eyes.

"Fuck," I heard the Master Assassin grumble as I tipped to the side.

Gray stones sped towards my face. At least my mind was spared another memory of pain because before it made contact, I had already slipped into unconsciousness.

19.

"Told you not to breathe it in," a smug voice said to my left.

A soft pillow greeted my cheek as I turned my head. Shade studied me from a chair nearby. He had his feet slung up on the table and a stack of papers in his hand.

I managed a strained snort. "Right."

Wood creaked underneath me as I drew myself up against the headboard and scanned my surroundings. I was in a large room filled with things too expensive for me. The paintings had frames of silver and the bed I currently occupied was the softest one I'd ever slept in. This place screamed of the Silver Keep. I looked back at the assassin lounging by the desk and drew my knees up to my chest.

"Why?" I asked.

He tilted his head slightly to the right. "I said I'd help you out when you needed it. You needed it."

"Yeah, that I did," I said with a small sigh. "But this was a lot more than just passing on some information." I hesitated before continuing. "What do I have to do to square this debt?"

Shade crossed his ankles on the table and just continued looking at me with unreadable eyes.

A tired smile crossed my face. "Come on, you never do anything unless it serves your cause. Whatever that is," I added under my breath. "So, what do you want in exchange for my life?"

"Some help would be nice."

I nodded. "Anything you want."

The dark-eyed assassin arched an eyebrow at me while a smile tugged at the corner of his lips. "Anything?"

I blew out a noisy breath and rolled my eyes at him. "Within reason."

"The elves," he said. "We could really use the elves on this one. And they don't exactly trust me enough to let me just stroll into their town and sit down for a meeting. But you, you they trust." I opened my mouth to ask what he needed their help with but he held up his hand. "The king will explain." He jumped to his feet and started towards the door.

"Can I...?" I began and motioned at my battered and dirty body.

"Oh, right, yeah there's a basin and some pitchers of water through there." He pointed towards a doorway next to the bed. "Come find us when you're done. Down the stairs, third door on the right."

"Got it."

He started out and had almost made it out of the room when I spoke again.

"Shade," I said in a soft voice. He stopped with his hand on the door handle and looked over his shoulder. I held his gaze with steady eyes. "Thank you."

He cracked a lopsided smile and gave me a slow nod before slipping out the door.

I don't think I'd meant anything, ever, as much as I meant those two words. Obviously, I'd come close to dying before. Several times in the last few weeks, actually. But nothing like this. Dying at the end of rope and dying in a fight were two very different things. At least to me. When I die, I want it to be on my terms: free, out in the open, fighting back. Not shackled and gagged in front of a crowd. I shuddered. No. Something like this would never happen again. I'd make sure of it.

After sucking in a deep, bracing breath, I swung my legs over the side of the bed and stood up. Those pitchers of water sounded very inviting. I stripped out of my clothes and started wiping off the grime.

The cool water did more than just clean the literal dirt, it also washed away the tiredness. Energy bounced around inside me like lightning. I was alive. My body thrummed. All those years of potential were still there waiting for me to use them. Adventure, mystery, and excitement was still possible. And most importantly, I would get to see Liam again. I smiled. Yeah. I would get to see all the people I loved again.

Wet hair flowed through my fingers as I redid the braid. My clothes were in a much better state too. After washing the grime from my hair and body, I had wiped them down as much as possible. They weren't exactly pristine but I felt much better about putting them back on my now clean body. Of course, not everything was as easily washed off as the dirt. Bruises from my run-ins with fists, boots, knees, shackles, and stone streets covered my body. Worst was the handprint around my throat that turned darker with every passing hour. I studied my image in the mirror. Evidence of lost fights and sleepless nights stared back. And dark green eyes burning with life. My life. I smiled at the reflection. Now I only had to go downstairs and repay a certain Guild Master for that. As I strode towards the door, I realized that I was actually curious about what that scheming assassin had cooked up this time. Probably some kind of trouble. I grinned as I opened the door. Most definitely some kind of trouble.

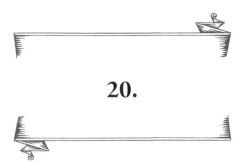

20.

"The Oncoming Storm," King Edward said as I walked in. "Glad to see you among the living."

"Me too. Your Majesty," I added after a brief pause.

The young king waved his hand in front of his face as if to tell me I could dispense with such formal titles here in this small dining room. It actually looked more like a dining room mixed with a kitchen and a library. I liked it. It had a homely feel to it. And it smelled of roast potatoes and steak.

"Please, join us," he said and motioned at the table at which he and Shade were seated.

The wooden tabletop was overlaid with pots and pans containing what I assumed to be King Edward's breakfast. When I lowered myself into one of the chairs, he got up and collected another plate and cup, as well as a pair of utensils, from a cupboard behind him.

After sitting down again, the black-haired king slid them towards me. "Please help yourself. There is more food here than I could eat in a day. And besides," he added with a smile, "I hear you parted with your previous meals down there in the square."

Shade chuckled and winked at me from across the table. My face flushed. Why did he have to tell him that? Bastard. It had been less than two hours since Shade had saved me from certain death and I already wanted to punch him in the face again. Guess some people just had that effect on others. I briefly wondered if I had that effect on other people as well. Maybe that was why so many of them were trying to kill me all the time. I gave myself a mental shrug. It certainly would explain a lot. With a slight shake of my head, I pushed my musings and previous embarrassment aside.

"Thank you," I said instead and started spooning food onto my plate. What? I'm not exactly someone who turns down free food. "So," I began and glanced at Shade before turning back to King Edward, "I hear you need help from the elves. What's that about?"

The king and the assassin exchanged looks, but then Shade shrugged as if to suggest that they might as well be honest. Edward nodded.

"What do you know about this situation with the Pernulans?" he asked.

"Honestly? Not much," I replied with a shrug. "I've been on bed rest trying not to die of some bullet and knife wounds most of the time they've been here. And when I wasn't stuck in that bloody room, I've basically just been busy dodging one attack after another."

King Edward studied me with an amused expression on his pale face. "People do try to kill you quite a lot, don't they?"

I chuckled and shook my head. "You have no idea. But yeah, anyway, so I don't know a lot about what's been going on with these Pernulans."

"And you haven't taken the time to get caught up on the situation?" Shade remarked and lifted an eyebrow at me as if that should've been my top priority.

"I am *under attack*!" I said and threw my arms up in frustration. "Someone is literally trying to kill me every time I set one foot out the door. So, no, I ain't got the time to get up to speed on politics."

"You should always know everything that's going on around you," the assassin said. "That way they can't blindside you. Or hang you."

I let out an indignant huff and stabbed a potato with my fork. King Edward stared up at the ceiling and heaved a deep sigh. "We're getting off topic..." he commented.

"Right, sorry," Shade said and leaned back in his chair again.

"This situation with the Pernulans," the king said. "It has become... complicated."

"In what way?" I asked between bites of steak.

"I'm not sure if you've noticed but they've brought a lot of pearls, and they use them as payment. Pearls are very valuable here, as you of all people no doubt know. That means it would be very easy for these Pernulans to, say, bribe people."

"Have they?"

King Edward paused for a moment, drumming his fingers on the table. It was Shade who continued.

"No," the Master of the Assassins' Guild said. "Not that we know. But let's just say there's a high risk of them doing it once they show their hand."

Staring into his intelligent eyes, I tried to read the mind behind them. "You don't trust them," I stated.

"Have you ever known me to trust anyone?"

I tipped my head from side to side. He did have a point. Running the death guild didn't exactly go well with being too trusting.

"So, why do you think they're really here?" I asked.

"Best case scenario," Shade began, "they're actually here for an alliance to help them stay out of a war. Worst case? They're here to start a war. You've seen the cannons on those ships, right? What do you think'll happen if they decide to point them at the city?"

Yeah. I had seen them. The sides of the ships were full of small hatches with cannons peeking out behind. If they fired them at us, large parts of Keutunan would soon lie in ruins.

"I see your point," I said before a sudden thought struck. "What about that Pernulan aboard the ship? He said he didn't want conflict, only peace and stability."

"Yeah, we've been considering that too," Shade said and looked to his king.

"It might mean that some of them want to bombard us," Edward said, "and others are trying to stop that from happening." He shrugged. "Or that conversation was about something else entirely. We don't know. And we need to find out."

I squinted at him. "How do the elves fit into this?"

"If the Pernulans do launch an attack, we need to know if the elves will fight beside us. With their archery skills, they would be invaluable in a long-range battle."

"I see. And you need me to go to Tkeideru and ask them." I studied their faces. "No, you need me to *persuade* them to help if the Pernulans attack Keutunan."

"That about sums it up," Shade said. "Do that and we're square."

"Besides," King Edward added, "it would benefit them too. If the Pernulans do attack, what's to stop them from turning on the

elves after they've defeated us? Both our civilizations would run
the risk of being conquered if we try to fight them separately. We
are much stronger together."

Tapping a finger to my cheek, I considered his words. I
would never try to make the elves do something they didn't want
to do; they were my friends and I didn't want them to get hurt.
But the king presented a convincing argument. If there was a
battle, we'd all stand a much better chance of winning if we
fought together.

"True," I said at last. "Alright, I'll talk to them."

The king and the assassin nodded in unison.

"There's just one thing," I began while tracing the rim of my
mug. "My knives."

All of my blades had been confiscated when I was arrested
and I felt their loss like the loss of a limb. It was embarrassing
to admit but an aching sadness seeped through my heart at the
thought of never seeing them again. Some of those knives had
been with me for so long that they felt like a part of me.
Ridiculous, I know. But it was true.

"The Hang Master has them," King Edward said. "Shade
figured that you'd need them back so I've already sent for them."

Relief flooded through my chest. "Thank you."

"It's not right!" a woman's shrill voice cut through the hall
outside. "You shouldn't be here!"

We all turned to look as Queen Mother Charlotte swept
into the small dining room. She clutched her skirts like her life
depended on it, and her eyes were wide and frightened.

"He shouldn't be here!" Charlotte turned her frenzied gaze
on us. "And neither should you! Who are you?"

Shade and Edward both got up from the table. The assassin moved towards the door and stuck a head outside. He whipped it from side to side before turning back with a shrug. King Edward moved closer to his mother while making calming gestures with his hands.

"Mother," he said. When she didn't respond he tried again. "Mother. Mom!"

Queen Mother Charlotte backed away, casting wary looks at her son. "Don't touch me! Who are you?"

"It's okay, Mom," the king said and put a gentle hand on her arm. She eyed it carefully but didn't pull away. "I'll get you back to your room. Some sleep and then you'll feel better, hmm?"

I watched the exchange from behind the table. "She doesn't recognize you? Her own son?"

Sadness washed over the young king's face. "No. She doesn't recognize anyone anymore. She hasn't for years. It's like she's looking at things but she's never really seeing anything." A small smile played on his lips. "Well, sometimes she does. I love those moments. But they're few and far between." He placed an arm around his mother's back and started leading her out. "I have to get her back to her room."

Shade nodded before returning to the table and plopping down in the chair again.

"Come on, Mom," Edward's voice drifted in from the hall. "You're alright."

"How sad," I commented.

The Master Assassin's face had taken on a strange look. There was a gloom in his eyes as he watched the doorway through which the mother and son had disappeared. "Yeah." He shook off the somber mood that had settled and turned to me. "Your knives should be here soon. You're heading straight to Tkeideru?"

"Yeah," I said. "But there's one more thing. The Hang Master." I locked eyes with Shade. "I want him dead."

The assassin watched me with an amused expression on his face but the nod he gave me seemed more impressed than anything else. "That can be arranged."

"Good." The food on my plate was getting cold so I started shoveling it into my mouth before it lost all its heat. "By the way, I've been thinking..." I said around the mouthfuls of food. "You can't be that much older than me. You're what? Twenty-two?"

"Twenty-three."

"Twenty-three," I repeated. "How did you even become a Guild Master this young?"

Shade studied me. He seemed to be weighing his options. "Let's just say that our method for choosing the next Guild Master is different from yours."

"What does that mean?"

"It means exactly what I said."

"Not gonna tell me, huh?"

The Assassins' Guild Master smirked. "Nope."

Hmmph. Assassins and their bloody secrets. Okay, fine, so I would never share our guild secrets with an outsider either. But still. My curiosity was far from satisfied.

"Uh-huh," I commented. "You know, you really–"

Shade slammed a hand on my arm and put a finger to his lips. I fell silent but frowned at him. He stayed in that same pose for another couple of seconds before pointing to the door. In one fluid motion, he detached himself from the chair and motioned for me to follow. That was when I heard them too. Soft footsteps coming up the hall. I followed Shade to the wall connecting the room to the hallway, and slipped in next to him. We were packed together behind a bookshelf in the corner.

"King Edward?" a smooth voice called.

Neither of us dared peek around the corner to see who it was, but it mattered little for I recognized the voice anyway. It belonged to General Marcellus, the leader of those visiting Pernulans. Shade put a finger to his lips again. I nodded. Running footsteps sounded outside.

"General," King Edward said, slightly out of breath, "what are you doing in this part of the keep?"

"I was looking for you, King Edward," Marcellus answered. "There was... well, I have been debating whether to say something or not, because I was afraid you would misunderstand my intentions. But... I am concerned."

"About what?" the king asked, still standing outside in the corridor.

"I have been seeing what I believe to be unsavory characters in this castle. I have seen nothing but shadows before, but a few days ago I was wandering the halls, as one does, and I saw a young woman slink past. It was close to that meeting chamber you spoke about and she seemed to be carrying a lot of knives, so I became concerned that you might have a security breach."

Even though my eyes only reached chest-height on the athletic assassin, I could feel Shade glowering at me. An iron glare met me when I tipped my head up. I grimaced and offered an unapologetic shrug. Or as much of a shrug as I could manage in that tight space.

"Oh, that is serious indeed," Edward said outside the door. "Could you show me where you saw her?"

"Of course," General Marcellus said. "So these dark figures sneaking around, they do not work for you?"

"Gods, no. I am glad you brought this concern to me," the king said in a voice that sounded further away than before. "I was going to pick up a package at the gates but I will have two others do that for me while you show me where you saw the intruder. Please lead the way."

Only when their footsteps had disappeared down the hall did Shade and I leave our hiding place. He crossed his toned arms over his chest and leveled an exasperated stare at me.

"Been spying, have we?" he said.

It was more of a statement than a question but I answered anyway. "Obviously. I've been trying to figure out who's out to get me, you know."

"You think it's someone from the keep?"

I pinched my lip. "Can't rule anyone out yet. You don't happen to know who it is, do you?"

"Who's trying to kill you? No." His mouth drew into a lopsided smile. "But I imagine there's quite the line."

Blowing out a noisy breath, I rolled my eyes. Well, he wasn't wrong.

"Come on," Shade said and started towards the door. "That last part was for us. Your knives are here."

Happiness flooded through my chest at the thought of getting them back. It's ridiculous, I know, but I couldn't help it. I cracked a grin as I followed the Master Assassin out the door. Soon, I'd be complete again.

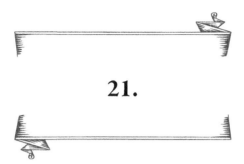

21.

Wind rushed in my ears and whipped through my hair as I ran along the Thieves' Highway. The air tasted salty and the smell of baking bread wafted up to the rooftops. I had never felt more alive than I did at that moment. My body was on fire. My soul sparkled. A gap between the buildings was coming up so I picked up speed and pushed off the tiles with all my might. I soared through the air. I felt lighter than I had in weeks. Being alive. It really was quite extraordinary.

After we'd left the small dining room in the Silver Keep, Shade and I had moved unseen through the halls until we'd arrived at the inner gates. The palace guards were part of King Edward's inner circle, of course, so they already knew about his connection to the Assassins' Guild. However, the king had wanted to keep his Underworld contacts a secret from the Pernulans, so we'd stayed out of sight until we'd reached the place where my knives lay waiting. While I'd continued making myself invisible, Shade had gone in and collected the box. He'd watched me in amusement as I'd strapped on the sharp blades with a wide grin on my face. After promising to head straight for Tkeideru, we'd split up and I had climbed onto the Thieves' Highway.

A figure I knew very well appeared in the distance, running towards me. He slowed down until he finally stopped a couple of rooftops away. I didn't. Closing the distance quickly, I ran straight at him and enveloped his body in a hug.

"You're hugging me," Liam announced, his tone filled with surprise. "What in Nemanan's name is going on?"

I drew back and gave his shoulder a soft push. "It's just good to see you, is all."

My best friend ran his eyes up and down my body while a deep frown settled on his face. "You're covered in bruises. A lot of bruises." He put a hand to my chin and lifted my head up and to the side, inspecting my throat. "Where did you get these?"

"It's a rather long story." I coughed. "Wanna go see the elves? And I'll tell you on the way."

Liam looked like he was about to protest my strategy of evasion but in the end, he just lifted one shoulder in a shrug. "Sure, why not?"

We took off straight towards West Gate. My heart beat nervously in my chest as we ran because I dreaded having this conversation with him. How many times had I almost died in the last few weeks? I didn't want to tell him about it almost happening again. After all, he had almost died himself last summer and he'd admitted that he was struggling with it. Every time he saw me almost leave the land of the living must've triggered his own painful memories. And now I had to do that to him again. I didn't want to. But there was no way I could keep it a secret from him either. I heaved a deep mental sigh as we drew closer to the city wall. This was going to be rough.

LIAM SAID NOTHING. He didn't even look at me while keeping pace beside me in the forest. During the whole story of how I'd come literally a finger's length from dying, he hadn't asked a single question. Not one. He'd only listened. Now that I was finished, my heart thumped in my chest as I waited for him to break the silence.

"How do you feel?" he asked at last.

I blinked. Out of all the things I'd expected him to say, that wasn't one of them. But perhaps it should've been. Liam's first concern was never his own emotions, it was how others felt.

"Honestly?" I said. "Alive. I've never felt this alive before." Twirling around, I swept my arms at the scenery nearby. "I mean, look at this. Look at the trees, and the bushes, and the flowers. Listen to the birds. Smell the damp moss. It's never felt more vivid. More real."

Liam nodded. "I know."

"I feel like there's a whole life waiting for me to discover it. Adventures to find and mysteries to solve. I feel like I can't waste this chance."

My friend grew quiet. I glance at him. His dark blue eyes had taken on a pained look. He almost looked... trapped.

"What's wrong?" I asked.

Spring birds chirped in the trees above but Liam remained silent. After a while, he heaved a deep sigh. "Imagine feeling like that, like you got a second chance, but only because *someone else* paid for it."

Walking beside him, I just continued to watch the pained expression written on his face. I had no idea how to respond to that. When I didn't say anything, Liam continued.

"Elaran paid for my life," he said. "Don't get me wrong, I'm incredibly grateful for what he did, but it's just... I don't know what to do anymore. I feel like I'm wasting my life. Wasting this life that Elaran gave me."

Pain seeped into my chest. Liam had spent almost half his life with me and he felt as if he was wasting it. I knew it was selfish but hearing that hurt. A lot.

"Do you wish you had a different life?" My voice came out sounding small and fragile.

"Yes."

A nail drove into my heart and I had to look away to keep the tears building in my eyes from spilling over. I focused on the squirrel scurrying up a tree nearby.

"Well, no," Liam added after a second and blew out a lungful of air. "I don't know." He grabbed my arm and forced me to stop and turn towards him. "Look at me. The years we've spent together have been the most exciting years of my life. I *don't* regret them. Not for a moment." He let go of my arm. "But I feel like I need to do more."

I wiped away a stray tear that had disobeyed me and fallen down my cheek. "Of what?"

My friend let out another deep sigh. "I don't know yet. But I need to start thinking about it." He drew me into a hug. "Don't worry, I'm not going anywhere."

While trying to swallow the lump in my throat, I nodded. "Good. 'Cuz I don't know what I'd do without you."

"I know," Liam teased and swiped his arms theatrically to the sides. "I am irresistible."

I gave him a playful shove to his ribs. "Moron." He just grinned at me so I shook my head and blew out an amused breath. "Yeah, well, may we only die twice, then."

Liam giggled and pretended to hoist a cup in the air. "To dying twice!"

His quick mood swings were still making me dizzy but I was glad the dreadful pain that had marred his face minutes ago was gone and now replaced by happy mischief.

As we continued deeper into the woods, I took stock of my own feelings. Slight pain from his confession still lingered in my heart but I felt a bit better. My best friend wouldn't be leaving me, and that was all that mattered. Earthen aromas drifted from the moss below our feet. It was a good day. A good day to be alive.

"Hej kollikokk!" someone called from our right.

Startled out of the comfortable silence that had settled, Liam and I both whipped around, ready for an attack. A short man with a walking stick emerged from the foliage. He cracked a smile, making the skin around his eyes crinkle.

"Hey colli-what now?" I said, frowning at our surprise visitor but relaxing my stance.

He just waved a hand in front of his face. "It's good to see you again, city girl. I hear you found the elves. Eventually."

"This is the man you told me about before?" Liam said.

I nodded. Last year, when I was out in the forest looking for Tkeideru, I'd run into this odd man. He'd given me some advice on how to find the elves. It had been good advice too, but I'd still gotten hopelessly lost.

"Yeah, I did find them," I said, shifting my eyes back to the man leaning on his wooden stick. "And I'm actually much less of a city girl now, by the way."

His light green eyes twinkled. "I know. You have made quite the journey, but you are not done yet. There are still plenty of roads to travel and decisions to make."

"How do you know that? What roads?"

"Change is not always bad. And bad is not always evil because good can also be evil and darkness can bring light."

Thousands of years' worth of wisdom seemed to swirl in his eyes but I understood none of it. He might as well have been speaking Pernish. I frowned at him.

"You're doing that thing again," I stated. "I ask something and then you reply to something else and what you say is so strange that I have no idea what you're actually telling me."

The man just smiled. "It was nice to meet you," he said to Liam before looking back to me. "A storm is coming. Make sure you are on the right side." With a swishing of clothes, he whirled around and strode away.

"That's what you said last time!" I called. "What does that even mean?" He was disappearing quickly between the trees. "Wait! You've never even told me your name."

The strange little man gave me no answer and before long, his body had become invisible among the greenery.

"That was... odd," Liam commented.

"You think?" I chuckled and then pulled at his shirt. "Come on, let's get going."

While we continued towards the City of Ash Trees, I thought about that befuddling man. I couldn't even begin to decipher his words, and his identity was equally puzzling, so I soon gave up trying. Whoever he was and whatever his words meant, I was sure I'd survive without that knowledge. I shook my head as we continued deeper into the forest. That was a mystery I seriously doubted I'd ever solve.

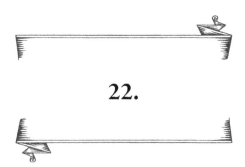

22.

Majestic trees as tall as the Silver Keep towered before me. Chatter, laughter, and the twang of bowstrings filled the air as people moved about on the different levels. On the ground, beneath the swirling staircases and decorated dwellings that wrapped around the trunks, stood a familiar figure with a radiant smile on her face.

"Storm! Liam! What brings you here?" Haela called across the grass.

I closed the distance between us and drew her into a hug.

"Oh, wow," she said after I released her. Surprise filled her yellow eyes. "Did so not see that coming."

"I just... nice to see you again," I said with an awkward flush on my face.

She smiled and drew Liam into a quick hug as well before her beaming expression disappeared. Scrunching up her eyebrows, she looked me up and down. "What did you do? Get into a fight with a bear?"

I snorted. "Close enough. How did you know we were coming?"

"We're kinda in tune with nature, remember?"

"Right." I did an internal facepalm. Obviously. "Is Faye here? Unfortunately, this ain't just a social trip. We're bringing business from Keutunan."

"Ah." A grin spread across Haela's striking features as she swept her raven hair back and executed a dramatic bow. "Our fearless leader awaits."

Liam giggled next to me. Typical Haela. I briefly wondered where in the world she got all that energy from but then I figured that if I didn't spend so much of it on being sarcastic and ducking people trying to kill me, I'd probably have lots of energy too.

Afternoon sunlight slanted in through the leaves as we crossed the city. A lot of the elves smiled and nodded at us as we passed. Well, okay, I think it was mostly directed at Liam. During our winter stay, they'd really come to love him. As most people did, so no surprise there. But still, they'd also come a long way from the guarded chill they'd shown me the first time I'd visited.

A familiar building rose up before us. The War Dancer. This tavern was my favorite place in Tkeideru because it reminded me a lot of the Mad Archer at home. A warm feeling spread through my chest.

"Faye's already here and the others should be on their way back soon too," Haela said before yanking the door open and striding in, with me and Liam in tow. "Look who I found!" she called and twirled around to point an arm in our direction.

The tavern's patrons looked up from their plates and let out a cheer. Liam beamed back at them as they raised their cups while I just managed to stay on this side of beet red. Barely. I knew they weren't cheering for me but I still felt uncomfortable being caught in the center of attention.

A silver-haired elf jumped up from the long table at the curved back wall and fired off a brilliant smile. "What brings you back so soon?"

I took a couple of long strides and saw her expression transform into one of confusion as I drew her into a hug.

"Hey, she did that to me too!" Haela pointed out in a baffled voice somewhere behind me. "What's going on?"

When I stepped back again, Faye studied me with yellow eyes that held amusement and surprise in equal measure. "Who are you and what have you done with the Oncoming Storm?"

I let out a *tsk* and glanced away. "Don't get used to it."

This hugging spree was quite uncharacteristic for me, so I understood the bewilderment. And I wouldn't exactly start doing that to people all the time, but surviving an almost-hanging warranted a couple of hugs at least.

Both elves laughed at my muttered comment before dropping down into the chairs. Liam and I did the same.

As soon as we were seated, Haela got straight to the point. "So there's trouble?"

"Yeah," I began. "Well, of a sort. More like, there might be trouble coming."

"What kind of trouble?" a soft voice asked beside me.

"Keya," I said as a brown-haired elf sat down across from me and swung her leaf-decorated braid over her shoulder.

She gave my arm a short squeeze before shifting her gaze between me and Liam. "Good to see you."

"You too," Liam said while I nodded my agreement.

"Is there a problem in Keutunan?" Keya asked again.

"Well, not yet," I began once more before being interrupted by boisterous laughter bouncing off the ceiling.

"Did you see that last shot? That was insane," Elaran said and gave Faelar a shove. "Well done!"

Faelar straightened and pushed his flowing blond hair back behind his pointed ears. He never showed much emotion but he seemed very satisfied with Elaran's praise.

"Hey, look who it is," Haemir said, motioning for the other two to look at the table we occupied.

"Liam," Elaran said and clapped a hand on my friend's shoulder. "Good to see you."

"You too," Liam replied with a smile.

The auburn-haired archer then turned to me. "Storm."

"Elaran."

I wanted to laugh out loud. Elaran and Faelar, who disliked humans the most out of our small group, had both warmed up to Liam but I was still on the receiving end of their grumpiness. Granted, I didn't exactly help the situation by being a sarcastic smartmouth myself but at least the outright hostility was gone. And to be honest, I quite liked the banter.

In a flurry of long limbs, they pulled over a couple of chairs and joined our now crowded table. When all three of them were seated and the commotion had quieted down, Faye spoke.

"Right, so now that we're all here, why don't you go ahead and tell us about this trouble?"

"There's trouble?" Elaran said and whipped his head towards me.

"*Potential* trouble," I said, drawing out each syllable. "And if you just shut up, I'll tell you about it."

The silver-haired Elf Queen held up her hand before Elaran could retort. "Go ahead, Storm."

I knew they were already aware of some parts, since I'd explained them during my meeting in the cabin with Elaran and the twins, so I picked up the story from there. A couple of empty wine cups later, I finished the tale and leaned back in my chair. I hadn't left anything out, even my near-death experience, because I wanted them to have all the information so that they could make an informed decision.

"Whoa," Haela commented. "You almost died? Like, for real this time?"

"Yeah," I said.

She nodded slowly. "And now I understand the hug."

Elaran frowned. "What hug?"

"Nothing," I said quickly and changed the topic. "So, basically, all King Edward wants to know is, will you fight beside us if the Pernulans attack?"

The table fell silent. All elves present looked to their queen. Faye seemed to ponder the question.

"Your king does have a point," she said at last. "If they were to attack your city, they probably wouldn't stop there. They'd come for us too." She tapped a finger to the sturdy wooden table. "*But*, we are not close to the coast. Their cannons can't reach us in here and they would have a lot of trouble even finding us."

A valid argument. However, I stayed quiet. I had delivered the information and asked the question, it was not up to me to persuade them to do one thing or the other. This had to be their decision.

"True. But you say they come from somewhere else, some place on what they call *the continent*?" Elaran said and looked to me.

I nodded.

"What's to stop them from going back and getting more warriors after they've conquered Keutunan?" he continued. "If they're here to colonize then we'd have a war on our hands anyway."

Faye studied her loyal archer. "And then we'd have to fight it alone," she finished. "You're right. If the Pernulans attack and we decide not to get involved, we'd only screw ourselves in the long run."

The table fell silent again. I sipped at the wine in my cup and exchanged a glance with Liam. It sounded like they were on board.

Faye slapped a hand to the wood, making the cups jump on the tabletop. "Come war and hurricanes, we're in!" Her fierce eyes blazed with conviction. "Tell your king that if these newcomers should attack, we will fight alongside you. Together we are strong."

I smiled at the fact that King Edward had said something similar. Those two were probably more alike than they realized. "I'll tell him," I said to Faye.

"Good. Now, let's drink and talk of happy times and good hunts."

"Hear, hear," Haela chimed in and banged her cup on the table. "Faldir," she called to the blond tavern keeper. "More wine, please!"

As Faelar's brother drifted over with another pitcher of wine, conversation moved away from the grim reality that faced us and towards funny stories and interesting discussions. Afternoon turned into evening as we ate and drank and reveled in each other's company.

"You're staying the night?" Faye asked when night had finally fallen.

"If it's alright?" I said. "I mean, we can find our way here and back again on our own but only when the sun's up. I don't know what's up with *your* special vision but *I* can't see shit in the forest when it's dark."

"Same here," Liam added with a shrug.

Elaran turned a smug smile in my direction. "Just one of the many perks of being an elf."

"Uh-huh," I muttered.

"Of course you can stay," Keya said before turning to her queen. "Their rooms are still the way they left them, right?"

Faye nodded. "Yep. All yours."

"Thanks," I said with a smile before drawing my eyebrows down. "It feels so weird to sleep during the night."

Liam let out a chuckle. "Trying to sound like a real underworlder, are we?"

"I am a real underworlder," I grumbled.

"Yeah, but you've also got the most messed up sleeping schedule of anyone I've ever met. Hey, let's go stalk someone during the day and then sleep at night. Sure! Hey, let's do a twenty plus hour stakeout and then sleep for two days. Why not? Hey, let's–"

I threw a stray breadcrumb at him. "Okay, fine, we get the point. I don't sleep like a normal underworlder and I was trying to sound normal, alright?"

The others burst out laughing. I shook my head. Idiots.

"We should probably start heading to bed too," Haemir said once the table fell silent.

"Yeah," the other elves chimed in.

Chairs scraped and cups clattered as our company of eight rose and made for the door. We all called out thanks to Faldir on our way out.

"We've all got stuff to do tomorrow," Faye said and ran her hands over the three braids gathering up the hair around her face. "So if we don't see you in the morning, stay safe and try not to die and all that."

I snorted. "Yeah, will do. And if trouble starts, one of us," I said, pointing from me to Liam, "will come let you know right away."

"Sounds good."

After some goodnights and some backslaps among the guys, our group broke apart. The elves returned to their homes and Liam and I went back to our temporary rooms on one of the higher levels. When we reached the right platform, we drifted towards the railing instead of heading straight inside to sleep. Tkeideru was beautiful from up here and we wanted to drink in the sight.

"Have you ever thought about how lucky we are?" Liam asked as he leaned against the railing.

Lucky? I had gotten my best friend killed when I was eleven and Liam was the reason his family was dead. And every time we did our job, people tried to hang us for it. In fact, I could barely remember a time when someone wasn't threatening me, blackmailing me, or outright trying to kill me over one thing or another. And now some unknown person was waging a war against me. So no, I didn't feel particularly lucky. However, I decided it best not to voice all that out loud. Instead, I settled for a bewildered stare and a counter question.

"How so?"

"We got to see all this." He swept a hand at the scenery in front of us.

I gazed at the view. A bright moon bathed the tree city in silvery light, and countless stars glittered above our heads. Spring had brought back the green leaves and colorful flowers that clung in vines around everything. I rested my chin in my hands. Yeah. It really was a sight like none other.

"And I don't just mean the view," Liam continued. "We actually got to live during a time when all of these extraordinary things are happening. Like, we've met the elves – and even become friends with them. Visited their city and learned from them. And now this whole new civilization has sailed right into our harbor. How many people can say that? Like, what are the odds of it happening during our lifetime?"

While continuing to drink in the beautiful night in the forest, I nodded to my friend. "You're right. You're absolutely right." I lifted my chin and removed my elbows from the wooden fence. "I've been so caught up in the shitstorm life's been throwing at me lately, I've forgotten there're actually good parts too."

"Well, given how many times people have tried to kill you these last few weeks, I think life will excuse you for not stopping to smell the flowers."

I chuckled. "Yeah."

Apart from an owl hooting in the treetops, silence reigned for a while as we continued to admire the scenery.

"What are we going to do when we get back?" Liam asked eventually.

Drumming my fingers on the wood, I considered for a moment. "I think we should head back to the guild first and let the Guild Masters know what's going on. And then I have to go see Shade again. It's probably best if I do that on my own."

"You still don't trust him?"

"Nope." I smiled before shaking my head. "Well, in a way, I suppose I do. But only if what we want is the same as what he wants. And since I'm never really sure what that is, it's hard to say."

Liam nodded. "Yeah, he's a complicated one, for sure."

"Uh-huh. Come on, let's go get some sleep."

After taking one last look at the silver-colored trees, we went to our separate rooms. I didn't know what tomorrow would bring but at least we now had help if hell were to come raining down on our heads. Pulling the cover over my body, I settled in to sleep and hoped that there would be no more nasty surprises waiting for me tomorrow. We'd see. We would see, indeed.

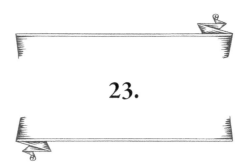

23.

"When the green-clad gentleman laughs," I said to the door. It was shoved open and panicked eyes stared out.

Keutunan had bustled with life on our return. Since I hadn't stopped at the guild to pick up my cloak before heading into the forest, my knives drew curious looks when we stepped through West Gate. Before we could draw too much attention, Liam and I had ducked into a side street and scaled the walls of the nearest building. From there, we had set course for the Thieves' Guild but now that we were outside the door, danger flashed up my spine. Something was wrong.

"Storm!" Bones hissed on the other side of the door. His gray eyes darted around the area. "Damn, I'm glad I was the one on guard when you got back."

"What the hell's going on, Bones?" I asked. "Why didn't you respond with your half of the password?"

"Listen, we don't have much time. The bosses know about you almost getting hanged but miraculously escaping."

I furrowed my brows at him because I didn't see why that would be a problem. "Okay?"

"Listen," he hissed again. "You know they've got people watching the king's inner circle, alright? And word is you sold out the guild to save yourself from getting hanged."

"What?!"

"Shh!" Bones threw worried glances down the staircase behind him. "Look, I know you didn't do it but people, important people, have been overheard talking about how great it is to have the Oncoming Storm on their payroll now."

"And the Guild Masters believe them?" I asked, incredulousness coloring my voice.

"You know them, they take these kinds of accusations very seriously. If you come inside, they'll keep you locked up until they can figure out the truth. And if they can't, you know what'll happen."

Yes. Betraying the guild was a mortal sin. No one caught doing that lived very long and their death was beyond horrible. I gulped back the panic spreading through my chest. Liam had just been stuck staring at our muscled gatekeeper during this entire exchange.

"Look," Bones continued, "they still haven't made up their minds if you're guilty or not, so they won't send out hunting parties for you. Yet. But you should stay away from guild controlled areas." He shifted his eyes to Liam. "Same goes for you. They know you're with her, so they'll pick you up and make you tell them where she is."

My head was spinning. "I don't understand... how the hell did this happen?"

"I don't know, but you have to figure it out." Bones threw a panicked glance over his shoulder. "Someone's coming! When you've got proof, get word to me and I'll try to sort things on this end. Now go!"

He drew the door shut in a quick but quiet motion. I stared at it for a second, not being able to comprehend what had just happened, until Liam snatched at my shirt. "We need to leave!" he hissed.

My brain snapped into survival mode and we both darted from the door. Awful dread and intense panic seared through my body but I pushed them down. I didn't have time to feel right now.

"Worker's End," I called to Liam as I veered right at the next cross street.

He nodded back. Before we left the Merchants' Quarter, I managed to swipe an unattended cloak from a nearby bench. I drew it around my shoulders as we ran. Once we had put some distance between ourselves and the guild, we slowed to a brisk walk to avoid drawing attention. Only when we had disappeared into the twisting alleys and narrow roads of Worker's End did we stop. It was deserted at this time of day since most people who lived here had a job to get to every day. We slipped behind a wooden fence and hid on someone's back porch.

"What in Nemanan's name is going on, Storm?" Liam asked.

"I don't know," I whispered.

My guild thought I was a traitor. They actually thought I had sold them out to the Upperworld. Hot tears pressed against my eyelids. This was worse than dying. The Thieves' Guild had been my home for most of my life, and now I couldn't go back. I couldn't go home. My heart felt like it was going to shatter and my mind threatened to shut down. Everything ached.

I slumped back against the wall and hugged my knees. "It's over. They've won. Whoever it is that's been out to get me, they've won. I have no idea who they are and I'm cut off from the guild. This is it. I've lost." Tears streamed down my cheeks.

"Don't say that." Liam crouched down in front of me and put a hand on my arm.

"Why not?" I snapped. "It's true. I might as well have died at that hanging."

"Don't you *ever* say that," Liam growled and pushed off from the ground. "What the hell has happened to you? Huh? One setback and you break down and cry? Pathetic."

"One setback?" I shot to my feet. "One? I've had *nothing* but setbacks in weeks!"

"So, deal with them instead of just sitting here moping like a kid. The Oncoming Storm?" Liam made a mocking sound. "Don't make me laugh."

My eyes went black and the darkness surged out of the deep pits in my soul. Dark tendrils whipped around my skin, crackling like lightning. To my utter astonishment, Liam broke into a triumphant smile.

"There," he said with that victorious grin still on his face. "Feel better?"

I pulled the darkness back and shook my head to clear out the anger. "Wait... that was an act?"

"Yep." Liam shrugged. "You were sinking fast into panic and hopelessness and I needed to make you snap out of it. And I know you too well to try cheering you up with motivational speeches."

I snorted. "Yeah, I guess you do."

"So, making you angry was the best way out." He gave my shoulder a soft shove. "And I do know what makes you angry. I didn't mean any of it, though."

"I know." Loosening the braid, I tipped my head up to the sky and ran my hands through my hair. "But you were right, I *was* acting like a child. It's just, there's been so much shit lately and I just got... overwhelmed."

"Understandable."

"But I need to stop staring blindly at the problems and start actually figuring out solutions. And I can't do that if I'm bawling my eyes out on the street." I looked down again and bumped my shoulder into Liam's. "Thanks."

"Anytime."

I narrowed my eyes at my best friend. "When did you even get this good at pretending?"

"Oh, you know, you pick things up."

"Uh-huh." I shook my head but dropped the subject since we had more pressing matters. "Alright, we need to make a plan. I have to figure out who's behind this and get proof to the Guild Masters, and we both need to stay away from the guild." I tapped a finger to my lower lip. "How'd you feel about going back to Tkeideru on your own?"

Liam frowned at me. "To do what?"

"Lay low until I can figure this out?" I could sense him about to protest so I held up my hand to stop it. "Look, I know you don't want to. I know you'd much rather stay here with me and help me figure this out but it's difficult enough for one person to gather information while ducking the guild. If both of us are moving around the city, the risk of us being picked up by the guild is twice as high. And if they get one of us, they've got us both."

Liam fell silent, studying me with even eyes. At last, he blew out a deep breath. "True. And I know I'm not a world class sneaker – not the way you are. I'd probably be the one to get us caught." He sucked his teeth and then stabbed a finger in my direction. "Alright, I want it stated on the record that I don't *want* to leave but... I will leave."

"Noted."

"The fact that you didn't even try to contradict me when I said I wasn't all that good at sneaking kind of hurt my ego but I guess I'll survive," Liam said and leveled his best imitation of an angry stare at me.

I offered him a sheepish smile and a shrug. "Sorry."

What he'd said had been true. Liam could hold his own but he was much more gifted in the art of charming people than he was at sneaking. And fighting, for that matter. Until we had someone who needed charming, I'd work better on my own. I know that sounds awfully pretentious and ungrateful but with stakes this high, we simply couldn't afford to spare each other's feelings. We were skilled at different things and in this situation, we needed my skills.

Liam drew me into a hug. "Just be careful, you. I mean it. If I get back and find that you've gotten yourself killed, I'm going to drag you back to the living and kill you myself."

"What happened to only dying twice?" I said with a slight chuckle.

He released me. "You know what I mean. Don't die."

"Promise."

Liam nodded and started towards the street. "If the Pernulans attack, come get us straight away. I'll make sure the elves are ready."

"I will." I watched him slip around the corner. "See you soon, Liam," I whispered to the empty porch.

Now, I only had to plan my next move. While redoing my braid, I considered my options. There were three orders of business that seemed most pressing, though they varied in importance and difficulty.

For one, I had to find somewhere safe to sleep. My Harbor District safe house was a bust since some of my attackers had already tracked me to that place. Not to mention that I had left two dead bodies there, which would probably have made the landlord complain and call the Silver Cloaks. No, I had to find somewhere else to stay for now. I also needed to let Shade know that the elves would back us up in a fight and last but not least, I needed to figure out who had caused all this trouble for me.

Not exactly a piece of cake but I had my knives, and thanks to Liam I had my wits about me again. Despite it being an act, his harsh words had been exactly what I needed. I shook my muscles loose. It was time to get to work.

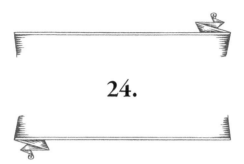

24.

The black metal door looked very uninviting so I skipped it and snuck around the back of the building instead. If I came in through the front door, I had a pretty good idea of what would happen and I had no intention of letting Shade subject me to another power play. This time, I'd be the one dropping in on him, on my terms, and there was a window to an upstairs study that I had my eye on for this particular operation. I started climbing up the side of the building.

There were no balconies on the Assassins' Guild headquarters so I had to make do with window ledges and tiny cracks in the wall.

Halfway up, I realized that I'd have to get up on the roof first and then climb back down to reach the window to Shade's study. Straining my muscles, I grabbed a hold of the roof tiles and rolled over the edge and onto my knees. The point of a sword pressed into my throat.

"The hell do you think you're doing?" an exasperated voice said.

Still on my knees, I gave the blade a disinterested stare before tilting my head up to look at the man attached to it. The Assassins' Guild Master raised his eyebrows at me, waiting for an answer.

"Look down," I said with a sly smile.

Shade frowned at me but did as I asked anyway. When he finally noticed the stiletto blade that had materialize in my right hand and now rested high up on his inner thigh, I had the pleasure of seeing his black eyes widen slightly.

Ha! He hadn't seen that coming. I smirked and arched an eyebrow at him. As long as his sword stayed at my throat, my knife would stay between his legs.

In a swift stroke, his blade disappeared and he returned it to his shoulder. He blew out an amused breath. "You're getting better."

"I've always been better," I said and rose to my feet while letting the stiletto vanish into my sleeve again.

"Humility isn't your strong suit, is it?"

"Neither is it yours."

Shade paused for a moment before replying. "No, it's not." He let out a soft chuckle and shook his head. "Let's go inside and talk."

"So you can go on another power trip in front of your guild?" I crossed my arms over my chest. "I don't think so."

Cocking his head slightly to the right, the Master Assassin studied me before his mouth drew into a lopsided smile. "You really *are* learning, aren't you?" When I didn't respond, he just nodded. "Alright, I assume this is about the elves. So, what've you got for me?"

"They're in. If there's a fight, they'll back us up."

"Good," Shade said. He looked genuinely relieved. "That's very good news."

"So, debt settled?"

He gave me a nod. "Debt settled. But continuing to work together would benefit us both. With your Thieves' Guild contacts and my connections in both worlds we'd have a much greater chance at figuring out what game the Pernulans are playing – and who's trying to kill you."

So, he didn't know about my situation with the guild. That was interesting. Very interesting indeed. Apparently, there were blind spots in his perceived omniscience.

Realizing that he wasn't all-knowing about what happened in the Underworld was great, but the confirmation that he wasn't behind my trouble with the guild was even better. As I've said before, I can never really tell what he's up to, so I had considered his involvement a possibility.

"What do you say?" he asked. "Partner up for a while?"

A strong wind blew across the rooftops, snatching at our clothes while I considered the proposition. I wasn't sure who would be using who in this arrangement but I knew I needed all the help I could get.

"Sure." I gave him a slow nod. "So, no threatening and blackmailing each other while we're doing this."

The deadly Guild Master raised his eyebrows at me.

"Fine." I heaved an exasperated sigh and threw up my hands. "No *excessive* threatening and blackmailing each other. Agreed?"

Shade's eyes glittered mischievously. "Agreed."

"Alright." I stuck out my hand.

The Master Assassin eyed it for a moment but then reached out with his own and gave me a firm handshake.

"So, do we have some kind of plan?" I asked once he let go.

"We do." He ran a hand over his jaw. "Know any forgers?"

"Maybe. What kind of forging are we talking about? Because if it's documents, I can do it myself. And so can you, if I remember our first encounter correctly."

A slight chuckle escaped Shade's lips. "Yeah, you really fell for that, didn't you? But no, we're not talking documents. I'm thinking more like jewelry forging."

"Jewelry?" I squinted at the white clouds in the distance before nodding. "Yeah, I might know someone. Why?"

"We're going to undermine the Pernulans' means of bribery before it can turn into a problem."

A grin spread across my face as the details of his plan dawned on me. "Ohh, I like it."

"So, can you get it done?"

"For sure."

"Good. Come see me here when you've got confirmation. I'll let the guild know so they'll let you through or send word to me if I'm not here." A smile flashed over his lips. "And so they won't be threatening you... excessively."

I snorted and rolled my eyes. "Right. And you let me know if you find out anything about who's targeting me."

Shade gave me a nod in confirmation.

"Alright, I'd better be off then," I said and started down the side of the building again. "Be seeing you."

Silence followed me as I made my way down towards the street again. As soon as my boots reached the stones beneath, I took off at a sprint.

That was one mission accomplished. Next, I needed to find somewhere to stay until night fell. Since Worker's End was no man's land among the Underworld guilds, I figured that was my best bet.

Setting course for Keutunan's main residential area, I put my mind to work on finding a suitable location. Once that problem was solved, I'd have a certain jewelry forger to visit.

MERCER STREET LAY DESERTED before me. A sickness had swept through here years ago but people were superstitious and barely anyone had dared live here since. In other words, it was the perfect place for a hunted thief to hide out.

Wooden window shutters creaked in the wind as I started towards a tall building on the left. There was no need to pick the lock on the door because it was already open, and when I pulled it outwards, it let out a quiet moan. Dust and sand covered the floor and the abandoned furniture in the hall. The rest of the ground floor was much the same. Dirty and empty. I moved towards the staircase. On quick and soundless feet, I examined the upper floor as well. Open cabinets and gaping drawers met me in the two bedrooms that made up the whole floor. The rooms had been stripped of everything valuable, even the mattresses on the beds, but there were working shutters on the windows and space on the floor. It was dry and empty, and most importantly, it was safe. I nodded to myself. This would do. My partly healed bruises from the past week weren't exactly happy but I'd definitely slept in worse places.

Spreading my stolen cloak on the wooden floor, I settled in to wait. Outside the window, daylight still reigned and my next move was better suited for the dark of night. I shifted my weight and put my hands under the back of my head. Burglary, bribery, and threats did require a certain atmosphere, after all.

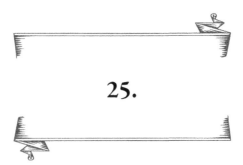

25.

Candles burned brightly in the windows of the mansion at the edge of the plaza. I stole across the manicured lawn and pressed my back against the smooth marble. One breath, two breaths. No alarm rang out. Ducking under the window, I moved towards the back door.

A thin curtain of fog hung in the air, making it harder to spot any potential intruders. It mattered little, though. When I arrived at the back of the house I noticed that the guard stationed there had dozed off in a chair near one of the large flowerpots. I sent a prayer of thanks to Nemanan. After sliding out a pair of lockpicks, I got to work on the door. It let out a soft click as it unlocked. I threw a glance at the guard. Still blissfully ignorant. Letting out a slight chuckle, I slunk inside.

The mansion was huge and a rookie burglar would've had no idea where to go next. But I was not a first-time intruder. In fact, I had been in this house several times before, so I knew exactly which route to take. The smell of roasted duck drifted from the great dining hall to my right. I hugged the wall and crept closer.

"Charles, it's time to eat," a woman's voice said. "Please come and sit down."

"Yes, Mama," a young boy answered.

This was the most dangerous part of my path. My destination lay on the other side of the house and I'd have to pass the doorway to the dining room to get there. I threw a quick glance around the painted doorframe. Lord and Lady Smythe sat at a massive table in the middle of the room, along with their son who had just finished seating himself in the decorated chair. The white linen cloth was already overlaid with silver dishes so I doubted I'd run into any servants right now. Aromatic smells were everywhere. I drew back.

"How was the lunch, my dear?" Lord Smythe said. "I am sorry I could not attend."

"It was very lovely," the lady of the house replied. "Except at the end when Lord Fahr got into quite a row with the others."

"Lord Fahr? That does not sound like him at all."

"Oh no, I meant the younger Lord Fahr."

"Ah," Lord Smythe said. "Yes, of course. That makes much more sense. He has not been himself since that awful business last year."

"What business, Papa?" their son said.

I dared another peek around the corner. Both parents were looking away from the door and towards their child. Perfect. I dashed across the opening.

"Oh, nothing you need to worry about, darling," Lady Smythe's voice spilled out of the door. "Nothing at all."

Moving away from the gathered family, I slipped around the corner and got to work on another locked door. While plates and cups clinked in the dining room my lockpicks helped me through the barrier and let me disappear into a dusky basement. I had discovered this room after I'd broken in here to snoop when I was bored one day. It had made my list of curious findings but I'd never expected it to be something I actually needed to use. Until today. Plopping down in the chair, I settled in to wait.

Evening dragged on until, at last, footsteps sounded down the stairs. I jumped up from the chair and moved behind the door while drawing a hunting knife from its sheath. The door creaked open. Flickering light from an oil lamp spilled across the walls as the owner of the lamp strode forward and placed it on a side table. I followed close behind. As soon as the lamp touched the table, my knife shot out. A startled inhale sounded but before it could turn into something louder, I hissed a warning.

"If you make a sound, one loud noise, you won't live to see tomorrow. Understood?"

"Yes."

"Good," I said and removed the blade. "Now, please take a seat, Lady Smythe."

The elegant lady stepped forward on careful feet before gathering up the flowing, orange skirt of her dress and sitting down in the chair I had previously occupied. She turned towards me as I leaned back against the door.

"Do you know who I am?" I asked.

Light danced over her beautiful features and made the exquisite jewelry she wore around her neck and in her hair sparkle. She seemed nervous but not afraid. Not yet.

"No," she said and placed her delicate hands in her lap.

"I am the Oncoming Storm."

Lady Smythe drew a sharp breath and then tried to cover it with a cough. But her emotions had already betrayed her.

"I see my reputation precedes me – good. That should make this conversation rather efficient."

"What do you want?" the well-dressed lady asked.

Lounging against the door with my ankles crossed, I twirled the knife in my hand. "Does your husband know you're one of the best jewelry forgers in town, Lady Smythe?"

The lady let out an indignant huff. "*One* of the best? I am *the* best jewelry forger. And no, my dear husband has no idea. He thinks I'm meditating in here, bless his heart."

I raised my eyebrows and let out a chuckle. "I see. Well, you're gonna have to put those skills to the test because I've got a job for you."

"And what makes you think I'd be interested in this job of yours?"

"Because you don't have much of a choice." I spread my arms. "And besides, you'll be very generously compensated."

Her eyes narrowed. "How well compensated?"

"Agree to do the job and we'll discuss it."

Silence fell as she considered my offer. Somewhere above us, running footsteps thumped back and forth across the floor, followed by juvenile giggling. "What is the job?" she asked at last.

"Pearls. We want you to make pearls."

"How many?"

A grin spread across my face. "Boatloads."

She drew back in the chair and frowned at me. "You're serious?"

"Very."

"In necklaces or earrings, or what?" When I shook my head, her dark eyebrows drew down deeper. "Why in Skapjanan's name would you need that many loose pearls?"

Ignoring her question, I leveled an even stare at her. "Can you do it?"

"How soon do you need it?"

I stroked my chin. "Like, yesterday."

The dark-eyed lady studied me. "I want twice my normal rate." I arched an eyebrow at her but she just jutted her chin out before elaborating. "Making *boatloads* of tiny balls that all look the same is dreadfully tedious. Besides, I have to dissuade my suppliers from asking too many questions about why I need these specific materials in such large quantities *and* I have to bring in a little outside help to get it done on such short notice."

"Fair enough," I said with a nod. "So we have a deal?"

Lady Smythe smoothened her skirt and rose from the chair. She strode across the room until she was right in front of me and then held out her hand. "Yes, we have a deal."

I cracked a smile. Making counterfeit jewelry and shaking hands? She sure was a rebellious one, this Lady Smythe. After I'd shifted my blade to the other hand, we shook on the contract.

"Oh, and before you go getting any ideas of calling the Silver Cloaks on me," I added, "you do know that jewelry forging is a hanging offence, right?"

"Hmmph. I have been making jewelry since before you were old enough to join a guild. I know what I am doing."

"Just a friendly reminder," I said and slid the hunting knife back in its holster. "A pleasure doing business, Lady Smythe."

"Mm-hmm." She picked up the oil lamp and strode past me. "Wait five minutes and then leave by the back door. The rest of the household will be elsewhere." Without waiting for an answer, she started up the stairs.

Flames danced on the walls until the upper door clicked shut. I let out a soft chuckle. She really was an interesting one. Lady Smythe was a noblewoman and as such she would want for nothing. Food, clothes, whatever she wanted she could have. And yet, she spent her spare time contacting suppliers, forging jewelry, selling it to gods know who, and no doubt making lots of money. I wondered what her story was. Why had she decided to become a jewelry forger despite not having any economic need for it? And when she cursed, she had done it in Skapjanan's name, which was even more interesting. Skapjanan is the God of Craftsmen. Not exactly the recommended first choice for a noble lord or lady. I shook my head. We all had our secrets, I suppose.

When I judged that roughly five minutes had passed, I tiptoed up the stairs. Edging the door open, I peeked out. The house was silent. I slid out and closed the door behind me before continuing towards the back door I'd used to get inside. It was unguarded but I threw wary glances around the area anyway.

Cool mist met me outside when I finally left the unexpected jewelry forger's house behind and took off across the grass. Jumping the short stone fence at the end, I bolted for the next building. I couldn't use the Thieves' Highway because of my trouble with the guild so I had to settle for skulking around the Marble Ring like some kind of civilian.

Fortunately, I didn't have too far to travel because my next destination was located in the Marble Ring as well. I stayed in the shadows as I moved towards it.

The sound of soft footfalls drifted to my ears. I took a sharp right. The footsteps sped up. Shit. I was being pursued. The person hunting me followed me around the corner but I had already disappeared behind the next one. It could be one of the armed men who attacked me every chance they got or it could be someone from my guild. There was also a possibility that it was a Silver Cloak or one of the guards from the prison. Or a Pernulan who'd seen me on their ship. Man, why did I have so many enemies? Soon I'd have to start making lists to keep track of them all. I ducked behind the next corner but then stopped. It was time to find out who it was.

I drew a hunting knife and then pressed up against the wall. The footsteps moved closer. My muscles tensed. Any second now. As soon as the first foot rounded the corner I threw my arm out and grabbed a hold of the stalker's shirt. Yanking them around, I slammed their back into the wall and raised my knife. Terrified eyes stared back at me from across the blade.

"Please don't kill me!"

"Cat?" I said, surprise coloring my voice.

"Hi, Storm," she answered while eyeing the knife at her throat.

I stared at my fellow Thieves' Guild member but didn't remove the blade. "What the hell are you doing?"

"They're saying you betrayed the guild. They're saying you sold us out to the king."

"It's not true." I shook my head. "Whatever you've been told, it's not true."

Cat studied me with big eyes. "But the Guild Masters–"

"The Guild Masters have been lied to!" I snapped. "I'm being set up."

My forceful outburst made her shrink back against the wall but her words came tumbling out regardless. "But you were sentenced to die and then you were saved by the Assassins' Guild. Why would the Assassins' Guild save you unless the king told them to do it? Especially now with the new king, the rumors are stronger than ever that they work for him so that has to be what happened." She shook her head, making her black bob sway. "And why would the king save you unless you gave him something he wanted?"

"Uhh…" I began. These were all valid points. Very valid, unfortunately. The king and Shade had saved me because they'd needed me to give them something they wanted. Only, it had nothing do to with the guild. How was I supposed to explain my way out of this without blowing Shade and Edward's connection and their plans wide open? If I did that, I was pretty sure I'd have to add the Master of the Assassins' Guild to my list of enemies and that would not work out well for me.

I heaved an exasperated sigh. "I didn't sell out our guild, okay? The assassins saved me because Shade owed me a favor."

Cat's eyes went from showing nervousness to disbelief. She scrunched up her eyebrows. "The Assassins' Guild Master owed *you* a favor?"

"Well, yeah. And he needed me to do something too so…" I trailed off. This wasn't helping my case. "Look, I know there's a lot of stuff right now pointing to me being a snitch but it ain't true." I removed my knife from my fellow thief's throat. "I'm being framed, Cat. Tell the Guild Masters I'm being framed and that I'll get them proof of it."

"I'm supposed to bring you in," Cat said.

I let out a chuckle and shook my head. "You know that's not gonna happen." Sticking the knife back in its sheath, I lifted one shoulder in a shrug. "And you can't take me in a fight so just tell them what I said, alright? Don't follow me."

In a burst of speed, I took off down the street again. No footsteps followed. Annoyance built in my chest as I weaved through the Marble Ring until I wanted to yell in frustration. Of course I looked guilty. Being saved by the death guild for no apparent reason screamed of inside dealing and the fact that I'd been spotting sneaking around the Silver Keep didn't exactly help my case. All of this, combined with someone powerful and close to the king actually articulating that I was on their payroll, left little room for interpretation. Damn. I needed to figure this out.

As my intended destination rose in the distance, I filed away all the information I'd received in the scheming part of my brain. I'd have the rest of the night to think that through and decide on a plan but first, I needed to finish this jewelry forging business. I had a killer to meet.

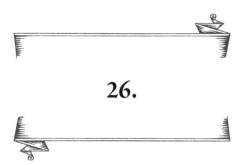

26.

"How is this not classified as excessive threatening?" I muttered and gestured with one hand at the sword against my throat. I had wanted to use both hands but my other arm was pinned behind my back by the owner of said weapon.

Shade shook his head at me from across the room. "You seriously need to stop sneaking around our building, and start knocking on the front door when you want something."

"Yeah but see, I'm not a knocking-on-the-front-door kind of girl," I replied, my mouth drawing into an unapologetic grin.

"Mm-hmm." The Assassins' Guild Master crossed his arms over his chest and ran his eyes up and down my body. "Strip her."

"You what?" I exclaimed and pulled against the hand locking my wrist in place.

Another assassin appeared from the side and started removing my various knives. *Oh. That.* Shade arched an eyebrow at me with an amused smile on his face. Damn assassin and his damn power trips. One day. One day I'd get back at him.

"She's clean," the man announced as his companion released my arm.

"Is she?" Shade said, fixing me with a calculating stare.

I rolled my eyes and magicked one more knife from my sleeve. While flashing a satisfied grin to the blond man on the left, I dropped the blade on the pile in front of me. The assassin who had missed it threw panicked looks between his Guild Master and the stack of knives.

"I'm sorry, Master," he said. "It won't happen again."

Shade glanced at him from the corner of his eye. "No, it will not." Shifting his gaze back to me, he jerked his head towards the staircase behind. "Let's go."

I hated it when he ordered me around but refusing to follow him up the stairs would only make me seem petty, so I trailed behind him until we reached his upstairs study.

"You sure have a talent for making enemies," Shade said after he'd lowered himself into the chair behind the large desk.

I dropped down into the one across the table. "What do you mean?"

"Slim, the blond assassin by the door," he began and nodded back the way we'd come, "you made him look like a fool. In front of *me*."

Leaning back in the chair, I crossed my arms. "Well, if he didn't want me to embarrass him he shouldn't be so damn incompetent, should he?"

"He's not going to forget this. But don't worry, no one in my guild will touch you." A smirk settled on his face. "Unless I tell them to, of course."

I threw up my hands and blew out a sigh. "Again with the threats. I came here on business, do you wanna get on with it or not?"

Shade stared at me with an unreadable mask on his face before flicking his hand. "Go ahead."

"I met with the forger and she's on board."

"She?"

"Yeah."

He raised his eyebrows. "Your forger's a woman?"

"That's what I said. I told her we need a boatload and we need it sharpish and she agreed." I held up my hand. "And before you go all attack mode on me again, she has no idea who the 'we' are. Now, she's good, she'll keep quiet, and she'll get it done. But she wants twice her normal rate because of the volume and the rush job. I'm assuming His Majesty the king is bankrolling this? 'Cause I ain't got that kind of money."

Shade nodded. "Yeah. Whenever you have the number, just let me know and I'll pass it along."

"Alrighty then." I jumped out of the chair. "Now, if you'll excuse me, I have to go figure out who's trying to kill me."

"Actually," Shade said, stopping my progress towards the door, "I was going to head to the keep and see if I can overhear something useful among our guests. I'll be focused on their potential hostile takeover but if they're the ones targeting you, you might pick something up."

Turning back around, I squinted at him. "I could just go to the Silver Keep on my own."

The Assassins' Guild Master pushed out of the chair and strode past me to the door. "Suit yourself. I can get us into places you can't, but if you don't want my help then so be it."

He pulled the door open and stepped into the hall. I hated asking others for assistance or relying on them to do stuff for me. It went against my every instinct. But he was right. Damn.

"Wait," I called, tipping my head up towards the ceiling. His footsteps came to a halt. I heaved a deep sigh. "I'll come with you."

He glanced at me as we started down the stairs. "How about a thank you?"

"Don't push it."

The blond assassin by the door, whose name I now knew to be Slim, cast venomous looks at me while I strapped on all my knives again. Shade disappeared into a room just off the corridor for a while and then returned with two slightly curved short swords behind either shoulder blade.

"Ready?" he said.

After securing my boot knife in its proper place, I stood up and nodded.

"Alright, let's go," the Master Assassin said.

Without sparing a glance behind to see if I followed, he stepped out on the stones outside and took off towards the Silver Keep. I shook my head. There he was again, giving me orders. But I'd tolerate it. For now. His help would make it easier for me to eavesdrop on potentially important conversations. I took off after him. I had a good feeling about tonight. Tonight we might actually learn something crucial.

MY HEART SKIPPED A beat and I dashed into the nearest doorway. "There are guards here," I whispered while trying to melt into the door.

Shade gave me an amused look as he strode past. "Yes, there are." He continued straight for the two armed men blocking the narrow hallway. "Good evening, Albert. Frank," the assassin said in a casual voice before calling back up the corridor. "Are you coming or what?"

Simply strolling up to a couple of Silver Cloaks went against my every instinct so it took a moment to detach myself from the door. Deep down, I knew that these guards were part of King Edward's inner circle and therefore wouldn't arrest Shade or anyone accompanying him, but my mind still screamed at me to run in the opposite direction. I cast wary glances at them when I walked past but they didn't even look at me. They were probably paid well enough, or threatened well enough, to stop them from asking questions and remembering faces.

"Nervous, are we?" Shade said when I caught up.

"You might not have experienced it because your little guild is in league with these people but the rest of us have spent our whole lives ducking people like that, so yeah, excuse me for being somewhat cautious."

"My *little* guild?"

I threw a quick glance at him. Yeah okay, that probably wasn't the best choice of words. Man, one of these days I really needed to start working on those social skills. Oh well, today was not that day. "You know what I mean."

"Uh-huh."

A soft carpet muffled our footsteps as we continued further down the hall. I'd never been in this part of the Silver Keep before. It was too well guarded and I hadn't felt the need to risk detection just to snoop, so I hadn't even tried. There were no decorations along the hallway, only the fluffy red carpet beneath our boots, and it was rather narrow which made me think it was more of a servants' corridor than an official one.

"Alright, I have a question," I said, breaking the silence that had settled.

"Okay."

"So, if we're going to eavesdrop on the Pernulans, why didn't we bring one of the scribes? I don't know how to speak Pernish and neither do you, I assume."

Shade turned to look at me before shaking his head. "Yes, Storm, why didn't we bring a civilian translator on our super-secret spy trip?"

"Don't talk to me like I'm soft in the head," I snapped. "It's a valid point. Why are we bothering to listen in if we don't even understand what they're saying?"

"Watch that tone," the Master Assassin said, not taking his eyes off the path ahead.

Watch that tone? In my head, I gave him a very thorough lesson on what I thought about that comment but outside the safely of my own head, I had to settle for a grumbled curse.

"Besides," he continued, "we're not going to be eavesdropping."

"We're not?"

"Nope. I was thinking something a bit more direct." His black eyes glittered. "We're going to break in."

An excited smile spread across my face. "I'm listening."

"The Pernulans never leave their room completely unguarded so we haven't wanted to risk it before. But now..." he trailed off and looked at me expectantly.

And suddenly I realized that I'd been manipulated. Gods damn it. He hadn't asked me to come because he thought it might benefit me too. He'd done it because I was a thief, and a great one at that, and *he* needed *my* help. And I'd fallen for it. Damn, he was good, I had to give him that.

"You manipulated me," I stated flatly.

"Hey, you should be flattered. I could've brought one of my people for this but I wanted a professional."

"Flattered?" I snorted. "Yeah, sure, let's go with that."

We continued along the barren hallway in silence for a while. Only the soft rustle of boots on a carpet disturbed the peace.

"You did that earlier too, didn't you?" I said at last as a sudden thought crossed my mind.

"Did what?"

"Manipulated me." I glanced at the assassin from the corner of my eye. "Into searching the Pernulans' ship for you."

The corner of his mouth quirked upwards. "Yeah. I didn't want to risk anyone connecting it to my guild and then to Edward. But you're just some random thief. If you'd gotten caught, no one would've known about the king's hand in it."

I opened my mouth to inform him exactly how I felt about being used in this way, and about being called *some random thief*, but before I could do that, Shade pressed on.

"Besides, you were already planning on looking into the Pernulans." He offered me a light shrug. "I just nudged you in a direction that would benefit us both."

Arching an eyebrow, I turned my head to stare at him. Well, wasn't that just ingenious? I mean, absolutely infuriating for me because I'd fallen for it, but I couldn't deny that he was incredibly cunning. And in my book, that wasn't necessarily a bad trait. I might even find it a bit attractive.

Something between a sigh and a chuckle made it past my lips before I shook my head and switched back to the problem at hand. "So, what's the plan?"

"For the break-in?"

I nodded. He seemed satisfied that he'd won our brief argument about manipulation because he cracked a confident smile. One day I'd get back at him. One day.

"I'm going to create a distraction that makes the guard chase after me and while he's doing that, you're going to search their room."

A smug expression settled on my face. "So, you're bait."

Shade huffed and threw me a dirty look. "I'm the distraction, get your terminology straight."

"Uh-huh." A chuckle slipped from my lips before the flashing eyes of the Master Assassin next to me shut me up. I cleared my throat. "Okay, so while you're distracting him, what am I looking for?"

We had arrived at a nondescript wooden door. Shade put a hand to the handle but didn't open it.

"Anything you can find that proves they're not just here to make an alliance," he said in a soft whisper. "Look, there's just too much suspicious stuff going on around them for it to be a coincidence. They've given us more knowledge in the past weeks than we would've gotten on our own in the next decade and all they want is the promise of an alliance. How does that sound?"

"Too good to be true."

"Exactly. And you and I both know that when things sound too good to be true, it's because they are. But Edward, he..." Shade trailed off. "Let's just say he has a lot riding on this so he doesn't want it to be a trap, which makes him reluctant to call their bluff and break off the contract."

Silence fell over the hall as I studied the Assassins' Guild Master. He covered it well with manipulation, threats, and snide remarks, but underneath it all, he looked worried. How odd. I wondered why.

"Why are you so personally invested in this? In him?" I asked and nodded back the way we had come.

"Oh I had no intention of being invested. I had a plan, other plans, but then I... I never expected to care about him this much."

The words had come tumbling out of his mouth without a pause to consider. Cocking my head, I studied him with curious eyes because that was probably the most honest thing I'd ever heard make it past his lips.

When he noticed the expression on my face he seemed to realize what he'd actually said. Lightning flashed in his eyes and before I'd had time to react, I found myself up against the wall with a sword to my throat. He leaned in, his forearm across my chest, until I could feel his breath on my skin. When he spoke, his voice was quiet and deadly, like poison.

"If you ever repeat that to anyone, *ever*, you will die begging for the sweet release of death."

I swallowed. There was no mistaking the lightning storm in his eyes, he was dead serious. Dead serious. What a ridiculously ironic choice of words at this particular point in my life.

Meeting his blazing eyes with an even gaze, I decided that this was neither the time nor the place to be a smartmouth. "Understood."

With a slight push of his forearm, he withdrew and returned the blade to his shoulder. "Good. Now, we have work to do. Outside that door," he said and nodded towards the plain one in front of us, "is a broad hallway with three large doors. We're hitting the one in the middle. I'm going to head out first and pretend to attack and then escape in the opposite direction. The rest of the Pernulans aren't here so the guard outside the room will have to pursue me and leave the room unprotected. While he's following me, you'll get inside and do your thing."

After filing all of this information in my brain, I nodded.

"Once I open that door there'll be no more talking so if you have any questions, now's the time," Shade said.

"Am I stealing or just looking?"

"Just looking. We don't want them to know that we know."

"How much time do I have?"

"I'll try to give you as much as possible but count on little to none."

I snorted. "Great."

Shade put his hand on the handle again. "That dining room we met in last time, can you find your way there?"

"The one that looks like a library kitchen?"

"That's the one."

Flicking my eyes to the smooth ceiling, I calculated a route in my head. "Yeah."

"Alright," Shade said with a nod. "Wait for the scream and the sound of running feet." He pushed the handle down. "Show time."

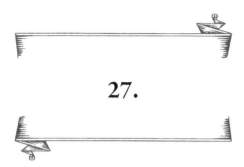

27.

The screaming started within seconds. An earsplitting roar and a string of what I assumed to be foreign profanities bounced off the marble walls and made their way through the thin wood. I lifted my ear from the door. That had been an entirely redundant precaution; the signal had been loud and clear. Boots slapped against stone as the cursing drew further away. Edging the door open, I peeked out. The corridor was empty. *My turn.*

I dashed for the huge door in the middle. While sliding out my picks, I eyed the metallic lock. It was a standard type of lock, similar to the rest of the Silver Keep, so my picks and tension wrench got it open in no time. After a hurried glance over my shoulder, I slipped inside.

A cacophony of bright colors met me on the other side. Pillows and curtains of every color were draped across the room but there was no bed or anything that would give it the semblance of a bedroom. It looked more like a meeting room. Between the windows at the back, a large desk had been pushed against the wall, making room for the cluster of tables that occupied most of the floor space. Overflowing bookcases lined the walls. Shit. This was going to take time.

After sparing a quick glance at the door, I put my mind to work on the problem. I didn't have enough time to search the whole room so I had to decide on which parts to focus.

If I was a super-secret incriminating battle plan, where would I be? The tables in the middle were out. Anyone with brain capacity greater than a seagull wouldn't leave documents like that lying around. Following that reasoning, the bookshelves would be a waste of time as well. Attaching documents to the underside of chairs, desks, and drawers was way too common, as was hiding valuables in random pots or between pages of a book. These were among the first places people from my guild checked when breaking into a house.

If I decided to search all those spots in this room, it would be all I had time for and I had a feeling that these Pernulans were smarter than hiding it there. But where?

Resisting the urge to cast another glance at the door, I scanned the room. What stood out? Time was slipping away and I would have to make a decision right now. A sudden thought struck as a flash of lightning. Of course. It had to be. I sprang across the room and pulled out a chair. Jumping up on it, I stuck my fingers inside.

Smooth paper met me. I wanted to laugh out loud. The answer had been staring straight at me the whole time, flashing its bright colors. Who in Nemanan's name needed this many curtains?

With nimble fingers, I drew out a roll of paper from the rod pocket of the orange curtain in front of me. After placing it on the desk underneath, so I'd remember which scroll belonged in which curtain, I moved to the next one.

The pink drape was empty but the dark red one and the green one held two more rolled-up documents. This time I did allow myself a look over my shoulder. I didn't have time to go through all the curtains so I decided I should start checking the documents as I found them instead of trying to locate every single one.

Paper rustled faintly when I spread open the first roll. I squinted. It was a map. One look was enough to confirm that the depicted building was the Silver Keep. Tiny crosses dotted it. I knew exactly what those were as well because I had created a similar map in my head. They were guard locations. I rolled open the next document and drew back frowning.

Unrecognizable squiggles filled the whole page. Damn. It was all in Pernish and since I could neither speak nor read that language, I snapped it shut again. Trying to figure that out would be a colossal waste of time. Just as I spread open the third document, a small sound make me look up.

My ears pricked up. Footsteps in the distance. *Shit*. I ran my eyes over the last paper and concluded that it too was a map. However, this one was of Keutunan. There was a line drawn across it in a curving fashion, like the edge of a hand fan. My mind calculated the possibilities. The starting point appeared to be out in the harbor. On the ships. My head jerked up. The cannons.

The sound of the footfalls grew louder. *Crap*. I scrambled back up on the chair and pushed the papers back in, taking care to leave them exactly as far in as I'd found them. My heart thumped in my chest. *Hurry*. The guard outside drew closer. I jumped down from the wooden chair and lifted it back to its original position before sprinting to the door. After one last look to assure myself that every tiny detail was precisely the same as when I'd arrived, I slunk out the door.

Heavy boots sounded down the hall. Blood pumped in my ears as I dropped to my knees in front of the lock. I had to finish relocking it before he rounded the corner. Exhaling a soft breath, I got to work on the lock. I was nervous and under pressure but Shade had been right: I was a professional. My hands were steady and my mind focused.

The lock clicked into place. With not a second to spare, I bolted for the servants' corridor we'd arrived through. I held my breath as I skidded to a halt and pushed the thin wooden door closed behind me. My heart beat rapidly in my chest. No alarm came. Closing my eyes, I allowed myself a deep sigh of relief.

My mission had been a success. Well, if you could call finding out that your so-called allies were planning to attack your city a success. The second map had shown the calculated range of the cannons and the line indicating it had been drawn high up. Very high up. And they had lots of cannons on their three ships. If they gave the order to fire, about half of Keutunan would be destroyed. I rested my head against the door.

This had certainly complicated things. Finding out who was trying to kill me should be my top priority but if the Pernulans conquered Keutunan, I'd be in an equally bad position. I let out an annoyed sigh. There was too much going on at the same time and it was getting harder each day to prioritize which event was more pressing. My mouth drew into a smile. At least Liam was safe with the elves.

I pushed off the door. It was time to get moving. Shade had most likely already reached the strange dining room filled with books and I had to share what I'd found as soon as possible. I still didn't know what my next move would be after sharing my findings but I needed to figure it out. Before this night was over, I had a lot of decisions to make.

"YOU WEREN'T SEEN, WERE you?"

"Hey, Shade, nice to see you too," I said in an overly cheerful tone and narrowed my eyes at him.

Albert and Frank had followed me with their gaze when I passed them on the way back out of the long corridor but they hadn't stopped me so I assumed Shade had instructed them earlier to let me pass. To be honest, I'd been nervous about it but I hadn't had a choice because that was the only way out. Well, except for the thin door at the other end. But an angry Pernulan waited on the other side of that one so I'd put my faith in the presumably well-paid and well-threatened Silver Cloaks. Navigating through the rest of the keep had been relatively easy so I'd ended up in the kitchen library without further trouble.

"Were you seen?" the Master Assassin reiterated.

"Of course not," I said, plopping down in the chair across from him. "What do you think I am, some kind of amateur?" Shade opened his mouth to reply but I held up both hands. "You know what, don't answer that. Is King Edward coming or should I start briefing you straight away?"

"He'll be here in a couple of minutes."

Leaning back in the chair, I crossed my arms. "Alright."

For a moment, we just studied each other. Green eyes meeting black eyes. Then, Shade broke the silence.

"Why didn't you tell me?" he asked.

I frowned at him. "There are a lot of things I don't tell you. Anything in particular on your mind?"

He held my gaze with an even stare. "About your guild. Why didn't you tell me they think you're a traitor?"

How had he managed to find that out? Well, it mattered little, I suppose. He knew, so there was no hiding it now. It was embarrassing, though. I glanced away and instead occupied myself with studying the large cast iron pot in the corner.

"Can you do something to fix it?" I said.

"Yes."

"Would you?"

The Assassins' Guild Master paused for a moment. "No."

"And that's why I didn't tell you. I know you can't go telling my Guild Masters about your secret plans with the King of Keutunan. If you start explaining things to them then they'll have ammunition to use against you, which you'd never allow." I shifted my eyes back to the assassin in front of me. "I might know shit-all about how the Upperworld's run but I do know a thing or two about guild politics."

Shade drummed his fingers on the table before offering me a nod in acknowledgement. I just shrugged and went back to studying the room. The bookcases were filled to the brim but it didn't look like they contained any useful books. Nothing that could teach you anything. Based on their titles, they appeared to simply be stories. How odd. Imagine living a life where you had time to sit down and read stories. I wondered what that would be like.

"Where are you staying?" Shade asked, his fingers still tapping the tabletop.

"Oh, you know, here and there."

"Is it safe?"

Knitting my eyebrows, I watched him for a moment before answering. "More or less."

He fell silent for a while before resuming. "You could stay here in the keep, if you want?"

I blinked at him. "Stay here? With the Silver Cloaks and the noblemen and the Pernulans? Why in Nemanan's name would that make me feel safer?"

The Master Assassin lifted one shoulder. "Just a thought."

We continued waiting for the king, both of us drifting off into our own minds, until a thought popped into my head.

"What's the vault?" I asked.

My question had been so unexpected that the assassin didn't manage to cover his reaction in time. A look of shock flashed over his face for a brief second before his cool mask slammed back in place. "What vault?" he said, drawing his eyebrows down in an attempt at confusion.

"Oh don't give me that," I said. "I saw that look on your face. You know exactly which vault I'm talking about."

The Assassins' Guild Master leveled hard eyes, dripping with authority, on me. "I suggest you drop this subject. For your own sake."

Right as I was about to reply, soft footsteps rounded the corner and a frazzled-looking young man appeared through the doorway. "Sorry to keep you waiting. Herding fourteen Pernulans through the garden was more difficult than I expected." He raked his hands through his glossy black hair. "Especially when all they wanted to do was return to their room."

Shade shot to his feet. "Your Majesty," he said before shooting me a hard stare, presumably to keep me from bringing up the vault again. I lifted my hands to show that the message had been received. Loud and clear.

King Edward waved Shade back in his chair before rounding the table and sitting down next to him. After exhaling a deep breath, he flicked his eyes between us. "Were you seen?"

Before I could once again question whether they had any confidence at all in my skills as a thief, Shade cut me off with a look. "Only by Frank and Albert," he said.

Shifting my eyes from the assassin to the king, I shrugged. "Same."

The black-eyed king cocked his head slightly to the right and leveled a piercing stare at me. "What did you find out?"

"I... uh..." I began as both of them studied me. "Maps. I found maps. One of the Silver Keep that shows the location of all the doors and where the guards are positioned and how many there are, and... yeah, well, all that. Then I also found a map of Keutunan where they've measure how far their cannons reach." I hesitated before continuing. "It's about half the city."

"Fuck," Shade swore.

King Edward folded his hands in his lap and leaned back in the chair. The silence stretched as his gaze drifted to the ceiling. "Are you absolutely sure?" he asked at last.

"Yeah."

A heavy atmosphere blanketed the room but after that last confirmation, I held my tongue. This situation was the same as the one in Tkeideru. I had delivered the information but it was not up to me to make the decision. That was up to the ruler of Keutunan.

"In other words," Shade began, "they say they're here to help and to make an alliance but it's really an occupation."

The king closed his eyes. A pained expression lingered on his young face. I wondered what that was about but given how Shade had responded to my previous queries, I figured it best not to ask.

At last, King Edward opened his eyes and gave us a wry smile. "Well, every good occupation deserves a resistance, right?"

Shade mirrored the expression. "Indeed."

After nodding to his assassin, Edward turned his gaze on me. "And you? Are you with us?"

I opened my mouth and then closed it again. Was I with them? Getting involved in yet another power struggle wasn't exactly high up on my to-do list for the day. However, our guild relations were favorable with this king, as was the relationship between him and the elves. He wasn't trying to exterminate us underworlders and there was a peace treaty between Keutunan and Tkeideru. If the Pernulans took power there was no telling what they'd do to the city. Either of our cities, in fact. In order to ensure my own safety and the welfare of the people I cared about, it seemed as though I would once again have to get involved in the business of monarchs. I heaved a deep sigh. Hurray.

"Yeah, I'm with you."

"Good," King Edward said. "First things first. Do we have a pearl forger?"

I nodded.

"Perfect. Can you tell him to give us each batch as soon as it's done so we can start flooding the market with them right away?

"Her," I corrected. "And yeah, I'll tell her."

The king raised his eyebrows but didn't ask any further questions about the gender of my forger. "Good, good. I'll give you enough money to cover the first few batches right now so you can take it to her and then you can just let me know how much additional payment is required." He peered at me from across the table. "I can trust you to give that money, *all* of that money, to the forger, can't I?

I rolled my eyes. "Of course. Who do you think I am?" When the king opened his mouth I realized that I didn't want an answer, so I held up my hand. "Never mind. Yes, you can trust me."

Edward gave me a satisfied nod but Shade's calculating eyes never left my face. After the inquiry into my trustworthiness had been dealt with, we moved on to practical plans on how to distribute the fake pearls. Night turned into early morning before we had settled on a plan.

"I should get going," I said and pushed to my feet. "I'll visit the forger later and give her the money and get an update on the situation, so I'll let you know afterwards. Should I come here or to your guild?" I asked, nodding at Shade.

The king and the assassin exchanged a look but it was Edward who answered. "After the fake attack on the Pernulans today, it's probably best if we have as few... shady people here as possible. At least until I can assure them that it was just a random attack."

"The Assassins' Guild it is," I said.

"Knock on the front door this time!" Shade called at my retreating back.

"Yeah, yeah," I muttered before slipping around the corner.

Grumbled curses followed me out the door. Liam had been right about my messed up sleeping schedule. Last time I'd slept had been in Tkeideru and now I'd gone a whole day and night without sleep. Besides, a lot had happened in that time span, so it was safe to say that I was exhausted. I'd have to cram in some sleep in the next few hours because then I had another full day and night ahead. There was a jewelry forger to meet, money to give, and pearls to distribute. Well, that was of course in addition to figuring out who was trying to kill me and gathering evidence to prove to my guild that I was innocent while also ducking unidentified armed men, Pernulans, Silver Cloaks, and my own guild members. Right. Who needed sleep anyway?

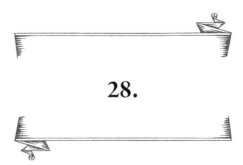

28.

"If you do that for me, you can keep three of the pearls," I said, rattling the precious contents inside the soft pouch.

Well, the allegedly precious contents, anyway. The boy in front of me studied me with cautious eyes. I adopted my best friendly face, hoping that it would convince him, but I had a nagging feeling that the knives peeking out from under my cloak were working against me.

After getting a couple of hours of restless sleep early this morning, I'd returned to Lady Smythe. She'd made good on her promise of a rush order and already had a few batches of pearls ready, which she had happily parted with in exchange for the bag of money I'd brought. My next stop had been the Assassins' Guild. I *had* knocked on the front door this time but only to shove two pieces of paper into the hands of the closest assassin. The first one contained Lady Smythe's bill and the second specified which drop point they should visit to pick up the coming deliveries of fake pearls. After that, I'd taken off again because I didn't have time for another power showdown with Shade. I had servant boys to bribe.

"I just tell them Lady Windone wants a dress and give them the pouch?" the blond boy in front of me asked. "And then I can keep *three* pearls?"

"Yep."

He squinted at me. "What 'bout the dress?"

"You can pick it up and give it to your lady. Or not." I shrugged. "It's up to you."

Lady Windone's servant tipped his head from side to side while sucking his cheek. "Alright, I'll do it," he said at last, transforming his previous head motion into a couple of quick nods instead.

A broad grin spread across my face. "Excellent." I dropped the pouch into his open palm.

After one last nod, he scurried off towards the high-end dressmaker's shop up the road. I needed to get the fake pearls in circulation as fast as possible and the best way to do that was to buy pricey stuff. However, my Underworld-looking self couldn't exactly just stroll into an upscale boutique and place the order. That would be far too suspicious. Instead, I had to convince more legitimate-looking people to do it for me and the young servant boys of various lords and ladies made for both strategic and easy targets. The blond teenager disappearing up the street had received the last pouch of pearls from this batch. Watching him from the shadows of a side alley, I grinned. Inflation was coming.

"This Underworld your city has, it is very disturbing, is it not?" a vaguely familiar voice said.

When the correct memory snapped into place, I shrank back into the shadows. I held my breath as General Marcellus passed by the mouth of the alley. A finely-dressed gentleman walked beside him on the main street.

"Oh, uhm, yes, I suppose so," the Keutunan lord said.

"Very troubling, indeed," General Marcellus continued. "Only yesterday was my fellow countryman attacked inside the palace, *inside*, by an... an... underworlder. What is your king doing to rid himself of this most foul plague?"

Foul plague? I drew my eyebrows down and I would've harrumphed if not for the fact that I was trying to remain unnoticed. Who was he calling a foul plague?

"Oh, I don't know," his walking partner responded. "I'm not on the Council so I don't really know."

"I see," the general said. "I spoke with Lord Raymond earlier and he..."

His voice drifted out of range as they continued down the street. Hmmph. The nerve of these Pernulans. I shook my head and then glanced at the sky. Pink and purple streaks lined the heavens. I had gotten to that last servant boy just in time because now that evening was fast approaching, most Upperworld shops would be boarded up and closed. My work was far from done, however. I needed to get some kind of lead on who was targeting me so that I could deliver proof to my guild. That was easier said than done, though.

The best plan I'd been able to come up with was breaking into some mansions in the Marble Ring. Not just any mansions but the ones I knew housed some of the biggest gossips in the well-fed part of the Upperworld. My plan was to eavesdrop on these noble ladies who seemed to know as soon as someone sneezed inappropriately. That way, I might stumble onto something that would help my investigation. At least, I hoped so. After checking for potential threats, I pulled up the hood of my stolen cloak and vanished into the falling darkness.

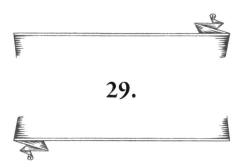

29.

A cloaked figure stood motionless in the alley. I drew up short. Night had fallen while I'd circled back up to Worker's End with the intention of hitting the Marble Ring from the north, so I couldn't make out the face of the person waiting for me a few strides ahead. Because he had to be waiting for me. There was no logical reason for anyone to simply be standing there, at this hour, doing nothing. I narrowed my eyes at the surprise visitor. If this was meant as an ambush, it was a terrible one. Feeling the comforting weight of the stiletto blades in my sleeves, I moved forward.

"The Oncoming Storm," the figure said as I approached. "You're a hard woman to track down."

The voice was vaguely familiar but I couldn't quite place it. I squinted at the brown-haired man blocking my way. "Who are you?"

"I work for the man who's been trying to kill you these past months."

At that extremely unexpected announcement, I only managed to jerk back and stare at him for a moment. He worked for the man who had been trying very hard, and nearly succeeding several times, to kill me. I blinked at him. I'd set out to eavesdrop on gossip in the hope of picking up some kind of clue as to the identity of my attackers and now there was a man standing right in front of me telling me it was him. What in Nemanan's name was going on?

A stiletto blade shot out of my sleeve as I grabbed his shirt and drew him towards it. "Who. Are. You?" I pressed out between clenched teeth while resting the point of the blade against his throat.

"Uh, uh, uh," he said and wagged a finger in my face. "You really don't want to be doing that. You want to know why?" He didn't wait for an answer but instead pointed towards the second floor of the building to my left. "Look at that window."

Still keeping the stiletto at his throat and his shirt in my fist, I glanced at the upstairs window. The contours of a person filled the space. I shifted my stare back to the ambusher in front. "So what?"

"Keep watching," he said before holding up one finger in the air.

Shadows danced in the window as a light source bloomed. With knit eyebrows, I studied the figure in the now lit window for a moment before realization struck me like a basher's bat. Drawing a sharp breath, I stepped back and released my hold on the man's shirt. *Not possible*. I whipped my head between the mysterious ambusher and the person in the window. This could not be happening. Again. Light flickered across Liam's face as he stood rigid in the opening with a pistol hovering a short distance from the side of his head.

"So, now you underst–" the brown-haired man began.

My eyes went black as the darkness ripped at my soul and I lunged for him before he had time to finish. A heavy thud echoed through the alley but my strange ambusher remained calm despite now being pushed up against a wall by a maniac with black eyes.

He shook his head and made a tutting sound before holding up two fingers in the air. "Watch."

Twisting around, I looked over my shoulder. The pistol moved forward until it pressed against Liam's temple. My friend closed his eyes. Panic washed over me like an ocean wave and I backed away from the man giving the orders while raising my hands. My stiletto had disappeared into my sleeve again.

"Okay, okay, I get it," I said. "I'm sorry, okay? Just... I'm sorry."

The man smoothened his rumpled clothes. "Good. Now that we have established the premise for this conversation, we can get started. You can call me Lord Makar."

"You're a lord?"

"No." His thin lips drew into a smirk. "But you can call me that anyway."

"Lord Makar?" I cast a glance at the window. Liam had opened his eyes again and was watching the scene. "Okay. What do you want, Lord Makar?"

While continuing the conversation with the lord pretender, I kept my eyes fixed on Liam's face and flashed him the Thieves' Guild hand signal for *hurt*: a stretched out thumb and pinkie, followed by a stretched out thumb and forefinger, followed by a fist. That signal could of course have different meanings depending on the circumstances. It might inform someone that you are hurt, or tell them to hurt someone else, but I knew Liam would understand that I was asking if *he* was hurt. My friend gave me an almost imperceptible shake of his head. Good.

Lord Makar snapped his fingers in front of my eyes. "What I want is for you to look at me when I'm speaking to you."

My first reaction was to punch him in the face but I managed to suppress it and instead shifted my gaze back to the pompous man. If I opened my mouth, I was pretty sure something highly inappropriate would spill out so I kept it shut and just stared at him instead.

When I didn't offer a reply, Lord Makar pressed on. "We have a job for you."

To say that I was sick of people having jobs for me was the understatement of the year. A frustrated howl built in my throat, begging to be released. Why couldn't they carry out their own missions every once in a while?

"We want you to kill two people for us," Makar continued. He pulled out a folded piece of paper from inside his vest and shoved it in my hands. "The first lives with his family in the house marked with the number one on this map. He's the only grown man in there so you should have no trouble identifying him. The second one lives alone at the place marked with the number two."

Opening the neatly folded paper, I studied the hand-drawn map inside. A house in the Artisan District and one in the Marble Ring were marked in black ink. "Who are the targets?"

"That's irrelevant," Lord Makar said. "I tell you to kill them and you do it. Or we kill Liam."

The darkness screamed in my soul, making me fight to keep it locked up. "Why me?"

"Because my employer wants you to hurt." A wolfish smile spread across his thin lips. "He realized that death is too easy a way out for you. Getting you exiled from your guild and making you a puppet, forced to perform actions for him, is so much better."

I could feel my eyes going black and had to draw a deep breath to push it back. "And the action he wants me to perform is to kill these people?" I said and waved the piece of paper in my hand.

"Yes." Eyes that gleamed with satisfaction matched the smirk on his lips. "So, I guess the question is, would you take the life of two innocents to save the life of your friend?"

Loosening the grip on my self-control slightly, I let the darkness seep into my eyes before fixing them on the blackmailer. When I opened my mouth, I drew out each word until they dripped with malice.

"You know nothing about me. I would slaughter whole cities. The lives of strangers mean nothing to me." A grin steeped in madness flashed across my face. "And if that's what I'm willing to do to innocent strangers, what do you think I will do to my enemies?" The self-confident smirk on his face faltered but before he could say anything, I went on. "I will kill these guys for you but you remember this day, for this was the day you signed your own death sentence as well."

Lord Makar recovered and flicked his hand dismissively. "Toothless threat from a collared dog. Get it done before sunset tomorrow and then get back here. Or your friend dies."

Before I could do something I would come to regret, I spun on my heel and stalked up the alley. It hadn't been true. The part about slaughtering cities, I mean. Well, at least I didn't think so but since I'd never been in a position where I had to find out, I couldn't be entirely certain.

As I passed the two-story building on my left, I glanced up at Liam and threw him an apologetic look but I didn't show him any hand signals. There was nothing to say. It was my fault that he was once again in danger and I didn't have a plan for how to fix it. I turned right at the nearest side street and jogged back towards Mercer Street. The sounds of people getting ready for the evening drifted from the windows. Pots clanked and children giggled as their mothers prepared dinner. I pulled up the hood of my cloak and tried to remain invisible among the shadows.

They must've grabbed Liam after we split up two days ago and been trying to locate me to stage this scene ever since. All this time I'd thought Liam was safe with our friends in the forest when he was really being held at gunpoint by some jumped-up commoner pretending to be a lord. And it was all because of me. Again.

When I reached my temporary residence, I slammed the door shut behind me and released that frustrated howl that had been stuck in my throat since the ambush. Loud crashes echoed into the night as I went on a rampage and shoved and kicked over every loose piece of furniture I could find on the ground floor. When everything not bolted to the floor had been overturned, I took my fury out on the wall.

Knife after knife hit the wood as I hurled them against the living room wall. Peeling paint and sharp blades flew across the area until I had nothing left to throw. I slumped down against the opposite wall and closed my eyes. My chest heaved.

Why was stuff like this happening all the time now? I used to be just a thief, but lately, people had been dragging me into one mess after another and the ones I cared about always got caught in the crossfire. I leaned my head against the cold wood behind me. How had it come to this?

Once my anger had simmered down and my breathing returned to normal, I drew out the map I'd been given. There was no time to figure out a counterstrategy to Lord Makar's blackmail right now. I would just have to get to the Artisan District and the Marble Ring and kill whoever lived in those houses. But I couldn't help wondering who Makar's employer was and why that person wanted the owner of these particular houses dead, and why he wanted me to do it.

What could I possibly have done to make an enemy out of someone as powerful as whoever it was that Makar worked for? It had to be a lord. But breaking in and stealing stuff from their house didn't usually warrant this level of hatred. I let my legs slide to the floor and kicked a chair out of the way. Half-broken furniture littered the room. I heaved a deep sigh.

That question was a problem for another time because right now, I was on the clock. Filing away my list of unanswered questions in the scheming part of my brain, I pushed to my feet and stalked towards the cluster of knives still sticking out of the wall. I had some assassinations to plan.

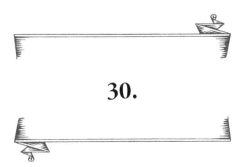

30.

Strong winds whipped through my hair and pulled at my clothes. I had left the cloak behind in the building on Mercer Street because I needed my moves to be unobstructed. Perched on the roof of the building across the street, I peered into the windows of the Artisan District house that was marked on the map.

It looked like any other home in Keutunan. Most commoners lived in Worker's End, of course, but quite a lot of people who worked in the Artisan District lived here, in their part of town, as well. In fact, it was the same with the merchants; a lot of them lived in the Merchants' Quarter. That meant whoever lived in the building across the street was an artisan of some kind. I had no idea why in Nemanan's name someone would want a random craftsman dead but I didn't have time to figure it out so I pushed my concerns aside and continued studying the building.

Figures moved about inside. A woman paused and wiped her brow while cleaning pots in the kitchen on the ground floor. She arched her back and stretched her arms before diving back in. In the room next to her, a young boy jumped around with something made of wood in his hand. He ran towards the back of the room and disappeared from view before reappearing in the upstairs window moments later. The boy ran straight for a heavily muscled man. Lumbering forward, the man lifted the boy in his arms and spun him around. A weight pushed against the walls around my heart. Whoever this man was, he clearly had a family who loved him. And I would have to take that away. This was going to be rough.

From atop the roof, I watched the family of three move around the house until the last candle had been blown out and the house was left in darkness. Once I was sure they had all gone to bed, I started down the side of the building. My feet barely produced a sound when they hit the stones. After casting a quick glance in every direction to make sure the area was empty, I stole across the street.

Kneeling down in front of the door, I took out a pair of lockpicks and got to work. The lock clicked open in less than ten seconds. I slid inside. With the door closed behind me, the house was once again left in darkness. For a moment, I remained rooted in that hallway, listening to the silence. No talking or sounds of movement drifted through the rooms. The occupants were asleep. I let out a soft exhale before starting up the stairs.

I walked on the balls of my feet and stayed as close to the wall as I could in order to reduce the risk of accidentally making the wooden planks creak. While drawing soft, shallow breaths, I scanned the area at the top. It was empty. I took the last few steps in quick strides and drew myself up against the wall. My investigation had revealed that the upstairs room closest to the street was some kind of study, and the three family members had disappeared further into the house before blowing out the last candle, so I assumed that their bedrooms were at the back of the second floor. I released another soft breath and started forward.

There were two rooms down the hall, one on either side. The one to the right was a little further in than the one on the left but there were no other distinguishing marks to show me which room belonged to the parents and which belonged to the child. I had to check them both. Deciding to start with the room on the right, I tiptoed down the wooden hallway. A soft groan escaped the planks under my feet. I froze. My heart pattered against my ribcage.

Excruciating seconds crept by but none of the occupants seemed to have heard it. After sending a quick prayer of thanks to Nemanan, I started out again. Once I reached the door of the far room, I slowly pushed down the handle and edged the door open. Thankfully, it moved quietly. When I peeked inside, I immediately realized that it was the wrong room.

Wooden toys lay scattered across the floor and a chest filled with stuffed animals stood gaping against the opposite wall. Next to it was a bed. The small boy in it lay on his back, his chest rising and falling under the covers. I drew the door shut. With my back to the wall I closed my eyes. That little boy would wake up with only one parent. My heart bled for him. But at least it was one parent more than I and everyone else in the Underworld had ever had when growing up. And we'd made do. He would too. I steeled my heart and snuck back towards the door on the left.

This one opened without a sound as well but revealed a slightly larger room with a double bed that occupied most of the floor space while drawers and closets lined the walls. The master bedroom. Under the covers, a man and a woman lay sleeping, their rhythmic breathing almost in sync. This was going to be tricky. I slunk through the doorway and tiptoed to the man's side of the bed. For a moment, I just stood there in the darkness, watching them sleep in blissful ignorance of the awful events waiting for them. The man snored a couple of times and then rolled over on his side. I briefly wondered who he was and what he had done to deserve such a fate but then I realized that these thoughts would not make my job any easier so I shook them out and instead stuck my hand inside my belt pouch. After cutting off all my emotions, I drew out a syringe.

In the empty house on Mercer Street I had formulated a plan for the assassinations. I didn't want to simply slit their throats, and there were two reasons for that. Firstly, slitting someone's throat is messy, and if something goes wrong, it can get pretty loud as well. That was something I couldn't afford. The second reason was that having a blade cut through your windpipe was a violent way to go. These two men had done me no wrong so I could at least give them a peaceful death. I owed them that much.

Before coming here, I'd stopped at an Underworld contact who I'd gotten to know early on but only used sporadically. He wasn't part of any guild and only those who already knew about him, knew about him, so to speak. With money I'd stolen on the way, I'd paid for two syringes filled with fast-acting poison. Now I stood with one of the deadly needles in my hand and watched my first target draw what would become his last breaths.

The muscled man before me groaned and then continued his snoring. If I hadn't already cut off all my emotions, I would've remained rooted there next to the bed, staring at him forever, but without my troublesome feelings, I moved mechanically. His jugular vein was prominent so I located it without much effort. My hands were soft and my moves delicate as I stuck the needle into his exposed vein and pushed down the plunger. The clear liquid disappeared into the deoxygenated blood rushing towards his heart. I withdrew the syringe.

In a minute, his heart would stop beating and he would leave the world of the living. It was quick and painless and his wife and son would not wake up to find a shocking scene filled with blood. No nightmare-fueling trauma. They would be devastated, of course, but they would believe that his heart simply gave out as he slept.

I watched the rise and fall of his chest while the poison worked its way to his heart. When it finally stilled, I sent a prayer to Ghabhalnaz, God of Death, on his behalf. I couldn't do much to change the awful hand fate had dealt him but I'd done what I could to give him a peaceful passing. Leaving my cut-off feelings there by the bed, I turned around and strode out the door. I still had work to do.

BRIGHT MOONLIGHT BATHED the Marble Ring in silver. The second mark on the map had led me to a building on the outskirts of the city's wealthy area, close to the Artisan District. At the end of the wide street lay my target. It was more of a compound than a house and when I crept closer to the fence surrounding the area, I realized where I was. This was the Court of Knowledge. I drew up against the stone wall and furrowed my brows. Why did someone want a scribe dead?

The compound on the other side was the place where the Scribes' Guild lived and worked. Though, given what I'd overheard at the Council of Lords, it was probably full of

Pernulans as well. I wondered if the person my mysterious blackmailer wanted dead was one of our scribes or one of the newcomers. Putting a hand inside my vest, I drew out the map. The hand-drawn number marked a freestanding building at the back of the enclosure but there was no way of knowing who lived there. It matter little, though. I'd find out soon enough.

There had been no time to scout the area beforehand. Lord Makar had told me to get it done before sunset tomorrow but I really only had tonight to carry out the bloody deeds. Assassinating someone in broad daylight was incredibly difficult and even though I was fairly competent in that most noble and deadly art, I was nowhere near as skilled as Shade and his people. Killing someone in the middle of a busy workday, and getting away with it, would be close to impossible for me. Therefore I had to get it done tonight.

Hugging the outside wall, I skirted around the area until I had the indicated building right on the other side of the barrier. I used the gaps between the stones to climb up and then peeked over the top. The streets of the compound lay deserted. My muscles tensed as I drew myself up and rolled over the wall before landing in a crouch on the other side. Barely a whisper had betrayed my moves but I scanned the area with quick eyes anyway. Not a soul in sight. I darted for the closest building. It was smaller than the others and it only had one floor. While the rest of the long buildings contained multiple rooms, and probably housed the majority of the scribes as well as their workplaces, this looked more like someone's private residence. Whoever lived here had to be important.

I snuck around the one-story house, looking for possible entry points. Since we were far into the night, the shutters were of course closed on the windows and the only other possible opening was the front door. I peeked through the slits of each shutter as I passed. There seemed to be only three rooms: a bedroom, a small kitchen, and something that looked like a study. The front door led to a hallway that connected the three rooms. I ducked back under the window.

Since I hadn't had time to map out any potential guard rotations, I wanted to avoid the front of the house as much as possible. I didn't like having to pick a lock with my back to the road if I was unsure whether someone would walk past while I was otherwise occupied. It was too risky and I couldn't afford to get caught so I opted for a window leading to the study instead.

Sliding a lockpick through the opening, I reached the latch and lifted it open. Now came the risky part. I didn't know how well-used these hinges were but I prayed to Nemanan that the shutters wouldn't make too much noise as I pulled them open. The God of Thieves must've heard me for they opened without as much as a groan. While bracing myself on the window frames, I climbed up on the ledge and into the room.

Bookcases lined the walls but most of the books and scrolls lay scattered throughout the room. I crinkled my eyebrows. It looked as though a storm had blown through and left the contents of the shelves in haphazard piles across every surface. How could anyone think in this mess? I shook my head and tiptoed towards the hallway, careful not to step on any of the items littering the floor.

The door to the bedroom had been left gaping inwards so I could stick my head through the opening without worrying about it making noise. This room was as messy as the study. Scrolls and books mixed with pieces of clothing occupied the set of drawers in the corner as well as the nightstand. I slipped through the doorframe and into the room.

A gangly figure lay sprawled on the bed, his long limbs tangled in the sheets. Reaching his jugular vein would be a bit more difficult since he was lying in the middle of the bed and on his back. He was also a lot skinnier so his veins weren't as prominent as they'd been on the muscular man in the first house. For a moment, I just stood there next to my sleeping second victim and considered how to best proceed.

"Aha!" the scribe called and sat bolt upright.

I jerked back before dropping to the floor and rolling under the bed. My heart beat against my ribcage. Gods damn it. Had he heard me come in and just been pretending to be asleep? But that didn't make any sense. If I caught someone breaking into my house I wouldn't sit up and yell 'aha!' like it was a game of hide and seek. I would get behind the wall and then stab the person as they walked through the door. But maybe that was just me.

"That's it! That's the answer," he continued.

Above my head, the scribe fumbled for something on the nightstand. I kept my breathing soft and shallow. After a few seconds, he tumbled out of bed and stumbled towards the door. He hadn't lit a candle so he tripped over a stack of books and slammed into the wall.

"Ouch! Who put all these books here?" he muttered as his legs returned to a vertical position. "Oh, right." He chuckled heartily. "That was me."

From under the bed, I saw his feet round the corner and disappear into the hallway. Well, this had taken an unexpected turn. From what he'd said, I assumed that he'd figured out the solution to a problem he'd been working on. That was good because it meant that he was still oblivious to the fact that an assassin lay waiting for him under his bed. However, it complicated my plan. I couldn't exactly stick a needle in his neck while he was walking around his house so I'd have to wait until he went back to bed. The half-healed bruises all over my body made their presence known as I tried to make myself comfortable on the floor. *And now we wait.*

Minutes had turned into hours and still the scribe hadn't returned to his bedroom. I stuck my head out and glanced through the slits in the window shutters above. Soon the early morning birds would sing and the sun would chase the darkness away. When that happened, my chances of success would drop rapidly. I had to do something. Right now.

I rolled out from under the bed and darted to the door. Sloshing water and the popping of a fire made their way from the kitchen. On light feet, I moved towards the sound.

"Tea," the scribe said. "Tea always makes everything better. That's what Mom says. Hmm, yes." He let out a pleased chuckle. "You were right, Mom."

The damn man was making tea. Tea! He certainly wasn't going back to sleep anytime soon. I heaved a deep internal sigh. How was I supposed to dose him now? Porcelain clattered as he removed a cup and saucer from the small cabinet near the table. *Wait. The tea.* I grinned. Yes, that would work. I only needed to create the right conditions for it to succeed.

A plan formed in my mind as I scanned the study and the kitchen from the hallway. His mess worked in my favor. I waited for him to pour the tea and then drew back as he crossed the hall and moved into the study. When I returned to my previous position, I saw him balance the cup on top of some books on the desk. After pushing his glasses back up his nose, he went back to reading whatever it was he'd been studying before the urge to make tea had taken him. I slunk into the kitchen and grabbed a small pot before sneaking back into the hallway. This had better work.

I lobbed the pot back into the kitchen. It created a terrible ruckus as it hit the floor and bounced under the table. The scribe jerked his head up and blinked repeatedly. When I heard the chair scrape against the floor, I dashed towards the bedroom.

"By all the gods, what was that?" he muttered as he stomped towards the kitchen. "Don't they know I'm trying to work here?"

As soon as his back had disappeared into the kitchen, I sprang forward and slid in through the door to his study. I only had seconds.

"Stupid pot," the scribe's voice drifted from the other room.

Skidding to a halt in front of his desk, I whipped out the second syringe. There was no time to be gentle so I jammed the plunger down and squeezed the clear liquid into his tea. A cupboard slammed shut in the kitchen. Shit. My plan had been to escape through the window before he came back but there wasn't enough time. Footsteps sounded behind me. I dove over piles of books stacked on a chest and hunkered down on the other side.

"Now, where was I?" the scribe said.

Wood creaked as he lowered himself into the chair again. I tried not to breathe behind my very flimsy cover.

"Where did I put my tea? Oh, there it is." He chuckled. "Come here, lovely. You're getting cold, aren't you? That stupid pot disturbing our special moment."

It took all my self-control not to burst out laughing. Man, these people were so weird. A slurping sound drifted over the stacks of books. Behind them and the chest along the wall, I listened to the tea-loving scribe gulp down his beloved drink and turn pages in a book. He had no idea that he was going to die a couple of minutes after finishing that cup. A dull sadness tried to wash over me but since I'd left my feelings behind in that other house, it sloshed uselessly against my hardened heart.

Time stretched until a heavy thud finally echoed through the room. I peeked out from my hiding place. The scribe was lying with his cheek pressed into an open book on the desk, his eyes glassed over and distant. I rose and walked over to him. An empty tea cup sat perched on a stack of books. At least he had died doing what he loved: drinking tea and reading books. That was more than most of us could ask for.

Two innocent people were now dead. The tea-loving scribe and the family man in the Artisan District would never see another sunrise because of me. I wish I could tell you that I felt horrible, that this was something that would haunt me for the rest of my days, but that would be a lie. Of course, I would never have killed them if I'd had a choice. Well, actually, that wasn't exactly true either. I did have a choice. A choice between Liam's life and theirs. And in that scenario, I would pick Liam. Any day of the week. It saddened me that these two innocents had to die but I would lose no sleep over it because if I hadn't done it, my best friend would've been killed. Sometimes there are no good options. And no heroic third way.

I closed the scribe's unseeing eyes before climbing out the window and into the dawn of a new day.

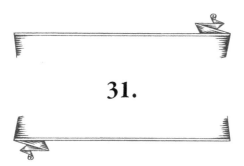

31.

Afternoon sunlight filtered through the white wisps of cloud above the teeming streets of Keutunan. Worker's End had been mostly empty but the Marble Ring saw lords and ladies taking their afternoon stroll while merchants and craftsmen hurried past with determined steps. I blended in with the crowd by adopting a carefree gait.

After leaving the Court of Knowledge early this morning, I'd used the last of my stolen money to buy some food and then I'd returned to the empty building on Mercer Street. It had been a while since I ate or slept. Again. So I'd spent most of the day catching up on some much needed sleep.

When I'd finally woken up, I'd figured it was time to check in with Shade to see how the pearl distribution was going. I'd let that slip since I'd been otherwise engaged last night.

A low whistle broke my wandering thoughts. Whipping my head around, I looked for the source. It sounded again from somewhere above me. When I tilted my head up, I saw a dark-clad figure atop the roof to my right. He jerked his head.

Bastard. I rolled my eyes at his presumptuous command but scrambled up the side of the building anyway.

"What, no ambush this time?" I said as I rolled over the side of the roof and got to my feet.

Shade chuckled. "No need. You already know I could if I wanted to."

"Hmmph," I muttered and crossed my arms over my chest. He was right but I didn't want to admit that so I changed the subject. "How's the flooding?"

"Good," he said. "Your forger's fast. She's had several batches delivered, all through the night and today as well. But it's taking longer to get it distributed so we can't expect any real drop in value until the next couple of weeks or so."

"So it's on track at least? That's good."

"Yeah," Shade said before a troubled look crossed his face.

I narrowed my eyes at him. "What's wrong?"

A seagull squawked and flapped past while the Master Assassin took to pacing back and forth across the roof. "There've been some disturbing developments."

"Okay?"

"Both the Master of the Builders' Guild and the Master of the Scribes' Guild died last night."

My stomach dropped and icy dread spread through my chest. Crap. So that was who I'd killed. This was bad. I had to tread very carefully now.

"Both of them?" I said and raised my eyebrows in surprise. "That's an odd coincidence."

The Master Assassin ran a hand along his jaw. "Yeah, but that's the thing. I don't think it's a coincidence. It looks like their hearts just gave out but what are the odds of that happening to those exact people on the exact same night?"

I offered him a shrug. "You're right, it does sound pretty suspicious."

"But that's not the end of it. Since they were Guild Masters, someone else had to step in to fill the position. And guess who that is?" Shade didn't wait for me to guess but instead stopped pacing and locked eyes with me. "Two Pernulans."

"What?" I jerked back and furrowed my brows. "But that's not how it works. I assume their guilds have rules for choosing the next Guild Master, same as we do? How could a Pernulan get that position?"

"As far as I can tell it's because they've wormed their way into the guild with all this new knowledge. Both the Builders' Guild and the Scribes' Guild have benefited greatly from the Pernulans' knowledge sharing so I guess that's the card they played."

"Damn," I swore.

Not only had I assassinated two of our own people, it had been highly important people, and now the Pernulans had control over both the builders and the scribes. That meant the person targeting me was most likely in league with the Pernulans. So, in the last few hours, I had apparently betrayed my allies and aided a foreign takeover while crippling our own defenses. Great. Just great. This could turn out terrible for us.

I glanced at the Assassins' Guild Master in front of me. This could turn out terrible for *me*. If Shade found out that I was the one responsible for it, that I was the one who'd betrayed them, then I would most certainly not live to see another sunrise either.

"Do you have any leads on who did it?" I asked.

"No. I can't even be certain they were killed but you've got to admit the timing is too suspicious to be a coincidence."

I nodded. "Yeah, you're right."

"That means two people *have* been assassinated and it wasn't by anyone in my guild."

"Are you sure?" Lightning flashed in his dark eyes. Alright, that had been the wrong question to ask so I tried to smoothen it over. "I just mean, they could've gotten to one of them and pressured them into doing it."

The Master Assassin fixed me with an iron stare. "You know nothing about our guild. None of them would betray me, even to save their own life."

I held up a hand to show that I didn't intend to argue the point. "Alright, got it, sorry I asked. But have you gotten started with trying to figure out who *did* do it?"

"No, we're spread thin as it is. I don't have the resources for it. And besides, it doesn't really matter who did it. The important part is that they're dead and we've got to deal with the Pernulans now running the Builders' Guild and the Scribes' Guild."

Inside the safety of my own mind, I breathed a deep sigh of relief. I would get away with this. But there was one last thing I could do to drive the last nail into my innocent coffin.

"I could look into it," I said and lifted my shoulders in a carefree shrug.

Shade turned his eyes to the white clouds above before nodding. "Yeah, that would actually be pretty good."

"Consider it done." I turned around to leave but stopped when a strong hand encircled my arm.

"Hey," he said, spinning me around, "we're not done. Did you find out anything about who's targeting you?"

I stared at his hand through narrowed eyes until he released my arm. "Nope. I eavesdropped on some of the noble gossips in the Marble Ring but I didn't get anything useful," I lied casually.

"Huh. If you do find anything out, let me know and I'll see if I can do some digging on my end."

"Will do," I said before letting mock formality fill my voice. "Now, may I leave?"

He answered with an exasperated sigh and a shake of his head. Before another sarcastic remark could slip past my lips, he threw a large pouch at my chest. I caught it with both hands.

"Get these pearls into circulation," Shade said. "We've still got a lot to do."

Pressing my jaws together, I leveled a hard stare at him. "You know, one of these days you've really got to stop giving me orders."

A knife materialized in his hand and he started flicking it between his fingers. "Or what?"

"Or I'm gonna start throwing knives at you. I'm serious."

He cracked a lopsided grin. "Now who's doing the excessive threatening?"

Blowing out an annoyed breath, I spun on my heel and stalked away. "I'll get them distributed. But not because you told me to," I called over my shoulder.

The Master Assassin's rippling laugh followed me as I climbed down the side of the building again. I had a lot to do before this day was over.

First, I'd make sure these pearls found new homes and then I had to return to Worker's End. Lord Makar had told me to be back before sunset and though I despised people ordering me about, I was reluctant to disobey because he had Liam.

But I had meant what I'd said to Shade. If people didn't stop giving me orders soon, I would start throwing knives. Consequences be damned.

However, deep down I knew that wasn't a viable solution to my problems. I needed to inventory my strengths and my advantages and then use them at the next possible opportunity. It was high time I started outsmarting people.

"NOT ONE MINUTE TOO early," Lord Makar said and tapped his foot on the stones.

Well, he wasn't wrong. Purple and dark red bloomed in the sky, giving evidence that sunset was only a few minutes out. I gave the lord pretender a nonchalant shrug.

"You said be here before sunset, I'm here before sunset. And I got it done, as you've no doubt heard."

Lord Makar nodded. "Yes, I did. I also hear you managed both assassinations before first light so perhaps I was too generous with my time frame."

He was baiting me, I knew that, so I didn't respond. Instead, I just crossed my arms and kept staring at him until he continued.

"We have another job for you," he said.

"That right?"

"Yes. And need I remind you to keep that tone polite?"

I struggled mightily not to roll my eyes and managed a smile instead. "No."

"Good. Now, as I said, we have another job for you. You're going to show me the way to the elves."

Panic flared up my spine. I took a step back. "You want me to what?"

"I want you to show me how to get to the City of Ash."

I licked my lips. "Why?"

"That is not your concern." Lord Makar held up one finger and light bloomed in the upstairs window.

Not again. I closed my eyes briefly because I didn't want to see that scene again. Slowly turning my head, I saw Liam once again stand there with a pistol to his temple. My heart ached. How many times had he ended up in dangerous situations because of me? He had gotten kidnapped by lunatics twice in the span of a single year. What were the odds of that? In a normal world, people didn't get kidnapped that often. It was ridiculous. But I guess I didn't exactly live in a normal world.

"What we do with the information is none of your business," Makar continued, unaware of the guilt and panic swirling around in my mind. "All you need to know is if you don't do this, we will kill your friend."

Every alarm bell inside my head blared all at once. I couldn't show him how to get to Tkeideru. Whatever it was that he wanted with the elves, I knew it was bad. It was one thing to kill two random strangers but the elves were my friends. I couldn't betray them. But if I didn't do it... I couldn't even finish the thought.

"Okay," I said. "When?"

"Right now."

I drew back and scrunched up my eyebrows. "Right now? You won't be able to see which way we're going, and neither will I, so none of us will be able to do what we're supposed to."

Lord Makar huffed. "Fine. First thing tomorrow."

"Alright," I said with a nod. "Meet me outside West Gate."

Once I'd seen him nod back, I turned around and made for the mouth of the alley. However, this time, as I passed the upstairs window Liam occupied, I touched my thumb to my ring finger and then touched my thumb to my middle finger before finishing the fast sequence with a fist. The Thieves' Guild hand signal for *I have a plan*. From the corner of my eye, I saw him give me a short nod.

The wheels in my brain spun as I made my way back to Mercer Street. I had a whole night to plan and carry out the scheme taking shape in my mind. There was no room for error; everything had to be perfect. If I failed, I would have no choice but to betray my friends. On the other hand, if I did this right, I would get everything I wanted.

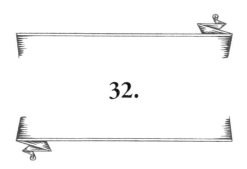

32.

The pale light of dawn trickled through the leaves outside West Gate. The forest floor smelled of morning dew and damp soil. Pacing across the grass, I waited for Makar to show up. I really hated waiting for others but there wasn't much I could do about it. It was probably the lord pretender's payback for me arriving so close to the deadline yesterday. While I waited, I prayed to Nemanan and Cadentia, and any god who would listen, that my plan had worked.

At last, Lord Makar came striding across the root-covered ground. Three people trailed behind him but since the pompous lord in front blocked the view, I couldn't yet make out who they were. As they all closed in and the leader stepped aside, my mouth dropped open.

"What's Liam doing here?" I asked, shock filling my voice.

Lord Makar made a tutting sound and wagged his finger at me. "Did you really think that would work?"

"What would work?"

"Don't play stupid," he said and shook his head. "We are watching your old contacts, we always have been. Did you really believe you could send them a message without us finding out?"

Dropping my gaze, I kicked at a stray rock. "I guess not."

"No, indeed. And what a pitiful plan you had concocted too. While you were keeping me busy in the forest you thought this," he said and waved my letter in the air, "this Starving Dog would be able to rescue your precious friend."

I could feel Liam's eyes on me but I didn't meet them. "Don't be so quick to judge. The Starving Dog would've been able to charm your guard with nothing but an armful of food."

"Perhaps," Lord Makar said. "But since we intercepted the letter, you will never find out." When I raised my eyes, I found him smirking at me. "And now I have brought Liam with us so that I can show you just how mean I can be when people disobey me."

"Don't," I said, throwing glances at the two armed men on either side of Liam. "I'll behave. I'll show you straight to the elves."

Liam frowned at me but I shook my head, urging him to keep silent.

"Yes, you will," Lord Makar said. "Now, let's get on with it."

Our odd party of five started into the forest. No one said anything for the first hour or two but I let them see my annoyance by stomping through the underbrush as loudly as I could. At last, Lord Makar snapped.

"Would you stop that?" he said and threw out his hands.

"I'm not doing anything," I retorted.

"Yes, you are. You're making so much noise I can't hear myself think."

Leaves rustled up ahead and a startled bird sped past us.

"Fine," I muttered before raising my voice again. "But see how light-footed you'd be if I kidnapped your best friend and threatened to kill him unless you betrayed your other friends."

A wide grin spread across Lord Makar's face. He'd been waiting for this. "It really bothers you, doesn't it?"

"Your people there," I said and pointed to the two silent men behind us, "each have a gun on Liam, of course it bothers me."

"I meant that you have to betray your elven friends," Makar said. "I thought you were above this having-feelings thing. After all, betraying and killing is second nature to you."

I narrowed my eyes at the lord pretender. "If your guards were dead, I could take you out in seconds."

Lord Makar showered me in another satisfied grin. "Good thing they're not, then."

Metal dinged against metal as two pistols spun through the air. I lunged for the grinning man in front of me. Two soft thuds sounded next to us, followed by two much heavier, but I didn't turn around to watch since my full focus was on tackling Makar. His face transformed into a mask of shock right before my shoulder connected with his chest and we both tumbled to the ground.

"Not him! I need him alive!" I called to the forest.

Lord Makar's arms flailed uselessly at his sides and his breath was driven from his lungs as I landed on top of him. Straddling his chest, I pulled a hunting knife from behind my back and pressed it to his throat.

"What the hell's going on, Storm?" the forest answered at last.

Flicking my eyes up, I smiled at the auburn-haired archer in front of me. "Elaran. Man, am I glad to see you."

"Faelar?" Liam called as another archer emerged from the trees.

The blond elf scanned the area before taking up position beside Elaran. Next to us, Liam twisted his hands out of the rope that had bound his wrists and then approached. On the other side of the blade, a suddenly very nervous-looking man licked his lips.

"This was the plan?" Liam asked when he reached my side.

"Yeah," I said before turning back to Elaran. "The other two?"

"Dead. Just like you said. Now, I ask again, what the hell is going on, Storm?"

Leaning down, I pressed the blade further into Makar's throat. "What's going on is that this worthless commoner thought he could blackmail me into betraying you." I flashed the outsmarted man a victorious grin. "But little did he know that thieves know a thing or two about the forest as well. Did you really think I was that stupid? You only intercepted that letter because I let you intercept it. I wanted you to bring Liam here so that I could both free him and capture you when my very-in-tune-with-nature friends got here."

"Yeah, we figured something was up," Elaran said. "It was impossible not to hear you coming because you were stomping around the forest like a *herd* of pregnant moose this time and that was unusually loud." He snickered. "Even for you."

I snorted but then locked eyes with the grumpy ranger so he'd know that I truly meant what I was about to say. "Thank you."

When Elaran nodded and then glanced away, I shifted my eyes to Faelar and did the same. The taciturn elf mirrored Elaran's nod.

"The rope, please, Liam," I said and hauled the captured lord to his feet.

He walked back and picked up the twisting coil from the damp grass. After he'd tied it around Lord Makar's hands, he gave me an amused smile. "The Starving Dog? Who'd charm someone with an armful of food?"

I grinned back at him. "I figured you'd appreciate that."

Liam giggled. "Yeah."

Lord Makar had been silent since he found me on top of him with a knife at his throat and now when he opened his mouth, the smug superiority was gone. "Look, I only did as I was told. You don't understand who my employer is. I couldn't say no."

"Oh, we are going to have chat about that exact topic right now," I said and pulled on his arm. "Remember that conversation we had that first night? When I told you what I'd do to innocent strangers? Today, you'll get to see what I do to my enemies."

"No please, you don't understand. I can't tell you who employed me. I can't."

"Oh, you will tell me everything," I said before turning back to my companions. "This'll get pretty loud. And messy. I'll go a bit further in so you won't have to watch."

A soft hand touched my arm. "Storm, don't do this," Liam said. "Please."

"What are you talking about? We need to know who he works for. His plan might've failed this time but he's gonna keep coming at us. At you." I looked at Liam and then threw my hand out and motioned at Elaran and Faelar. "At everyone I care about. I need to know who it is and why he's targeting me so I can stop him from hurting you."

Liam shuffled his feet. "Yeah, I know. But do you really need to use violence to get it?"

I shifted my gaze from my best friend to the suddenly hopeful-looking man next to me. Damn. This wasn't working in my favor. "Elaran, could you take him and... I don't know, tie him up by a tree over there?" Feeling that the grumpy elf was about to argue, I sent him a pleading look. I didn't want to have this conversation in front of Makar. "Please," I said.

"Fine," Elaran muttered and took charge of the prisoner.

Once Lord Makar and the two elves had disappeared into the trees, I turned back to Liam. "What's going on?"

My friend blew out a lungful of air and threw his arms up. "I feel like all I ever do is get kidnapped!"

I just studied him for a few seconds, my eyes filled with sympathy. "Yeah, and do you know why that is? It's because you have the great misfortune of being *my* best friend. And because I'm a shitty person, I've made enemies and when they want to get back at me they go for you. That's why I have to do this. Because if I don't, you will be in danger. Again."

"I get that you need the information but do you really have to hurt him to get it?" Liam dropped his arms in defeat and tilted his head up to stare at the canopy above. "I just feel like there has to be more to life than this endless cycle of violence."

A soft wind rustled the leaves while I considered his words. He did have a point, I suppose. There had been so much violence and death in my life, in our lives, that for me, it felt normal. But that was exactly it. Life in the Underworld, well, life in general really, was chaotic and messy. Choosing a path of pure righteousness was a luxury few could afford and I certainly wasn't among them. Don't get me wrong, I'm not saying everyone should be bad guys and go kill and hurt people whenever they want. It's just, life is a lot more complicated than simply good versus evil, which is why I don't like picking a side at all. I just do what I must to keep the people I care about safe.

"So, what do you want me to do?" I asked.

Liam tipped his head back down and shrugged. "I don't know. Maybe try talking to him? See if you can trick it out of him?"

That sounded like it would take much longer than what I had in mind but I figured I could at least give Liam's way a shot. "Alright, I'll try it."

He gave me a bright smile. "Thanks."

As we started towards the elves and our prisoner, I nudged an elbow in Liam ribs. "And you do a lot more than just get kidnapped, you know."

"Yeah, yeah."

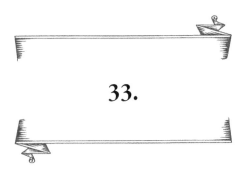

33.

Morning had turned into noon and then afternoon but the nervous lord pretender still hadn't said a word. I'd tried everything I could think of to trick him into telling me what I wanted to know but he'd remained silent. Whoever had hired him clearly terrified him. After stomping away in frustration for the third time, I'd even let Liam and then Elaran have a crack at him but neither of them had been successful.

"We can't just keep him in the forest forever," I said and blew out a frustrated breath.

Elaran ran a hand over his tight side braid. "No, you can't. Especially not if what you said about the Pernulans is true."

While I'd been trying to get Lord Makar to talk, I'd also filled in Liam, Elaran, and Faelar on the situation with the Pernulans and the documents I'd found. Now that we knew they were planning an attack, I'd asked the elves to be ready at a moment's notice and they'd agreed. A battle was coming and we both knew that we were stronger together.

"What if he works for this General Marcellus?" Elaran continued. "Getting you to lead them to us today might've just been the first scouting trip before they launch a full-blown attack on Tkeideru." He fixed me with a hard stare. "And I will *not* let that happen again."

The scars from the Great War between Keutunan and Tkeideru were still there, especially for the two elves present today since they'd both lost their parents to that war. Neither of these fiercely protective elves would allow a second war to lay waste to their home.

"Yeah, I've considered it," I answered to his first question. "But I don't understand why General Marcellus would want me dead. I don't even think he knows I exist." I tipped my head from side to side. "But then again, I can't really think of anyone else who'd want me dead either." Elaran's eyebrows shot up but before he had time to say anything, I held up both hands, motioning for him to stop. "This much. I can't think of anyone else who wants me dead *this much*."

"If all this is connected to the Pernulan invasion, we need to know," Elaran continued. "Fast."

Turning my head, I watched the tied up man by the tree across the clearing. The grass in front of him had been flattened by the many restless feet trampling it in search of answers. I shifted my gaze back to Liam.

"I'm sorry, Liam," I said and gave him an apologetic shrug. "We tried it your way but we're running out of time. I have to do this."

"No, you don't," my friend argued.

I was about to respond but Elaran surprised me by weighing in. "Yeah, she does." Deep understanding filled his yellow eyes when he looked at me. "To protect the people she loves, yes, she does."

Elaran had never been my biggest fan. In the beginning, he'd outright hated me and now we were, well, I didn't know what we were, but he tolerated me at least and deep down I had a feeling we might be friends. In a strange sort of way. But he rarely agreed with me on anything and he took every chance he got to throw snide comments at me. However, in some ways, we were very much alike. There was nothing he wouldn't do to protect his people. Just like me. So if anyone would back me up on this, it'd be him.

"I hear what you're saying," Liam said. "But if you have to go all attack mode, can't you at least start by only trying to scare him into telling you? Before you start with the blood and the screams again." His blue eyes held both sadness and exhaustion when he turned them on me. "There's so much of that already."

I heaved a deep sigh. How had a person as awful as me become friends with someone as kind and decent as him? After casting a glance at the afternoon sun filtering in through the trees, I nodded. "Alright. Wait here."

My best chance of making him fear me enough to betray his employer was to use the darkness. There was only one problem. I wasn't entirely sure how it actually worked. Sometimes when I called the darkness, it leaped from my soul straight away and sometimes it didn't. And then there were times when I didn't want to release it but it ripped from my soul anyway. I'd just have to hope it would come when I called this time.

"Time's up," I said as I closed the final distance and drew up in front of the tied up Makar. "Out of respect for my friend, I've tried to play nice but I've run out of patience." After pulling a throwing knife, I ran a finger over the blade while studying the gleaming edge. "This is your last chance before things get violent and messy." My eyes flicked up. "Talk."

Makar licked his thin lips and threw a couple of worried glances at the knife but remained silent. I wanted to scream.

Why did everything always have to be so gods damn difficult? All the anger, fear, and frustration of the past few days flooded my every vein. A raw howl ripped from my throat as I threw the knife. And then another. And another. I kept throwing until Makar's head was completely surrounded by sharp blades buried in the tree trunk. Lightning crackled over my skin as tendrils of black smoke whipped around me. Thunder roared in my eyes. The tied up man went from glancing at the knives around his head to staring at me with pure terror written on his face.

"You have one decision to make," I growled. "You have to decide who you fear most: your employer at some undetermined point in the future or me right now. Decide."

"Lord Fahr," Makar blurted out. "My employer, it's Lord Fahr."

Shit. Lord Fahr was a member of the Council of Lords. No wonder everyone was so afraid of him. He could make sure their whole family hanged with one signature. If he was involved in a larger conspiracy, we could be in some real trouble.

"If you're lying, I will know."

Lord Makar's narrow shoulders trembled against the tree. "I'm not. I promise. It's Lord Fahr. He hired me a couple of months ago to hunt you down and kill you and then his plans changed and he wanted me to do..." His eyes darted around the area. "This. To do this."

Standing dead still, I just continued watching the muscles in his jaw jump as he worked his mouth up and down. "Why?"

"Why did he hire me? Because I'm good at thinking and strategizing—"

"Why does he want me dead?" I cut off.

Lord Makar shook his head with short, jerky movements. "I don't know. I don't know."

"Why does he want me dead?" I pressed out between gritted teeth. When the lord pretender kept shaking his head, I drew a hunting knife and advanced on him. "Why?"

"Oh gods, please." He pulled at the restraints around his wrists. "I don't know. He never told me. Please, he never told me."

"Is he working with the Pernulans?"

Makar nodded eagerly. "Yes! I've seen him with them several times. But I don't know what they're planning. Lord Fahr only tells me about my part." He drew back slightly as uncertainty filled his voice. "Wh-which was you."

Panic welled up in my throat. Lord Fahr was in league with the Pernulans. A foreign force with maps of the palace was getting ready for a hostile takeover and they had a man from the king's inner circle on their payroll. Shade and King Edward were in more danger than they realized. Blood pounded in my ears but I still had to finish the interrogation so I pushed the panic out, for now, and filled my chest with rage.

Madness danced in my eyes as I pressed the knife to his throat. "Are you sure?"

"I'm sure, I'm sure. Please. If I knew anything else I would tell you. You have to believe me!"

Pure desperation bloomed in his eyes. He was telling the truth. I drew two fingers down his cheek and smiled. "I believe you."

He looked visibly relieved. What a fool.

"This is for Liam, for the builder and the scribe, for my guild, for the hanging, and for all the gods damn shooting and stabbing." In one precise slit, I drew the blade across his throat.

Blood spilled out and rushed towards his embroidered shirt neck, turning the garment red. Wet gurgles escaped his lips as he struggled to breathe. I watched the life dim in his eyes before pulling the darkness back. After yanking my throwing knives from the tree trunk, I dashed across the clearing.

"He had to die," I said with a hurried glance at Liam.

My friend just looked back at me with emotionless eyes. I knew he was disappointed in me but there really was no alternative. What were we supposed to do? Keep him prisoner? Where would we keep him and who would watch him so he didn't escape? Who would make sure he had food and water for the rest of his life? No. It doesn't work like that. And if we'd let him go, he'd warn Lord Fahr and the Pernulans so this was the only way. Besides, we were on the clock now.

"It's Lord Fahr," I blurted out. "He's the one who's been targeting me and he's working with the Pernulans."

"We heard," Elaran said. The auburn-haired ranger seemed unfazed by my murderous display only moments before. "Who's he?"

"A member of the Council of Lords." Words tumbled out of my mouth in rapid torrents. We didn't have time for this. "But it doesn't matter right now. I've gotta warn Shade."

Elaran grabbed my arm before I could take off in a panicked hurry. "Stop. Explain."

"Fahr is part of King Edward's inner circle. They had maps of the Silver Keep, for Nemanan's sake. They're planning an attack and they've got an inside man. I've gotta warn them." I whipped my head around the glen. "A full-scale attack is probably coming soon. Can you post an elf in the cabin so we can send word as soon as it happens?"

"I'll stay," Liam cut in. "I'll stay in the cabin and then as soon as you send word I'll run for Tkeideru and let them know." He glanced away when I tried to meet his eyes. "I've seen enough bloodshed."

Terrible feelings of hurt and shame pressed at my chest but I forced them away. I didn't have time to feel right now. "Alright," I said and drew him into a hug. My heart almost shattered when he barely hugged me back so I drew back before that could actually happen. "Stay safe, all of you. I'll send word as soon as I know."

Without waiting for a reply, I spun around and sprinted for the city walls. I had to hurry. Lord Fahr was working with the Pernulans. The reason why didn't matter right now. All that mattered was making sure I warned Shade and Edward before the Silver Keep was under attack. If we lost the king and his assassin, the Pernulans would take the city in days. And then there'd be no hope for me. Or Liam. Or my friends in the forest.

Despite the hurt and shame that Liam's last words and non-existent hug had brought me, I couldn't help second-guessing my actions today. If I hadn't taken his advice to try talking, and instead just done it my violent way from the beginning, I would've found out about this much sooner. I just hoped that those lost hours wouldn't turn out to be critical. As I dashed over root and stone, I prayed to any god who would listen that I wouldn't be too late. I couldn't be too late.

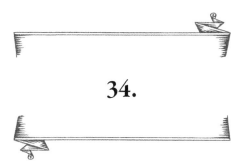

34.

Red carpets rumpled under my feet as I skidded to a halt in King Edward's throne room. Heavy boots smattered on the marble behind me.

"Tell them to back off but don't send them away!" I yelled at the two figures who had just appeared from the small door behind the throne. Two pairs of black eyes blinked at me in surprise. A rough hand tried to grab my arm but I twisted away. "Tell them!"

King Edward held up his hand, motioning for his guards to stop. The Silver Cloak who'd tried to seize me took a step back. The young king approached me with graceful steps, as opposed to Shade, who stalked across the floor. Lightning flashed in the assassin's eyes.

"You," he spit out. "What the hell–"

"Shut up!" I snapped. "Whatever it is, *this* is more important. Lord Fahr is working with the Pernulans. He's a traitor. He could get an army inside the castle at any moment without you knowing."

Shade whipped his head towards his king. Edward tried his best to remain calm and composed in front of his guards but I could see the panic swirling around in his eyes.

"Gather the rest of the guards," King Edward said to the Silver Cloaks positioned in the throne room. "Bring in the reserves. Find Lord Fahr. Secure the keep. Go."

Stamping feet and clattering metal rang out as the palace guards rushed to carry out the king's orders. King Edward shifted his eyes to me.

"How do you know?" he asked.

"I made his servant tell me." Frowning, I studied Shade. He still looked furious. "And what in Nemanan's name is wrong with you? I just warned you about a serious security breach."

The Master Assassin took a step forward. "And why should we believe you? After all, *you* betrayed us as well."

"I..." I hesitated. *Shit*. He knew it was me who'd assassinated the Master of the Builders' Guild and the Master of the Scribes' Guild. But how in Nemanan's name had he found that out?

"I swear, if you try to deny this," Shade said in a voice brimming with implied threats.

I jutted my chin out and threw my arms wide. "Try to deny what?"

Shade took another step forward and drew his swords. "You assassinated the builder and the scribe! You're the reason the Pernulans now control both those guilds."

"There are people here," a worried voice called behind us. "Why are there so many people here?"

The assassin, the king, and I all whipped our heads around. A woman in a silver dress as pale as her skin had wandered in through the gigantic marble arch that served as an entrance to the throne room.

"Mom?" King Edward said. "What are you doing here? You can't be here!"

The Queen Mother's gray eyes moved from face to face. She stumbled back. "You?"

Edward rushed forward. His mother did the same. "Mom, you have to leave," he said as he stopped her progress by gathering her in his arms.

"It's you!" Queen Mother Charlotte called. "It's you!"

Shade snapped his gaze back to me while the mother and son continued struggling next to us. "You betrayed us," he spat and leveled his right-hand sword at me. "You're working for the Pernulans."

I drew my hunting knives. "I'm not working for the Pernulans! Why would I come here and warn you about Lord Fahr if I was working for them, you dimwit?"

"No, let me go," Charlotte called to my right. "It's you. Let me go."

"I don't know what game you're playing," Shade growled at me, "but I'm going to kill you for this. All the knowledge we gained, all we know about shipbuilding, their language, their engineering skills, everything they shared, we've lost control of it all! Because of you. Because you decided to assassinate the leaders of the two most important guilds for our city's progress."

"I didn't *decide* to assassinate anyone!"

"Mom, calm down," King Edward implored beside us. "You're having one of your episodes again. Please, Mom, you have to leave."

"No!" Queen Mother Charlotte shrieked and struggled in her son's arms. "It's you. Can't you see it?"

Shade closed the distance between us and swung a curved sword at me. I deflected it with my knife and ducked back. Without a second's pause, he swiped at my ribs again but I twisted out of reach just in time. Lightning danced in his eyes while mine were going black like an oncoming thunderstorm. He lunged. I moved to slink away but he changed direction mid-motion and came at me from above. I barely had time to cross my blades over my head. The Master Assassin slammed his swords straight into my intersecting knives, forcing me down on one knee.

"Whose side are you on?" he bellowed at me.

My arms shook as he put his full weight behind the swords, driving them closer to my face. Metal ground against metal. "I'm on *my* side!" I yelled back at him. "Same as you!"

Silver-colored fabric swished to my right as Queen Mother Charlotte ran towards us.

"Mom, stop!" King Edward screamed. "Look out for the swords."

A smattering and a rumble came from our other side but before I could turn my head to see what had caused it, Charlotte rammed straight into Shade. She shoved him away from me. I blinked at her as the Master Assassin stumbled back. Why had she helped me? I was no one to her. Was I? However, before I could make any sense of it, a shot echoed throughout the cavernous marble hall.

Charlotte's body jerked back slightly as if pulled by an invisible string. She let out a sharp gasp before toppling backwards. Time seemed to pass in slow motion. I could make out every strand of her flowing light brown hair as it flew up around her head when she fell and every thread of her silver dress as it flapped on the floor once her body connected with the marble. With my mouth gaping open, I stared at the growing red stain on her chest.

King Edward released a heart-shattering scream and rushed forward. Shade stumbled back to his feet, casting frantic looks between the king and the marble arch. Men roared. A bullet zinged past my ear and exploded into the far wall. Boots slapped against stone.

A horde of Pernulans armed with swords welled through the entrance to the throne room but behind them stood a blond man in fine clothes. His raised arms each held a pistol. Lord Fahr snarled at me as he put the guns back in their holsters. King Edward had reached his dying mother and was lying bent over her with his arms around her narrow shoulders. One look told me she only had a few moments left in this life. Shade stood crouched in front of them, his swords out and ready, but when he threw a hurried glance at his king, his face showed signs of desperation. And fear.

While all of this had transpired, I'd remained kneeling on the floor, my mind just trying to process everything that had happened in the last few seconds. The mass of armed men closed in. People were attacking me. Again. Why were people always attacking me?

"Enough!" I bellowed with enough force to level cities. Darkness gathered around me like storm clouds. "I am so *sick*," I yelled as lightning boomed around me, "of people trying to kill me! All the fucking time!"

Black smoke whipped around me, matching the death that filled my eyes. The horde of attackers had halted their headlong rush and threw uncertain looks between me and the man in front, who appeared to be their leader. A ripple passed through the Pernulans as they whispered something in Pernish. Lord Fahr was nowhere to be seen. The lethal thunderstorm grew around me, crackling and swirling. When my black eyes, filled with rage and insanity, passed over Shade, he flinched. I kept them moving until they rested on the attackers.

"Die," I ground out between gritted teeth.

I let the darkness consume me. My feet moved on their own, speeding towards the forest of armed attackers. Blades slashed and stabbed. Screams of rage and desperation filled my ears as I twisted through the bodies. I flicked knife after knife until there were none left and then I continued the slicing and the cutting. Blood splattered the cold marble beneath our feet, making more than one attacker slip. I made sure they fell and never got up again. The black fog swirled around me as I rained hell down on everyone in my path.

Eventually, the screaming and shuffling of boots stopped. Eerie silence smothered the room only to be pieced by a muted dripping. A metallic tang floated in the air. I looked at the carnage around me. The floor was slick with blood and bodies littered it in a wide circle around me with a few corpses marking a trail towards the marble arch.

On the other side of the entrance, Shade still stood with his swords raised in front of Edward and Charlotte. He stared at me with an unreadable mask on his face.

Blood dripped from the knives in my hands. I heaved a couple of deep breaths as the darkness disappeared back into the pits of my soul. My blood-soaked blades hit the floor in a clattering of metal on stone. I wobbled slightly. Strength drained from me like a leaking boat. I blinked once and then my knees buckled. My body hit the marble hard and before I had time to worry about the consequences of blacking out right there, my mind shut down and darkness swallowed me.

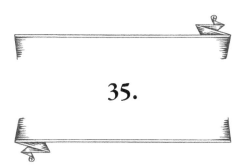

35.

My head throbbed. Light stabbed at my eyes so I closed them again for another few moments. When I felt ready to face the sunshine, I made another attempt at studying my surroundings. A room with expensive-looking furniture greeted me. I recognized the place. It was the same bedroom I'd woken up in when Shade had saved me from being hanged. This time, however, the assassin was nowhere to be seen. Good. I swung my legs over the side of the bed.

I had no way of knowing what had happened after I'd passed out but I assumed the men who'd attacked us in the throne room had been the only ones. Otherwise, I'd have woken up in hell instead of in a bed with soft pillows. Though, I had a feeling I might be heading to Ghabhalnaz's lower realm soon anyway. Shade knew I had done Lord Fahr and the Pernulans' dirty work and the Master of the Assassins' Guild didn't exactly forgive and forget. He'd probably only refrained from killing me while I was unconscious because he wanted to make sure I didn't have anything else to give him before he sent me to the God of Death.

The door opened behind me. I wanted to whirl around to see who it was but the pounding in my head prevented me and when I finally twisted around, they'd drawn the door closed again. Still sitting on the side of the bed, I heaved a deep sigh and scanned the room. My knives lay in a heap on the windowsill, illuminated by the morning light. Had I really taken out that whole group of Pernulans by myself last night? No wonder I'd been unconscious until after dawn. Pressing the heel of my hands to my temples, I remained seated on the bed until the pain in my head subsided.

When it had finally faded, I pushed myself up and walked over to the window but before I could spend any time gazing out of it, the door was yanked open again. This time, I'd recuperated enough energy to move at my usual speed so I whipped around to face the intruder. A black-clad man strode in. His lean muscular body stopped a few strides away and he fixed me with a calculating stare. Shade. I dove for the sharp pile next to me and snatched up two hunting knives. The Master Assassin pulled a gun and leveled it at my head.

"You betrayed us," he stated.

I stared back at him with an even gaze. "No. Lord Fahr's the one who's been targeting me all this time and a couple of days ago, his servant took Liam. Then he gave me a map and told me if I didn't kill the people living there, they'd kill Liam. So I killed them."

"What did you tell them about us?"

"Nothing. Only killed the builder and the scribe. And then when he wanted me to show them to Tkeideru, I set a trap and killed the servant and his guards. After I made him talk, that is."

Shade studied me from behind the raised pistol. "Doesn't matter. What you did crossed a line."

I gripped the handle of the knives so hard my knuckles turned white. "Crossed a line? Crossed a fucking line?"

"You worked for them, there's no coming back from that."

A clatter of metal rang out as I slammed the knives back down on the pile. Shade frowned at me and shifted his gaze from my face to the surrendered blades and then back again. I threw my arms wide and stalked across the floor. The Assassins' Guild Master kept his pistol trained on my forehead as I advanced but did nothing else since my outstretched arms showed that I clearly wasn't attacking. Only when I felt the cool metal of the muzzle between my eyes did I stop.

"Go ahead then," I snapped. "Kill me if you like. But don't you *dare* act as if what I did crossed some sort of line."

Shade kept his eyes locked on mine and his hand steady on the pistol but said nothing in reply.

"Cross a line?" I continued, blowing out an irritated breath and shaking my head. "There are no lines in our world. We do what we must to protect the people we love." I stabbed a finger at him. "You would've done the exact same thing if it'd been Edward. You know you would. So go ahead and blow my brains out then, but don't you dare tell me I did something unforgiveable." Jutting my chin out, I spread my arms wide again. "And besides, may I remind you that *I* am the only reason your precious king is still alive."

Silence fell. The assassin remained standing in front of me with his gun to my forehead for a good minute without doing anything. A battle seemed to rage behind his eyes.

"I know," he said at last, releasing a frustrated sigh as the anger on his face fizzled out. "Gods damn it, don't you think I know that?" Had that been embarrassment I'd seen flash past in his eyes? He took the gun from my head and let his arm drop to his side. "If you hadn't come back to warn us and then done...

well, what you did back in that throne room, Edward would be dead. Me too, most likely."

I crossed my arms over my chest. "So, are two life debts enough to square one act of forced betrayal?"

The Master Assassin stuck the pistol back in its holster. "Yes."

"Our temporary truce is back on?"

His mouth drew into a lopsided smile. "No excessive threatening and blackmailing."

I snorted. "Yeah, I think we got most of that out of our system in the last few hours, wouldn't you say?" I said before turning serious again. "How's the king?"

"He's in bad shape." Sadness passed over Shade's eyes and he heaved a deep sigh. "Charlotte's dead."

Tiny needles stabbed at my chest. I couldn't help thinking that maybe things would've been different if I hadn't wasted so much time doing it Liam's way when I interrogated Lord Makar. However, there was nothing I could do to change that now so I just pushed the uncomfortable weight off my chest and gave him a somber nod.

"Edward blames himself," Shade continued. "He thinks it's his fault because... never mind. It's not my secret to share."

Narrowing my eyes at him, I paused before replying. "This is about the vault, isn't it?"

The assassin ran a hand through his hair. "I still don't know how you know about the vault but–"

The door flew up. A distressed-looking Silver Cloak ran through the doorway and stopped in front of Shade.

"The Pernulans are here," he said.

"They're attacking?" Shade snapped.

"No, they... uh..." The guard scratched his beard. "General Marcellus and some others just walked up to the front door and demanded to see King Edward. They appear unarmed. What do we do?"

The black-eyed assassin stared at the palace guard for a moment while no doubt running through options in his head. "Escort them, under guard, to the throne room. Take your time. I need to get the king."

The Silver Cloak nodded and hurried back out the door. Shade took a few quick strides after him but then stopped and threw a glance over his shoulder. "Ceiling," was all he said to me before disappearing through the doorway as well.

Right. That had been my plan too. I strode towards the pile of knives still sitting on the windowsill. I had to hurry if I was going to make it to my favorite eavesdropping spot before the king and the Pernulans arrived in the throne room.

What in Nemanan's name were they doing here? They'd just launched an attack on the keep which had killed the king's mother and now they simply strolled up to the front door. The audacity of that was incredible. I wondered what kind of game they were playing. Apprehension spread through my chest as I shoved the last knife in place and took off towards the throne room. Nothing good. Nothing good at all.

"YOU HAVE SOME NERVE coming here today," King Edward said.

I shifted my weight on the beams up in the ceiling. King Edward sat straight-backed on his obsidian throne. His hard face was devoid of all emotion. At that moment, I realized that he looked nothing like the anxious boy I'd seen the first time I'd met him. He hid the pain of his mother's death well and presented a face of calm composure to the small group of Pernulans in front of the dais but I could feel the hatred brimming underneath the surface. Shade stood on the king's right while an army of Silver Cloaks surrounded General Marcellus and his people.

"Not at all," General Marcellus said. "We simply want to share some information with you. Information that will lead to a calm and peaceful transition."

"Speak plainly. Why have you come?"

"If you wish," the general said and swept his arms to the sides. "Before I leave here today, you are going to agree to abdicate the throne and hand over power to me."

The silence that followed his statement was deafening. King Edward stared at him with incredulity written all over his face while Shade's eyes roared like wildfire.

King Edward gave his head a short shake and then composed himself. "I have another idea. I will have my guards shoot you and your people here. Right now."

General Marcellus flashed a smile of brilliant white teeth. "I can see that you are still confused. Allow me to explain the situation you currently find yourself in. Since the day I arrived here, I have been infiltrating every part of your city. Have you been outside lately? My people are everywhere. They are inside every tavern, every house, and every garrison. They have made friends with fisherman, farmers, merchants, and soldiers. They are inside the houses of your nobles, either as lovers to the very romantically deprived noble ladies or because we bribed them and convinced them that a change of leadership was due." He flashed another triumphant smile and waved a hand. "Some did not even need to be bribed. They had scores to settle with you and your people so they came to me willingly. I also control your most important guilds when it comes to the city's technological advancement: the scribes and the builders. Do you see the problem yet?"

King Edward's hands were balled into tight fists but he said nothing. When he didn't respond, the self-satisfied general continued.

"Your city is mine," he said. "Did you really think that we wanted an alliance with your underdeveloped city? We are decades, if not centuries, ahead of you in technological development so what kind of assistance could you possible offer us in a war?" General Marcellus gave a derisive snort. "No, the only thing your backwater island is good for is as a last resort for us to retreat to if we were to lose the war." The general's face turned hard as he locked eyes with King Edward. "Now, I have an ultimatum for you. Abdicate your throne and name me your successor in front of your entire nobility *or...* I start killing everyone in the city."

The King of Keutunan drew back with a look of utter shock on his face while Shade's hands twitched at his sides. Then the storm broke. King Edward flew across the platform and launched himself at the foreign general. The ringing of steel filled the vast hall as the Silver Cloaks drew their swords and leveled them at the group of Pernulans.

"What did you just say?" King Edward growled in General Marcellus' face.

I had never seen him like this before. He'd always been calm, collected, and compassionate. Come to think of it, the compassion for his people, mixed with the heartbreak over his mother's death, was probably the reason he was filled with rage right now. Shade appeared by the king's side and put a hand on his arm but Edward didn't release his grip on Marcellus' shirt.

"I said that if you do not abdicate, I will kill everyone in your city," General Marcellus said matter-of-factly. "As soon as I give the word, every one of my people in every part of your city–the taverns, the garrisons, the farms, the mansions in the Marble Ring–will kill everyone in sight. Then, I will fire every cannon on my warships and reduce your city to ashes."

King Edward yanked the general's shirt forward. "Why don't I just kill you now then?"

General Marcellus gave him a patronizing smile and answered in a voice one might use to explain something very simple to a child. "Because if I do not return from this meeting, that exact order will be given as well. Just as the same will happen if I *do* return from this meeting, but with the wrong answer."

The furious king dropped General Marcellus' shirt as if he'd been burned, and stumbled back a couple of steps. Marcellus smoothened his rumpled clothing with a patient smile on his face.

"At last, you understand," he said. "You only have two options: abdicate or watch your city and its people be destroyed. You have to choose which one it will be. Right now."

King Edward's mouth gaped open without producing any sound while he stared at the leader of the Pernulans. Morning light streamed through the tall windows and fell across the king's speechless face, making it look paler than usual. Shade slipped in front of him and blocked his view of the Pernulans.

"My king," he said and gestured with his hands close to his chest, "you can't agree to this. You can't roll over for these people."

King Edward composed himself again by giving his head a short shake and then drew up to his full height. "Who are you to tell a king what he can and cannot do? Step aside."

Despite the heavy atmosphere and the grave topic being discussed on the floor below me, I had the urge to chuckle. The Assassins' Guild Master was probably not at all accustomed to people addressing him in that manner. I wished I could do that someday. Shade stepped back and took up position behind the king's shoulder again. I knew it was petty and highly inappropriate at this momentous moment but it was so satisfying to see someone put him in his place.

"I will abdicate," King Edward said with his head held high. "I will not bring death and destruction to my people for the sake of holding on to power. General Marcellus, *you* may be prepared to be king of the ashes but I am not. I shall host a grand reception at the end of the week where I will announce my abdication."

"Tomorrow," General Marcellus said. "You will announce it tomorrow."

King Edward threw out his hands in an exasperated gesture. "General, it is not possible to organize a reception that all the nobles will attend in such short time. If you want me to hand over power in front of all the nobles, I need more time."

Marcellus gave him a dismissive wave. "There is no more time. If the clock strikes midnight tomorrow and you have not relinquished your throne, my orders will be carried out. Do you understand?"

The young king opened his mouth to protest but then closed it again. He nodded reluctantly in reply.

"Good. I am glad we could come to an understanding. After all, we do not want war, only peace and stability." General Marcellus held up one finger as if he'd just remembered something. "Oh, speaking of conflict. I would advise you not to resume hostilities against Lord Fahr and his supporters. Lord Fahr is with us now so we would see that as a breach of contract." He flashed a self-satisfied smile. "We will see you at the reception, King Edward."

With those final words, the group of Pernulans swept out of the throne room, colorful clothes swishing behind them. The king and the assassin started arguing below me. Edward looked like he was about to throw something. Or murder someone. Or throw something at someone to murder them.

Wood creaked as I shifted my weight on the beam. Damn. This was bad. Actually, the word *bad* was woefully inadequate to describe the situation in which we currently found ourselves. The Pernulans had figured out the king's weakness: his great concern for the wellbeing of his people. And they knew exactly how to use it against him. They had pushed him, pushed *us*, into a corner. I heaved a resigned sigh and started back down to join King Edward and Shade on the floor. There was no way we would win this.

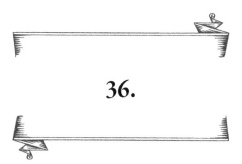

36.

Green foliage whizzed past as I raced through the forest. There was a lot to do and not much time. A flock of birds flapped away in a startled flurry of black wings when I jumped a creek and landed on the other side but I didn't stop. As soon as my feet touched grass again, I picked up the pace and I continued my sprint towards the cabin.

After I'd climbed down from the beams above the throne room, King Edward, Shade, and I had met in the king's study to formulate a plan. What Shade and Edward had decided in that room was more of a desperate hope than a convincing scheme. I don't like hastily thrown together plans but I had agreed to go when Shade sent me on a mission to contact the elves, which was why I presently found myself dashing through the leaf-covered outdoors.

Liam whirled around as I crashed through the branches and skidded to a halt in the clearing surrounding the cabin. He stared at me. I wasn't sure how to behave since last time we'd seen each other, he'd been upset with me. So I simply remained standing there, a few paces away. With a few quick strides, he closed the distance between us and drew me into a hug. A real hug, this time. Tears threatened to spill from my eyes.

"You're not still mad at me?" I mumbled into his shoulder.

His body shook as a laugh rippled through his chest. "I could never be mad at you, you lunatic." He let go and locked eyes with me. "I'm sorry, Storm. I didn't mean what I said yesterday. Well, I did, in a way. But I didn't mean to direct it at you. I was just frustrated with the world and what we need to do to stay alive."

I dropped my eyes and instead occupied myself with studying a root while I poked at it with the toe of my boot. "So you're not ashamed of me? Of who I am?"

Liam put a hand to my chin and lifted it until I met his kind eyes again. "Never."

Choking back a sob, I managed a grateful nod. Relief flooded my chest. The thought of Liam being disappointed in me and ashamed of who I was and what I did, had almost broken my heart. I knew that he wanted more from life than what we had in the Underworld. I did too. Our near-death experiences had changed us both in that regard, but in different ways. Liam wanted to live another kind of life and I wanted more of life. Maybe there was a way we could both get what we wanted someday. However, first we had to survive the deadly power struggle around us.

"The Pernulans have attacked?" Liam asked when he saw my eyes turn somber.

"Yeah, they've finally shown their hand," I said and motioned at the cabin. "Let's go inside. I've got a lot to tell you."

Liam nodded and started for the door. We were short on time but there were some things he needed to know before I sent him to get the elves. And some things he didn't need to know. Once we'd sat down at the table in the one-room cabin, I explained what had happened at the Silver Keep and what the plan was. Well, parts of the plan at least.

"She's really dead?" Liam asked after I'd finished speaking. When I nodded in affirmation, his dark blue eyes filled with sadness. "How's the king taking it?"

"He blames himself." Squinting at the cold fireplace, I tapped my chin. "Though, I'm still not sure why." However, we didn't really have time for psychoanalyzing the King of Keutunan in the wake of his mother's death, so I tore my eyes from the ashes of the dead fire and shook my head. "Anyway, you're clear on the plan?"

"Yeah," my friend said with a nod. "Get the elves to the edge of the forest but don't engage until we see the signal."

"Exactly." I pushed to my feet. "Alright, we've gotta go. It's gonna take some time for you to get there and for Faye and Elaran to get their people prepared, so no time to lose. You ready?"

"Ready," Liam said and jumped out of his chair before following me out the door.

I'd been about to take off into the forest again but stopped and turned back to my friend. "Be safe. Don't take any stupid risks, alright? Next time we see each other, all of this will be over."

Liam nodded but before he had time to say anything, I sprinted into the woods and ran for West Gate. I'd told him the plan but not the whole plan. It was better if he didn't know what I had to do next because I knew he'd disapprove. My mind churned while the wind whipped through my hair. I didn't exactly like it either but there was no other choice. If we were to survive this onslaught, it had to be done.

WOOD VIBRATED AS I pounded on the door. It was still daylight so I pulled the stolen cloak tighter around my shoulders to hide my ensemble of knives. The door opened and a young man peered out.

"Yes?" he said while casting suspicious glances between me and the empty back porch around us. "Who are you? This is not the front door."

You don't say? I gave him an internal eye-roll. What an amateur. If I'd been there to kill him, or anyone else in that house, I could've just walked straight in now that he'd opened the door. These people put way too much faith in the Silver Cloaks.

After withdrawing my hand from inside my cloak, I stuck a folded piece of paper under the servant's nose. "Tell your master to meet me at this location one hour after sunset tonight. There will be no change of time or place because there's a deadline that has to be met. He will understand what I'm talking about. Don't drag your feet with this. Give him the information right away."

The young man scrunched up his eyebrows and crinkled his narrow nose but took the offered paper. "Why would he be interested in this?" he said, waving the note in front of his face. "Who even are you?"

I pulled up the hood of my cloak and fixed the servant with an iron stare. "Tell Lord Fahr that the Oncoming Storm wants to cut a deal."

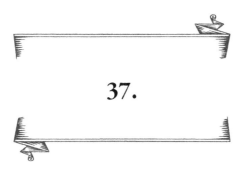

37.

Night had fallen and with it, waves of fog had rolled in from the sea. The damp mist clung to my clothes, making me shiver in the absence of a cloak.

After I'd finished the rest of my preparations, I'd gone back to the empty house at Mercer Street and dropped off my cloak and most of my knives. I'd figured that showing up to the meeting fully armed wouldn't exactly help my case when I'd asked him there to cut a deal. Since I was at a disadvantage in this conflict, I needed to show him I understood that he was in control. So I'd decided to show up unarmed as a sign of good faith. Well, *unarmed* might be a bit of a stretch. I felt the comforting weight of the stilettos in my sleeves. I never went anywhere without at least one knife.

Footsteps echoed up the alley. Five men strode through the mist and took up positions on the other side of the small courtyard I'd chosen as our meeting place. Lord Fahr stood in front with his hands on his hips while three armed men spread out in a semi-circle around him.

Next to Lord Fahr was another blond man that I recognized instantaneously. It was the one I'd seen aboard the Pernulans' ship. The one who'd been there to make a deal. Before I could dwell further on that, the three men behind Lord Fahr drew their swords.

"I'm unarmed," I said, spreading my arms wide and turning in a slow circle.

When I once again faced forwards, I saw the armed men nod among themselves. My clothes were tight enough that hiding weapons in them would be difficult for most people and there were no suspicious bulges in my garments so they seemed satisfied. Idiots. I said difficult, not impossible. And besides, when had I ever been *most people*?

"The Oncoming Storm," Lord Fahr said in a voice as well-oiled as his hair. "I was surprised to receive your message."

"I've come to cut a deal," I said.

"William," the other blond man said in his deep voice and put a hand on Lord Fahr's arm.

So, Lord Fahr's first name was William. I didn't know that. William Fahr took a half step back and motioned with his hand for his companion to proceed. It seemed as though Lord Fahr was giving over control of the conversation to this other man. I wondered how he was connected to this.

A vicious smile flashed across the lips of William Fahr's mysterious companion. "If you are here to beg for a truce, you should be on your knees."

The darkness pulled at my soul. Good thing I hadn't brought my throwing knives, because otherwise I might've hurled one at him. My fingers twitched while I leveled an even stare at him but he just raised his eyebrows and gestured expectantly.

Gods damn it. Who even was this man? I didn't want to do this but if Liam and I were to survive this battle, it had to be done. While keeping my eyes fixed on his, I got down on my knees, one leg at a time. The stones were cold and damp beneath me. I felt sick to my stomach.

"I've come to cut a deal," I repeated.

The malicious grin on the man's face broadened. "Have you finally accepted that you are outclassed, girl?"

"Yes." I had to force the word out of my throat.

"Good. Now, what is it that you want to beg of us?"

Heaving a deep sigh, I tipped my head up. "My guild." I ran my eyes over the rooftops around us. The Thieves' Highway. I'd spent so much time traversing it when I was a member of the Thieves' Guild but had barely been up there since I was framed. I really missed it. "You got me kicked out of my guild." I shifted my gaze back to William Fahr. "I want you to undo it. You can have whatever you want in return."

Lord Fahr adjusted his hands on his hips but said nothing. He only flicked his eyes to the man on his left, as if to see what he would say. A look of superiority settled on the unidentified man's face. "How does it feel?" he said. "How does it feel to be thrown out of your precious guild?"

Uncontrollable heartbreak filled my chest. I tried to push it down but was only partly successful. "It's awful. And that's why I wanted to meet." I flicked my eyes between the two men. "I want you to take it back," I said. "Tell people it was a mistake, or something, anything, just tell them it wasn't true. You know it isn't true."

The mysterious man ran a hand over the top of his blond head and bestowed a look of mock pity on me. "Aw, you want to go home?"

"Yes, I want to go home!" I let my arms fall to my sides. "I want to go home. And now with the Pernulans taking power there's no way in hell I'll survive outside the guild. So just take it back. I don't care what you tell people but fix this."

"Fix this, what?"

I took a deep, calming breath through my nose. "Fix this, *please*."

"And what would you have to offer us in exchange?" the nameless man said.

"What do you want?"

"What do I want?" The venomous smile was back on his lips. "Now we come to the heart of the matter. There is only one thing I want and I shall explain it to you shortly. But first, a question. Who am I?"

Squinting at him, I shrugged. "I don't know."

"My name is Eric Fahr."

"Okay?" I furrowed my brows at the blond man in front of me because that name didn't ring a bell.

"You really don't know who I am, do you?" He let the silence stretch, savoring the moment.

I was telling the truth; I had no idea who he was. When I thought I finally knew who'd been trying to kill me, there had turned out to be another layer. The attack on me hadn't just been by Lord Fahr, as his servant had said. William Fahr had a relative and this Eric Fahr seemed to be the real reason people had been trying to kill me. But I had no idea what his connection was to me and why he hated me this ferociously. As Eric Fahr fixed me with a stare that dripped of poison I realized that I was about to find out. At last.

"I am Frederick's father," he stated.

Frowning, I tried to connect the name with a face. A distant memory drifted across my vision. Dark stone walls of a storage room and a trembling figure backing away with his hands raised. A young man's pleading voice telling me, *you don't have to do this*. The gleaming knives in my hands and the grin tinted with madness flashing across my lips as I reply, *oh, but I want to*. The memory snapped into place. Rogue. I drew a sharp breath. Fuck. My chances of surviving this negotiation had just plummeted like a stone in the sea. I had to keep him talking.

"I see," I said carefully.

"No, I don't think you do." Eric's eyes were as hard as the stones I knelt on. "You killed my son. *My* son."

"I..." I trailed off. What was I supposed to say? I had killed his son. In a rather violent way too. Damn. Realizing that bargaining would get me nowhere, I jumped to my feet and raised my voice instead. Sometimes attack was the best defense. "Oh don't pretend he was some kind of hero. Your son infiltrated my guild, got my best friend kidnapped, and then had me blackmailed into killing someone else."

"My nephew worked for King Adrian," Lord William Fahr cut in. "The *rightful* king of Keutunan. The king sent him on a mission and because he completed it, you killed him."

Oh. So that was the connection. Lord Fahr wasn't just Lord Fahr. He was Lord Fahr the elder and the previously unidentified man next to him was his brother. Without realizing it at the time, I had apparently killed the nephew of one of the most powerful people in the whole Upperworld. Fantastic.

"His *mission* was to make me kill people I care about," I spat back at the brothers.

Eric snarled and shook his head at me. "You gods damn gutter rat. You think you're above the law and that you can just do whatever you want without any consequences. You didn't have to kill him, you could've just sent him away, but you chose to kill him. No one forced you to do it. You decided. On your own. To kill *my* son." He locked furious eyes on me. "Actions have consequences. These are the consequences."

As much as I loathed him for what he'd done to me, I was forced to admit that there was truth to his words. Frederick, or Rogue, as we in the Thieves' Guild had called him, had infiltrated our guild last summer and then had kidnapped Liam in order to blackmail me into killing the Elf Queen. After I'd gotten Shade to rescue Liam, I'd gone back to the guild and killed Rogue in retribution. Not because I had to, our plan would've worked anyway, but simply because I wanted to. And now the consequences of that decision had caught up with me. Damn.

"So that's why you targeted my guild?" I asked as another realization struck.

"Yes. I couldn't believe I hadn't thought of turning your own guild against you earlier." Eric Fahr bared his teeth. "And did you see how easy it was? How little they actually trust you? My brother only needed to whisper a few careful words in a few specific people's ears and your whole guild turned on you straight away. That must have hurt. All I want is for you to hurt until your heart breaks the way mine did when you killed my son. Tell me it hurt."

It had hurt. I knew that there had been way too many unexplained circumstances around me at the time but I still thought my heart was going to shatter when I learned that they actually believed I had betrayed them. But the younger Lord Fahr was wrong on one point. Not my *whole* guild had turned on me.

"Is that enough?" I called into the night.

"Is that enough for what?" Eric said. "Who are you talking to?" When I didn't reply he threw worried glances at the buildings around us but then his gaze passed over the three armed men. He snapped his fingers. "Take her. But don't kill her. She's mine."

When they advanced on me with raised swords, I threw nervous looks around me as well. The night remained silent. Then I heard it. One metallic ding at first and then a smattering. The brothers Fahr and their guards yelped in fear and surprise as bullets hailed down around them. With arms up to protect their heads, they sprinted for the alley mouth and disappeared back the way they'd come.

Dozens of heads popped up on the rooftops around me. I heaved a deep sigh and let out a giddy laugh of relief. It had worked. Three men that exuded authority landed on the street and strode towards me. The Thieves' Guild had come to my rescue.

I dropped to one knee and with my left fist on the ground and my right arm across my leg, I bowed my head. "Strength and honor to the guild."

"Strength and honor," my three Guild Masters replied. "Rise."

After breathing out another small sigh of profound relief, I did as they said and rose to my feet. When I met their eyes I could almost swear I saw traces of admiration in them. Guild Master Caleb's brown eyes looked slightly apologetic as well.

"The Oncoming Storm," Guild Master Killian said. "You did not betray the guild."

"No, Guild Master," I said.

He pushed his shoulder-length black hair back behind his ear and nodded. "We will let the rest of the guild know that you were framed and that you were innocent the whole time."

It wasn't exactly an apology but I hadn't been expecting one either. I was just grateful that I was once again welcome back to the guild. "Thank you," I said with sincerity.

Master Caleb regarded me with those observant brown eyes. "Bones was right. When he came to us and told us that you had brought word, we were skeptical. At first, we had no intention of coming here tonight because we were concerned it might be a trap. But he pleaded very valiantly for you and argued that if you said you'd bring proof of your innocence tonight, then you'd deliver it." His eyes twinkled. "You have a good friend there, don't you?"

I gave him a small smile. "Yes, I really do."

After I'd dropped off the invitation at Lord Fahr's house, I'd managed to contact Bones and share my plan with him. It had been a very brief meeting outside the Thieves' Guild's front door but it had been enough. He had really come through for me.

"Now, would you mind explaining why we couldn't shoot those lying bastards in the face?" Guild Master Eliot rasped in his grating voice. "Getting all of them," he gestured at the thieves still occupying the rooftops around us, "to shoot but not hit anything was no small feat."

"I understand," I said. "I'm sorry I couldn't be more specific earlier. There's actually a lot I have to catch you up on but I'll start with that." I shifted my weight on the stones and ran my hands over my arms a couple of times to get some heat back. The fog was still seeping into my clothing. "The Pernulans have delivered an ultimatum to King Edward: give up the throne to them or they'll start killing everyone in the city and then blast what's left of it to rubble with their cannons." My Guild Masters all drew back slightly at that but didn't interrupt me. "And I overheard General Marcellus talking earlier, the Pernulans *hate* us underworlders. He called us a foul plague. So even if we'd survive the cannons, we'd be fighting for survival as soon as they're in power anyway."

"That is indeed troubling news," Guild Master Eliot said. "But what does it have to do with not killing Lord Fahr and his brother?"

"It's part of the ultimatum. Lord Fahr... well, both the Fahr brothers, I suppose, work for the Pernulans so if King Edward were to kill them, the Pernulans would start slaughtering people."

"I see," Master Eliot said.

Guild Master Killian trained his piercing black eyes on me. "I sense that you have a plan for how to avoid this ghastly situation of being under Pernulan rule. What is it?"

Well, he was nothing if not perceptive. However, I couldn't reveal everything I knew because if I did, they would have questions about how I knew. And if I answered those questions, I'd have a very angry Master Assassin on my heels. That was something I wholeheartedly wanted to avoid now that he'd finally agreed not to kill me.

"It's not really my plan but I was contacted by Shade while I was setting this up." That was a harmless lie but the rest of my words were true. "He said he was sending it through the official channels as well but since there's a rush, he told me to tell you straight away too. He's calling an Underworld Conclave. Tonight."

My three Guild Masters stared at me for a moment but then Killian snapped his fingers and pointed in the direction of the guild. On the rooftops above us, the assembled guild members started trickling back towards our headquarters. Killian, Eliot, and Caleb all gave me a swift nod before returning themselves. Mist from the sea continued to roll over me as I took off in the other direction. It was time to visit the house on Mercer Street for the last time and retrieve the knives I'd left there. After that I would be heading home. My heart soared. Home. At last.

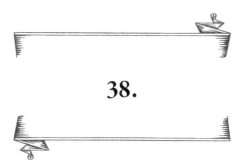

38.

Flames danced on the stone walls from the fires burning brightly in the four corners. Apparently, I wasn't heading home. Not yet anyway. I studied the stone-covered underground chamber. Thirteen people were gathered in the room. Eight were seated in ornate chairs around a large, round table while the remaining five stood behind them. I recognized six of the seated people but, besides myself, I only knew the face of one other person standing.

"I hereby declare this Underworld Conclave opened," Shade said.

He was sitting opposite my own Guild Masters, who occupied the three chairs in front of me. To my right, two more Guild Masters sat at the table. These were the only two seated people I didn't know beforehand. I knew which guilds they represented, of course, but I had never actually seen them in person.

Closest to us was a man in ragged clothing that seemed to consist of several different garments that had been altered and sewn together to form the outfit he now wore. His hair was matted and tangled but his blue eyes were sharp as ice, which had earned him the name Rime. He was the Beggars' Guild Master. A short distance away sat the only female Guild Master: Madame

Margaux, the Mistress of the Pleasure Guild. Her red hair hung elegantly braided with jewels down the back of her ornate dress.

To my left sat the two brawny brothers, Mick and Donnie, who ran the Bashers' Guild. I knew their faces because my smart mouth had managed to land me in some trouble with them a couple of years back. Fortunately for me, there were more muscles than brain on them so I'd managed to talk my way out of it before they'd started swinging bashers' bats at my head.

"Calling a conclave on this short notice is highly irregular, Shade," Rime said and turned his piercing stare on the Assassins' Guild Master.

"Yes, it is. But we are living in unusual times." Shade held up his hand and the man behind him placed a stack of papers in it.

The man behind Shade's chair was the only standing person I recognized. As I watched the tall, brown-haired man place his arms behind his back again, I realized that I still didn't know his name. We'd met several times but I'd never bothered to ask about it. I just called him Man-bun. With an internal chuckle, I added a mental note to ask Shade about it sometime. But whatever his name was, he had to be Shade's second-in-command.

Each guild was allowed to bring one extra member to the conclave. Usually, they brought their right-hand man. Or woman, for that matter. However, I was nowhere near being the second-in-command in the Thieves' Guild so I'd been extremely surprised when my Guild Masters had told me to accompany them. The only plausible explanation I'd been able to come up with was that they'd realized I was smack-dab in the middle of this and that's why they'd figured it was best to bring me along.

Shade put the papers in a neat stack in front of him. "Are you aware of the recent developments regarding the Pernulans?"

My three Guild Masters nodded, along with Madame Margaux, but the others shook their heads. Shade executed a businesslike nod in acknowledgement and then proceeded to catch them up on the Pernulans' ultimatum as well as their opinions on underworlders. Apparently, Shade had overheard them speaking about us on more than one occasion, and let me tell you, *foul plague* was among the least colorful expressions they'd used to describe us.

"I see." Rime knitted his fingers together and rested his chin on top of them. "At least the current king leaves us to ply our trade in peace, if done discreetly, but it sounds as though these Pernulans mean to cleanse the city of its Underworld inhabitants if they rise to power."

"That would indeed seem to be their intention," Shade confirmed. "Which is why I have called this conclave."

Guild Master Killian leaned forward in his chair in front of me. "You want the Underworld to band together and stop this foreign takeover. Why? Why is the king and his Upperworld army not enough to prevent this? Why do we have to get involved?"

"General Marcellus brags about having people everywhere in Keutunan. He says that the whole city is compromised and from his perspective, he's right. From his perspective," the Assassins' Guild Master repeated with a sly smile. "In his loathing, he has completely overlooked our world. He does not have people in the Underworld and we are not compromised. *We* are the only part of Keutunan that still remains free of these foreign invaders."

The crackling of the fires in the corners was the only sound interrupting the silence that had settled while the Underworld

Guild Masters considered Shade's words. The only uncompromised part of Keutunan was the much distained and terribly crooked Underworld. How ironic.

A snicker escaped Madame Margaux's red lips. "Their narrow view on morality has made them blind to the biggest threat of all." Her voice was silky smooth but her mouth drew into a vicious smile. "Us."

"Let us vote, then," Guild Master Killian said. "All in favor of a joint Underworld operation to stop this threat to our world, raise your hand." All eight Guild Masters raised a hand. "Unanimous. It is decided, then," Killian said before nodding to the man who'd called the meeting. "Shade, our guilds are with you. I assume you have a plan?"

The Master Assassin flashed a knowing smile. "I do indeed. My guild will do the heavy lifting in the killing department but we need help with certain areas where brute force works better than stealth. Can we count on your people for that?" he finished and nodded to the Masters of the Bashers' Guild.

Mick and Donnie looked at each other and broke into a grin. Donnie cracked his knuckles. "Yeah, we'll bash some heads, no problem."

Shade nodded and then shifted his gaze to my three Guild Masters. "We also need help with an operation that requires lots of stealth but no killing. I have a few of my guild on it but we need more people. Can we count on your guild?"

Killian, Caleb, and Eliot exchanged looks before they turned back to Shade. "You can," my dark-haired Guild Master confirmed.

"What about our guilds?" Rime said and nodded to Madame Margaux. "We are not fighters or sneakers. If we send our people on a mission that requires such attributes, they will die. And that I will not allow."

"I have no intention of asking you to send your people on any such mission," the Assassins' Guild Master said. "Your two guilds are very different from each other but you have one very particular skill in common: you are excellent at persuading people. We are going to need that skill for a different part of our plan. Can we count on you for that?"

Madame Margaux tipped her head in his direction. "My girls are with you."

"As are my people," Rime added.

"Good." A rustle of paper filled the room as Shade passed out various documents from the neat pile in front of him. "These are the specifics for each mission along with the time plan. Sticking to the time plan is crucial. One missed deadline and we're doomed."

The room fell silent as the other seven Guild Masters read through the documents spelling out their mission. While they were busy reading, Shade flicked up his intelligent eyes to me. *We need to talk*, he mouthed at me. I gave him a slow nod in reply.

When Mick and Donnie finally looked up from their papers, signaling that everyone was finished reading, Shade placed his hands on the table. "Any questions?"

"Yeah," Donnie said and scratched at a scar on his cheek. "What 'bout the Silver Cloaks? We gonna have any trouble from them while we do this?"

"No," Shade said with a swift shake of his head. "The Silver Cloaks are on our side for this."

"That's a first," Guild Master Eliot remarked.

"Indeed," the Master Assassin said. "So that means the Silver Cloaks who can't help us will at least stay out of our way."

Mick and Donnie exchanged a grin. "Good."

"Any other questions?" When no one spoke up, Shade nodded. "Then I declare this Underworld Conclave closed. Good luck and may the gods back our play."

Wooden chairs scraped on stone as the eight Guild Masters stood up and got ready to leave the underground chamber. Organizing this conclave, getting everyone to it, and then carrying it out had taken most of the night. Even though there were no windows in this meeting hall, I knew the sun would soon be up to mark the beginning of another day.

My bones ached with weariness. I'd pushed through another long couple of days with little sleep, and I need rest. And food. I knew Shade had said that we needed to talk but I had to sleep and eat to regain my strength first. As my Guild Masters filed out the door, I caught Shade's eye. *Tomorrow afternoon*, I mouthed at him. He rolled his eyes but then mouthed back, *Black Hand*. After a quick nod, I followed my three Guild Masters as they started towards the Thieves' Guild. Home. Now, I would finally be going home.

39.

"When the green-clad gentleman laughs..." Guild Master Eliot said into the slit in the door.

"...the whole manor disappears," a voice I knew very well finished from inside before the door was pushed open. "Guild Masters, welcome back," Bones said and ran his eyes over our small party. When his eyes reached mine, a broad smile spread across his lips.

"Thieves' Court, fifteen minutes," Guild Master Killian said to me before he and the others strode past and started down the stairs. Master Caleb clapped a hand on Bones' shoulder as he passed.

Once the three leaders of our guild had disappeared down the stairwell, I turned to Bones. I felt ridiculously awkward. Gestures of gratitude and appreciation had never been my strong suit. "Well, I just wanted to say... uhm... thanks," I said and gave his shoulder a soft push with my fist.

A rumbling laugh shook his massive frame. "Don't be an idiot," he said and drew me into a fierce hug.

"Thank you for believing me," I said into his muscular chest. "I mean it, thank you."

"Anytime, Storm. Anytime." Bones pulled back but kept his hands on my shoulders as he locked eyes with me. "How are you?"

I wanted to burst out laughing. *How are you?* Such a simple question for such a complicated time in my life. In these last few weeks I had almost died several times and my best friend had been kidnapped. Again. I'd killed dozens of people who were attacking me, killed some people I didn't want to kill, pretended to betray people, actually betrayed people, saved people, lied, plotted, and schemed until *I* had almost lost track of which side I was on. Despite my best efforts to stay out of other people's messes, I was once again caught in the middle of a dangerous power struggle that just might get me killed. How was I? I barely knew the answer myself.

"I don't know," I answered with a soft chuckle. "Ask me again the day after tomorrow. If I'm still among the living."

Bones seemed to understand the gist of it without me needing to explain so he just gave my shoulders a light squeeze. "It's good to have you back, trouble." He nodded down the stairwell. "You better get going. Don't want to make the bosses wait. We'll talk more later."

"Yeah." I gave him an appreciative smile. "Day after tomorrow. It's gonna be a long story so ale's on me," I called over my shoulder as I started down the stairs.

"Looking forward to it!" he called back.

His rumbling laughter followed me as I descended into the halls of the Thieves' Guild. Comforting warmth spread through my chest. I ran my hand over the rough stone walls. Home. Oh, how I had missed it. I glided effortlessly through the passageways until I arrived at the large gathering hall we called the Thieves'

Court. The room was packed but I managed to slip through one of the doors and take up position along the back wall without drawing too much attention. From their vantage point on top of the raised platform at the front of the room, our three Guild Masters watched people arrive.

Once the trickle of guild members coming through the doors had come to a halt, they got up from the high-backed, black chairs they'd occupied and strode to the edge of the platform. We all dropped to one knee, bowed our head, plated one fist on the floor and put the other arm across our knee.

"Strength and honor to the guild," we said in unison.

"Strength and honor," the Guild Masters replied. "Rise."

Clothes rustled as the entire Thieves' Guild stood back up.

"First order of business," Guild Master Killian said and locked eyes with me from across the room. "The Oncoming Storm. As you all know, there were rumors that she was a traitor who had betrayed our guild." He paused for a moment to ensure everyone was paying attention. "That was a lie. We have now received indisputable proof that the accusations were false. She was framed by influential people in the Upperworld. Let it be known that she is, and always has been, one of us."

Large parts of the crowd nodded enthusiastically. I may not be the most sociable of people and I wasn't exactly friends with a lot of my fellow guild members but people did respect me. As a thief, if nothing else. Eric Fahr had said that the whole guild had turned on me easily but since I hadn't been there myself, I didn't know for certain if that was true. I wondered how many of them had truly believed that I'd betrayed them. As I've said before, we strongly believe in honor among thieves.

"Second order of business," Guild Master Killian continued. "We are facing an invasion that will threaten our way of life. All the Underworld guilds have therefore decided to fight it together and you will all have a part to play."

While Master Killian continued to explain the plan that I had already heard, I leaned back against the wall. The cool stone against my back kept me from dozing off right there. Since the Guild Masters didn't know that I already knew the specifics of the plan, I participated actively when they divided up the areas of responsibility. I already knew which one I wanted so it was simply a matter of raising my hand when the correct question came along.

As soon as the meeting was over, I was among the first to slink out the door. There were probably some people who wanted to say welcome back and ask a question or two about the set up but I didn't have even a smidgen of energy left to talk to people. All I wanted was to sleep in my own bed. One day of peace before night fell. Then I would once again have to carry out missions for a higher cause that I'd tried very hard to stay out of. And all while hoping I didn't die along the way. Life. It sure wasn't dull, at least.

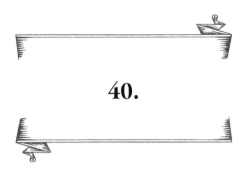

40.

A pistol pressed into my temple. I rolled my eyes and leveled an exasperated stare at the owner of said firearm. The assassin by the door kept his gun to my head until an authoritative voice called across the room.

"Let her through."

I hadn't been in a knocking-on-the-door kind of mood so I'd simply yanked open the door and strode right into the Assassins' Guild's exclusive tavern. The Black Hand didn't have any external security because no one, well, except me, was stupid enough to just stroll in. Once inside, however, an army of weapons and assassins trained to use them met any potential intruder. Since Shade had actually told me to come here this time, I was confident that none of his assassins would kill me when I walked through the door. Well, confident might be a bit much but I was pretty sure, at least.

Slim, the blond assassin I'd humiliated by hiding a knife from, cast venomous glances at me as I weaved through the tables. Shade was sitting on the wooden sofa in the fenced-in corner at the back, just as he'd done last time I was here. He motioned at a small side table outside the wooden barrier.

"Knives," was all he said.

Blowing out an exasperated breath, I shook my head before stripping my clothes of all the sharp objects hiding in there. Once I was done, he nodded to the chair in front of him. That godsawful chair that left me sitting completely unarmed with a room full of assassins behind my unprotected back. I don't think I'd ever hated a piece of furniture as much as I hated that chair.

For a moment, I entertained the idea of disobeying his instructions and sliding down next to him on the sofa but I decided against it. I was pretty sure that this power play wasn't just for my benefit. He probably needed to maintain a certain air of authority in front of his guild members. The wood creaked as I dropped into the chair of nightmares.

"Still think I'm gonna try to kill you, huh?" I said with a smirk on my face.

"It's just standard procedure," he said.

"Uh-huh. So, you said we need to talk. About what?"

Shade produced a knife from somewhere in his clothes and started running his finger along the sharp edge. And we were back to threats again. Every bloody time.

"I was surprised to see you at the conclave," he said while studying the knife.

"Yeah, me too."

His calculating eyes flicked up. "Then imagine my surprise when I found out you set a trap for Lord Fahr on your own. Without consulting me."

I crossed my arms over my chest. "It was actually the Fahr brothers, if we're being specific. And it wasn't your decision to make. I needed to set things right with my guild and that was the only way to do it."

"If Lord Fahr had been killed..."

"But he wasn't, was he?" I narrowed my eyes at him. "I'm not stupid, you know. I know what's at stake. But I needed to do this."

Shade regarded me for a moment before blowing out a short breath and giving me an approving nod. "Fair enough."

"So was that it?"

"No. I wanted to talk about tonight." He gazed at me with even eyes. "Which one are you hitting?"

"The middle one."

"Same. Was that a coincidence?"

Letting out an amused breath, I gave him a quick rise and fall of my eyebrows. "What do you think?"

His mouth drew into a lopsided smile. "I'm heading to the keep straight after. Are you coming?"

"Do you want me to come?"

The Master Assassin seemed slightly flustered by the question, which gave me great satisfaction. After a short pause, he finally responded. "Yeah, I do. With your skills, we could really use you."

I grinned at him. "Good. I mean, I was always planning on coming, I just wanted to hear you say it."

His eyebrows shot up and he stared at me for a moment before chuckling and shaking his head at me. "You really are an interesting one, aren't you? Are some of the elves coming too?"

"Most of them are hitting targets outside the city walls but I wouldn't be surprised if Faye, Elaran, and Faelar show up at the keep to make sure the plan runs smoothly. Probably the twins too."

Shade nodded. "I hope they do. We could really use them too."

Pushing to my feet, I nodded in agreement. "Alright, now I have some things to get done before night falls and this ridiculous plan of ours gets started." The Assassins' Guild Master watched me while I put all my knives back in their proper places. "Good talk," I said and gave him a mock salute once I was finished.

His black eyes glittered. "See you tonight."

Yes, I would see him tonight. Sunset marked the start of our desperate mission but at least now I felt physically ready to tackle it. I'd gotten a good day's undisturbed sleep in my own bed as well as a hot meal at the Mad Archer. My body would be up for the challenge. My mind, on the other hand, was screaming at me that this was foolishness worthy of ending up in history books as the actions of lunatics.

As I closed the door to the Black Hand behind me, I concluded that my mind was right. But then again, crazy was kind of my natural state so we might actually pull this off anyway.

Turning my head westward, I studied the afternoon sun hanging low in the sky. When the red light of dawn broke up the darkness tomorrow morning, we would either be victorious or dead. Not much room for error. This was going to be a long night.

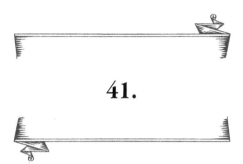

41.

A storm was coming. Wind whipped through my clothes as I stood watching the looming ships out in the bay. The wooden pier creaked beneath my feet.

"We're up next," a voice said from behind.

I nodded and tore my eyes from the ships' dark hulls. The small, hidden dock at the edge of the harbor was teeming with life. Rowboats packed with people dotted the water. Most of them held members of the Thieves' Guild but a few assassins were spread out among the vessels as well. I stepped into the empty rowboat that had just pulled up next to the pier. It rocked slightly as the rest of my fellow thieves and I climbed aboard and took up position on the narrow benches.

Shade directed the stream of people from atop a crate a few paces away. He looked calm, composed, and in control. I wondered how he really felt.

"Alright, listen up," the Master Assassin said once the pier was empty. He barely raised his voice but the sound carried to each rowboat waiting in the harbor. "You all know the plan so I'll be brief. Stealth is paramount. Right now, most Pernulans are either at the Silver Keep or at the various locations they've infiltrated in and around the city, which means that only a skeleton crew remains on the ships. However..." He paused and

273

swept his gaze around the silent boats. "If any of the crew members spot us and they manage to raise the alarm, things'll go sideways. Fast. Don't get spotted. But if you are, don't panic. There are assassins on all ships so let them sort out the mess while you get your job done as fast as possible. As soon as you're done, leave. Don't wait for the other ships. Get everyone into your rowboats, get back to the harbor, and scatter. Clear?"

The gathered thieves nodded.

"Good." He jumped down from the crate. "Move out."

Shade stepped into the last boat by the pier while the ones furthest out started their journey towards the three ships anchored out in the bay. I put a hand on the railing when my rowboat moved out as well. Waves lapped against the side of the boat but under the cover of darkness and the approaching storm, we glided unnoticed towards our target. This would be the second time I snuck aboard one of the Pernulans' ships but this time we would need to do a lot more than just eavesdrop. We all knew our roles so when the rowboat finally pulled up at the side of the ship, no one hesitated. Once it was my turn, I grabbed the closest rung and started upwards.

A wave hit the hull and sprayed cold water over my clothes as I climbed but my hands remained steady on the ladder. Strong winds pulled at my hair. I peered over the top. Empty. The crew was probably below deck, seeking shelter from the storm. The Pernulans had no reason to think anyone would be attacking their ships because they believed they had eyes everywhere in Keutunan. No one in the city could move without them knowing about it. Or so they thought. Fools.

I pulled myself over the railing and rolled onto deck. The thieves who'd climbed ahead of me were already moving, slinking across the deck and hugging the shadows. I joined them. Our first mission was to locate the stash of gunpowder so we spread out across the ship in search of it. Thief after thief disappeared down the different ladders connected to the upper deck because we assumed the black powder would be kept somewhere below to protect it from rain and potential enemy fire. The ship rolled slightly underneath my feet as I descended the stairs located at the middle of the deck.

It was dark below but I could just barely make out another thief sneaking towards the left so I decided to head right. Large cannons lined the side. I ran my hand over the cold and deadly contraption. If anything went wrong tonight, the Pernulans would fire these on our city. I suppressed a shudder at the thought of the destruction it would bring. No room for error. A hand grabbed my shoulder. I spun around with knives ready but when I saw Pipes' alarmed eyes, I relaxed.

"We've found the stash," he whispered and pointed in the direction of the staircase. "There's another ladder down that way and then another that leads to the lowest part of the ship. There's a whole room full of barrels of gunpowder down there. Spread the word."

After giving him a brief nod in acknowledgement, I moved back towards the stairs and climbed up. When I met another Thieves' Guild member, I repeated what Pipes had told me and then they did the same. Before long, everyone knew the location of our target and had taken up position in the prearranged line. Since I stayed in the room with the cannons, just below the first ladder, I received a bucket shortly. Water sloshed in it as I passed it to the next person. While I watched the empty cannon room, another bucket appeared from my left and then disappeared into the hands of the person on my right.

Shade's plan had been simple yet brilliant. The Pernulans had threatened to blow our city to smithereens so to prevent that, we had to sabotage the cannons. These big guns relied on the same black powder as the pistols used in Keutunan which meant that we knew their weakness. Water. Water ruined the gunpowder. No gunpowder, no cannon. So we simply had to pour water into their barrels of black powder and their big guns would be rendered useless.

Since running up and down the different decks with a bucket each was both time-consuming and potentially noisy, we'd decided to form a bucket brigade. People at the top deck hauled up buckets of water and then passed them to next person, who passed it to the next, and so on until they reached the thieves stationed in the magazine. They poured the water into the barrels of gunpowder and sent the empty buckets back up the chain. Easy.

A door creaked open at the end of the empty cannon room and a man stepped through. He jerked back and blinked at the line of thieves hauling buckets through his ship. His mouth opened. *Shit.*

Not hesitating a second, I ignored the coming container and instead threw two quick knives. The surprised Pernulan put a hand to the blades now cutting off his vocal cords before dropping to the floor. His body hit the wooden planks with a couple of dull thuds. I winced. Hopefully, no one had heard that. Leaving my place in the human chain, I strode towards the dead man on the ground. Blood pooled in front of his lifeless face when I drew the knives from his throat and wiped them on his shirt.

"Damn," a voice whispered behind me.

After pushing to my feet, I turned around to face Shade. "What? Would you rather I'd let him sound the alarm?"

"No." The Master Assassin cocked his head slightly to the right as he studied the corpse. "But now we have to kill them all. With a crew this small, they'll notice someone's missing and know something's up. Let's go."

"You want me to help?"

"Yeah, we have to finish this quickly so we need all the assassins we can get. And you're obviously better at killing people than you are at hauling buckets." He raised an eyebrow at me. "Unless you'd rather stay?"

How could anyone be bad at hauling buckets? But I did see his point. One more person acting as an assassin would make sure we got this bloody business done before the rest of the crew realized what was happening.

"Nah, I'm in," I said with a shrug.

The Assassins' Guild Master nodded. "Then start with that door he came through. I have to brief the rest of my people."

"Aye, aye, captain," I muttered to his retreating back as he disappeared up the ladder again.

Stepping softly on the balls of my feet, I snuck closer to the door the unfortunate Pernulan had used. It had swung shut after he'd exited so I started by pressing my ear to the gap between the door and the doorframe. The sloshing water and the thieves moving behind me made my task harder so I had to strain my ears to pick up any potential sound behind the door. It was difficult to tell but I thought I heard pots clanking. With nimble fingers, I edged the door open and peeked inside.

Warmth from a fire and the smell of food drifted through the crack in the door. This had to be the kitchen. A young man hummed softly to himself while stirring something in a large pot. He had his back to the door so I drew a hunting knife and slipped through the opening. I'd only made it halfway across the room when a plank betrayed me by groaning under my feet. *Crap.* The man said something in Pernish and twisted around.

His eyes widened when he saw a woman covered in knives standing in his kitchen instead of the countryman he no doubt had expected. *Shit.* If I gave him even a second to breathe, he would raise the alarm. I sprang forward.

The young man yanked the ladle from the pot and swung it at my head. Soup flew overhead and splattered the walls of the kitchen as I ducked under the attacking utensil. I stabbed a knife at his chest but he slammed the large spoon down towards my wrist with such force I had to jerk back to avoid getting my wrist broken. While I was busy stumbling back he hurled the ladle at my head, forcing me to deflect it with my forearm.

Unidentified soup splashed across my face as the projectile slammed into my arm before clattering to the floor. I wiped broth from my eyes just in time to see the young man snatch a kitchen knife from the counter and rush me. With my free hand, I flicked a throwing knife at him but he ducked it and before I'd had time to throw another, he'd closed the distance.

He swiped at my ribs but I blocked it and drew the other hunting knife. While his knife hand was occupied elsewhere, I stabbed at his chest again. Pain vibrated through my arm. The blade in my left hand clattered to the floor as the Pernulan withdrew a copper rolling pin from my elbow crease. I kicked at his hip. He stumbled back as my boot connected, giving me time to reach for another throwing knife. My opponent dropped the rolling pin and seized a wide lid just in time. The thrown knife bounced off the makeshift shield and landed uselessly on the floor.

Without missing a beat, he resumed his attack and flew towards me, lid and kitchen knife in hand. I ducked under his arm and drove my fist down on his wrist. His blade went flying across the floor but while I'd executed that maneuver he'd swung the heavy lid around. It sped towards the side of my head with alarming haste. I barely managed to throw up my arm in front of my temple before it connected.

Another knife flew across the kitchen and clattered to the floor. This time it was mine. The near hit of the lid made my ears ring, forcing me to blink repeatedly to clear my head. In those precious few seconds, the man attacking me managed to land a shoulder tackle to my chest. We both crashed to the floor in a tangle of limbs. The hard fall drove the breath from my lungs. I gasped in air to refill them just as the young man brought both his hands over his head. The lid shone in the flickering candles. He drove the edge towards my throat.

In a burst of adrenaline, I shoved a knee into his backside, making him tumble over my head. I tried to scramble away and get some distance between us so I could catch my breath but a hand clamped around my ankle. My back scraped across the wood as he jerked me back. I kicked at him with my free foot. He lost his grip but launched himself at me anyway. His knees slammed down on either side of me but before he could stabilize himself, I grabbed his shirt and yanked him towards the floor.

We rolled across the wooden planks in a mad struggle for leverage until we hit the far wall.

When the barrier stopped our wrestling I found myself pinned to the floor with the Pernulan straddling my hips. Something gleamed in the corner of my eye but before I could reach for it, the young man snatched it up and stabbed it towards me. The sharp edge speeding towards my throat was something I knew very well. It was one of my own hunting knives. I threw my arms up and managed to grab his wrist before he could drive the blade home. He put both hands to the handle and leaned over my outstretched arms in order to force the knife down. A little more. Just a little more. The blade edged closer to my throat until his head finally moved into the right position.

A mechanism clicked in place. The young man drew in a sharp breath before it was cut off abruptly. His hands released the stolen knife and I had to twist my head away to avoid being hit by it when it fell to the floor. Blood spilled across my face and neck as I withdrew the stiletto blade piercing the Pernulan's windpipe. His body crashed down on top of me. I hadn't extended the stiletto all the way, so it was still attached to the mechanism inside my sleeve. After wiping the blade clean on his shirt, I retracted it and then shoved his lifeless body to the side. My heart pounded in my chest. Damn.

Since when were kitchen boys this good at fighting? These people were insane. A gods damn kitchen boy, for Nemanan's sake! I shook my head on the floor but stayed there for a few more moments, trying to catch my breath. Somewhere behind me, the door creaked open. I twisted my head around to look at the intruder.

"Damn," Shade said as he surveyed the room. "What a bloody mess."

"Shut up," I grumbled from my place on the floor.

"Maybe you *are* better at hauling buckets than you are at killing."

"Not. Another. Word," I pressed out while still heaving deep breaths.

A smile tugged at the corner of his lips as he watched me struggle to my feet. Once upright, I placed a hand on the counter and closed my eyes until my head stopped spinning. After wiping the blood from my face with a kitchen towel, I went searching for my four missing knives. One hunting knife was of course right next to the Pernulan, since he'd tried to kill me with it, and the other lay against the far counter. The first throwing knife I'd hurled was lodged in one of the overhead cupboards while I found the other one lying on the floor next to the still boiling pot of soup.

"If you're done playing in the kitchen, we have one more deck to search," Shade said once I'd shoved the last knife back in place. "Oh, and put out that fire."

I glanced back at the fire used to boil the broth and frowned. "Why?"

The Master Assassin leveled an exasperated stare at me. "Don't you think their ship going up in flames would kind of alert them that something's wrong?"

Tipping my head from side to side, I considered. "Good point."

After dousing the fire with the unidentified soup, I followed Shade out the door. My unexpected kitchen fight had only taken a few minutes so the thieves in the empty cannon room outside were still handing buckets back and forth. The Assassins' Guild Master and I slipped through the bucket brigade and moved down the next ladder. I had no idea what this deck was called but it was the last one before the lowest one where they kept the gunpowder.

A room filled with cables and what looked like miscellaneous spare parts met us when we left the ladder with the water-hauling thieves behind. They continued moving containers down the final ladder in the opposite direction. Shade and I exchanged a glance before sneaking forward. At the end of the room was another door. We pressed up against it. Cheerful voices drifted out from the cracks in the wood.

The assassin drew the two swords he carried behind either shoulder blade and then arched an eyebrow at me. I pulled four throwing knives from behind my own shoulders. His piercing black eyes found mine. I nodded in response to the unspoken question. He kicked the door open.

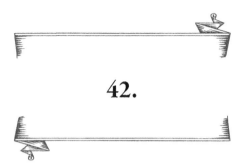

42.

Six men shot to their feet as Shade and I barreled through the doorway. Chairs hit the floor while the men scrambled for weapons. I flicked the two knives in my right hand, taking the closest sailor in the throat and eye. Shade swiped his blades upwards as the next man tried to get away. Blood bloomed from the slash that opened his chest.

The other four Pernulans had managed to get to their feet and draw their weapons on the other side of the table. They crouched down and hissed something in Pernish. Not wanting to give them time to discuss strategy, I resumed the attack and hurled my two left-hand knives at the group. The burly one in the middle yanked his sword up and deflected the blades. Metallic clattering filled the room as they bounced away.

Shade kicked at the study wooden table. It scraped against the floor as it rushed towards the Pernulans and slammed into their thighs. While they were busy shoving it away, I threw two more knives at the same time as Shade leaped atop the table. The sailor on the right ducked the first knife but the second one hit him in the shoulder. He drew in a sharp breath but then yanked it out and hurled it back at me with a growl. I ducked the flying projectile while blades clashed to my left.

From atop the table, the Master Assassin slammed his swords into the raised blades of the two defending Pernulans on the left. The two on the right stopped their attack on me as the burly one put his hands under the tabletop and began lifting it. Shade executed a backflip and vaulted off the table just as the two men on the right heaved it up and flung it towards me.

The large wooden rectangle raced closer at an alarming speed and I was forced to throw myself backwards to escape it. It smacked into the wall with a deafening boom. While flicking another knife at the man on the right, I rushed for the burly man. My throwing knife hit its mark with deadly accuracy and the rightmost man dropped to the floor. Shade stepped into my path and blocked the sword swung at me from the left. Metal ground against metal as he pushed the blade away.

As the burly man resumed his attack, I drew my hunting knives and slashed at him while keeping Shade's blind spots clear. Back to back, we twisted and danced to the rhythm of battle.

A sword raced for my head only to be stopped by the assassin's blade. While Shade kept the man's weapon trapped above, I shoved a knife between his ribs. The blade came back red as I withdrew it and the previously attacking man crumbled to the floor.

Metal dinged to my left. The Master Assassin drove his swords into the Pernulan's with furious strength while the burly sailor on my right released a howl and rushed me. I hurled a throwing knife at him, forcing him to dive for cover. Shade's right-hand sword disappeared into his opponent's chest just as my attacker got to his feet. I feigned a lunge for his throat and slipped under his arm. Metal rang above my head as Shade's swords took the blade meant for my head. He whipped it back and unleashed a flurry of thrusts. The burly Pernulan parried them and shoved him to the side.

While Shade was off balance, the sword-wielding foreigner managed to land a heavy boot to the back of the assassin's knee. It buckled and he hit the ground hard. The Pernulan raised his weapon to deliver the final blow.

The sword clattered to the floor as he gasped and stumbled sideways while his meaty hands swatted uselessly at his back. I yanked out the knives I'd rammed into his kidneys from behind. Wood vibrated under my feet as his gigantic frame toppled to the floor. Shade pushed to his feet and looked me up and down.

I grinned at him. "What was that about hauling buckets again?"

The Assassins' Guild Master released a surprised laugh.

All around us, overturned chairs and tables, blood, bodies, and weapons covered the floor. I swept my gaze across the mess before glancing back at Shade.

"So much for being sneaky," I said. "Someone's bound to have heard that."

The Master Assassin just shrugged. "Doesn't matter. I told you before we came down here, remember? This was the last deck we had to sweep. Everyone else is already dead."

Now that I thought about it, he had mentioned that. Good thing. Otherwise we'd have alerted the whole ship with this ruckus.

"Come on, let's get going," Shade said and started for the door.

"Hold on. I gotta grab my throwing knives. They're very–"

"–valuable," he finished and let out a low chuckle. "Yeah, I remember."

Shade's black eyes followed me as I rummaged through the room for my knives. What a fight it had been. I'd never fought as seamlessly with anyone as I'd done with him. Usually I'd have to keep constant tabs on my partner to make sure they didn't get in my way or get themselves killed, but with Shade I hadn't been worried for a second. He held his own without tripping me up and he had my back when I needed it. It was as if he could anticipate my moves without me having to tell him what I was planning. I watched the Master Assassin leaning against the wall. He sure was a professional, that one.

"Ready?" he asked once I'd pushed the final throwing knife down in its holster.

"Yeah."

When we returned to the ladder, we found it empty. My fellow Thieves' Guild members must've finished soaking the black powder while we battled the Pernulans. Despite no one being left alive to overhear us, we climbed the stairs to the upper deck in silence.

"Master," a somewhat familiar voice said as we emerged into the stormy night.

I squinted at the blond assassin striding across the wooden planks. *Ah. Him.*

"Did everything go alright?" Slim asked.

"Yeah, it did." Shade paused and then nodded towards me. "With her help."

Slim blinked in surprise and shifted his gaze to me. After the stunt I'd pulled at the Assassins' Guild headquarters, I knew he disliked me. To be honest, I was slightly worried I'd made an enemy out of him, and trust me, having a member of the Assassins' Guild as an enemy was somewhere between extremely dangerous and life-threatening on the risky scale. When his gray eyes locked on mine, the previously present hostility had almost disappeared.

Slim gave me a nod before turning back to his Guild Master. "The thieves have already gone back and the rest of our people are waiting for you in the rowboat down below." He motioned at the side of the ship. "Also, Curly's boat came by. They had to off everyone on their ship too but the other one managed without."

"So all three ships are done?"

The blond assassin nodded. "All their gunpowder's bust."

"Good. Then let's head off."

These assassins seemed to consider their Guild Master's welfare of outmost importance so thanks to Shade's comment about me helping him out, Slim's opinion of me appeared to have changed. While Slim turned around to lead the way, I caught Shade's eye and gave him an appreciative nod. He flashed me a brief, lopsided smile before following his guild member towards the rowboat.

Shade was such a difficult person to read. Some days, he was threatening me or even outright trying to kill me and then other days he was saving my life and doing... well, things like this. He gained nothing by helping me improve my relation to Slim. Or at least, I didn't think he did.

Man, I really had no idea what his end game was and trying to figure it out would be like trying to untangle a nest of highly venomous snakes. With fangs. And a penchant for surprise attacks. Nope. I was so not sticking my hand into that. After a short headshake to clear it of dumb ideas, I jogged to catch up.

Wind tore at my clothes and hair and the sea sprayed salt water over the railing as we rowed back to shore. At least it didn't rain. The waves rocked our boat but we made it to the hidden dock at the edge of the harbor without any mishaps. Another group of assassins stood waiting for us when we climbed onto the pier. I recognized a few of them, mainly Curly, the black-haired one with fierce eyes, and the tall man with brown hair tied into a bun. Man-bun. Or whatever his real name was.

"Master," Curly said and then pointed to a short man next to him. "Both our ships are done."

"I heard," Shade replied. "Ours too. The second stage begins now." He shifted his gaze to Man-bun. "Is everyone in place?"

"They are. I also sent two people into the woods to make sure the elves had arrived and some redheaded archer almost put an arrow through them thinking they were enemies." Man-bun shook his head. "But yeah, the elves are here and they're ready too."

On the inside, I let out a soft laugh. I knew exactly who the suspicious ranger with auburn hair was. Elaran. That meant Liam had been successful and our friends in the forest were ready to hit the targets outside the city.

"Good." Shade's mouth curled into a smile. "Then let's light up the night."

We took off towards the Silver Keep. Since I was shorter than them, I had to push myself to keep up with the group of assassins around me but I managed.

Dark clouds blew across the heavens, leaving the streets steeped in musky darkness. They were completely deserted as well, which was strange at this time of night, but I suspected that King Edward and his Silver Cloaks had made sure people stayed indoors. And the royal guards themselves were of course occupied elsewhere.

Before long, the gigantic fortress that was the Silver Keep rose up ahead. In contrast to the dark city behind us, it glowed like a jewel. Light bloomed in the fire pots outside while candles flickered in the windows. Music and chatter drifted from inside.

Shade flashed his guild members a couple of hand signals that I didn't understand but made them scatter in different directions while the two of us continued towards the front courtyard. When the Silver Cloaks stationed there saw Shade and me appear from the shadows they drew up slightly but then went back to scanning the area as if we weren't there.

"Have you ever done this before?" I whispered to the Master Assassin as he reached into a container and pulled out a small wooden box filled with thick sticks.

"Nope." He put it on the ground and shrugged. "But there's always a first."

Once it was all set up, he pulled a burning stick from the nearest fire pot and put it to the fuse. We ran for cover. Pressed together in a narrow archway, we watched them explode. Gold glittered in circular shapes before dripping down over the rooftops in a rain of sparkles. The next stick raced towards the dark sky. A bang rang out and golden stars filled the heavens once again. As far as covert signals went, setting off a batch of fireworks was both effective and beautiful.

"Alright, now it starts," Shade said and turned to me. "Let's get to the back garden."

In the true spirit of someone used to people obeying his every command, he didn't even wait for me to reply but instead just took off along the side of the keep. After releasing a frustrated sigh, I followed. Rain began falling from the sky in light drops as soon as we arrived at the manicured garden so we took shelter under one of the trees against the back wall.

"How long do we need to wait?" I asked while running my hands up and down my arms to get some heat.

"A few minutes or so should be enough to give everyone a head start," Shade replied.

I nodded. Strong winds ruffled the leaves above our heads but they kept most of the water out. Hopefully, everyone had seen the signal and was moving into position now. We just needed to give them some time to get their tasks started before we began ours. The Master Assassin next to me stood straight-backed as a statue, staring into the falling rain with a calm mask on his face. I'm not one for needless small talk and neither was he, it would seem, so we counted down the minutes in comfortable silence.

Three pairs of feet landed on the grass next to us, making Shade draw his swords and crouch into an attack position. Ha! I knew it.

"Come to make sure everything goes according to plan?" I said with a grin.

Faye threw her silver-colored ponytail back behind her shoulder and returned the smile. "Naturally."

"Besides, we couldn't exactly leave it in your hands, could we?" the elf next to her cut in. "Because everything you touch usually goes straight to hell, one way or another."

I graced his statement with a *tsk* and an eye roll. "Nice to see you too, Elaran."

"I hear you almost killed two of my people," Shade said and narrowed his eyes at the auburn-haired archer.

"Your people should know better than to sneak up on a group of elves," Elaran replied.

Before they could get into a very evenly matched fight about who was the grumpiest, Faye put a hand on Elaran's arm. He heaved a deep sigh but held up a hand in what I assumed was an apology. Or at least a ceasefire.

While the two grumps decided not to argue right now, the third elf who'd dropped down from the wall straightened and then strode over to our small group. Thousands of tiny droplets clung to his flowing, blond hair.

"Faelar," I said with a nod.

He nodded back, first in my direction and then to the black-clad assassin next to me. Shade returned the gesture. "Any more of you coming?" he asked.

"Nope, just us," Faye answered. "The rest are taking care of the farms and everything else outside the walls." The Elf Queen turned to me. "The twins are leading it."

"And Liam?" I asked, dreading the answer.

"Stayed behind in the cabin." Faye's yellow eyes filled with sadness. "He said he wanted to stay out of the blood and the screams."

Relief flooded through my chest. I wanted him to stay as far away from this fight as possible. "Good," I said. "He's seen way too much of that already."

Shade's analytical eyes scanned the area. "We should get going," he announced. "Follow me."

The Master Assassin darted across the wet grass. After another eye roll, I shrugged and followed him. The three elves did the same. We entered the Silver Keep through the narrow door Edward had used when he saved me from his father last year. Once we were inside, Shade led us through a series of twisting halls, stairs, and rooms until even I was unable to keep track of our route but we eventually wound up at a plain wooden door.

"The ballroom's through here," the Assassins' Guild Master said. "Spread out along the balcony but stay hidden until I give the signal."

Once he'd seen us all nod in acknowledgement, he pushed down the handle and slunk through. We slipped in after him. The other side of the door revealed a narrow balcony that ran the length of a vast hall. Hauntingly beautiful string music floated through the air. I peeked over the intricately decorated fence. It wasn't that far to the floor. Anyone who knew how to land properly would be able to jump it safely and if there was one thing you learned when you spent your days running across rooftops, it was how to land properly. My eyes continued scanning the room.

Lords and ladies from Keutunan and men from the distant nation of Pernula moved across the marble with graceful steps. Their expensive clothing in rich hues made it look like paint swirling across a white canvas. I snuck further down the gallery in the same direction Shade had gone. If I strained my eyes, I could just barely make out men in black clothes drifting through the shadows atop the balcony on the other side. Shade's assassins. I assumed they'd gotten word to King Edward because he cast a swift glance towards our location before returning his iron stare to General Marcellus.

The general had been conversing with a group of Keutunan lords but paused to throw an impatient look at the young king.

My blood boiled with fury at the sight of the noble gentlemen around him. The brothers Fahr.

In addition to my own seething feeling about them, they had some nerve showing up here after William Fahr had killed the king's mother. King Edward was showing more self-control this one night than I had displayed in my whole life put together. If it had been Liam... I shuddered at the thought. But if it had been, I would've ripped him to shreds the minute I laid eyes on him. Instead, the king, wise beyond his years, merely leveled eyes alight with cold fury at the traitorous lord.

Next to the two-faced blond man and his brother stood Lord Feger and the two other gentlemen I'd seen while spying on the Council of Lords. They were the ones who had accepted pouches of what I now knew to be pearls. I wondered what else the Pernulans had promised them in exchange for their loyalty.

General Marcellus raised his dark eyebrows at the king and motioned impatiently with his hand. King Edward met his eyes but simply gazed back at him with black eyes that oozed disinterest. The general threw his hands down by his sides and stalked across the floor. When he reached the raised dais the king occupied, he extended his leg and nimbly climbed up.

"Noble lords and beautiful ladies," General Marcellus called in his smooth voice. "I believe King Edward has an announcement for us."

The violins fell silent and the merry chatter died out. All eyes turned to the King of Keutunan and the foreign general on the platform. Up on the balcony, Shade mouthed at me to get ready. I repeated it to the elves on my other side. They nodded back. Down on the stage, King Edward drew himself up and swept black eyes filled with determination across the gathered crowd of Pernulans and Keutunan nobility.

This was it. In the next few minutes we would find out if the desperate plan we'd cooked up in the king's study was insane but brilliant, or just sheer madness. I sent a prayer to Nemanan. This had better work.

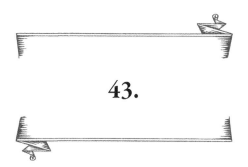

43.

"My people," King Edward called across the sea of silent spectators. "As you know, ever since these Pernulans sailed into our harbor we have been engaged in a fruitful partnership. They have shared their valuable knowledge with us, for which we are very grateful," the king added with a nod. "New information has now come to light which will change the dynamics of this partnership."

The young king paused and once again swept his gaze across the crowd. Satisfied smiles etched the faces of the Pernulans, with General Marcellus' haughty smirk taking the prize, while the gathered nobles of Keutunan looked to their king with confusion and slight apprehension on their faces.

The heavy, silver crown remained firmly placed in his glossy black hair as King Edward raised his chin. "These Pernulans are not our friends anymore."

General Marcellus jerked back slightly in surprise and stared at the calm king with wide eyes. "Choose your next words carefully," the general hissed.

King Edward gave him a disinterested stare before pressing on. "Ever since they arrived, they have been infiltrating every part of our city. They are inside our farms, our taverns, our shops, and our houses. *Your* houses. Yesterday, General Marcellus," the king threw an arm in the direction of the stunned general, "presented me with an ultimatum. Surrender our city to their foreign rule or they will kill all of us and bombard our city with their cannons."

A worried buzz spread through the crowd as the nobles threw nervous glances at the Pernulans mixed in with the throng. King Edward squeezed his hand into a fist. "But we will not let some foreign invaders just roll up and take our city."

"Oh, come now, King Edward. That is not the whole truth, is it?" The general seemed to have recovered from his surprise because the smirk was back on his face when he turned towards Edward. "After all, *you* are the one who invited us."

A ripple went through the crowd. I whipped my head towards Shade. King Edward had invited the Pernulans? Could that really be true? The Master Assassin gave me a quick nod in response to my wordless question before motioning for us to stay on the balcony.

On the floor below, King Edward tried to calm the anxious lords and ladies who'd broken into uneasy whispering.

"What does he mean?" someone called from the crowd.

"Yes, how could you have called them here?"

The young king held up both hands, motioning for them to quiet down. "It is true that I am the reason they found us."

"How?" a tall gentleman called from the middle of the crowd.

"There is a vault here in the keep. It contained magic, old magic, that no one knows how to wield anymore. There was an item that I and all my forebears believed to be the reason for our isolation. We believed it kept our island invisible or protected by some kind of barrier." King Edward paused and drew a deep breath before continuing. "I broke the spell."

Disbelieving murmur broke out and a few cries of outrage rose from the floor. On the other side of the balcony fence, I stared at the king in shock. So that had been the secret of the vault. No wonder he'd felt responsible for everything that had happened. He *had* been responsible.

"So you see," General Marcellus called across the throng. The gathered Keutunans quieted down and looked up at his self-satisfied smile. "We are not invading. We are merely responding to your foolish king's careless actions."

"You do not get to speak here," King Edward said and leveled eyes that burned with cold fury on the smirking general. He softened them slightly before returning his gaze to his people. "Because of my actions, our city's advancement has leaped forward by decades so I will not apologize for bringing economic growth and technological development to our city. As for the general's treacherous ultimatum, I reiterate: no outside forces will conquer us." The young king raised his chin and his voice. "Keutunan may be small compared to the land from which these intruders hail but we are a proud nation. We do not respond well to threats and we will *not* bow to foreign invaders."

A cheer rose through the air as the nobles hoisted fists and nodded enthusiastically. I had to give it to him, Edward sure knew how to move a crowd.

"A moving speech, really," General Marcellus said and smacked his lips. "But utterly useless. Do you want to know why? Because your situation has not changed. I still have people in every part of your city and I will start killing everyone unless you hand over power." He swept a hand at the nobles in the ballroom. "Starting with these fine people."

"See, there are two problems with that," King Edward said and shot a smug smile at the general. "First, you do not control every part of my city for you have missed the most dangerous one. Secondly, Keutunan does not stand alone."

King Edward threw up his right arm, balled his hand into a fist, and jerked it back down. Assassins poured over the balconies from every side of the room in a wave of black clothing. After giving the elves a sideways nod, I grabbed the top of the railing and followed the tide of assassins.

Gasps and shrieks echoed from the Keutunan nobility and the Pernulans as rows of assassins, a thief, and three elves landed on the ballroom's smooth marble floor. Rolling to my feet, I drew four throwing knives. To my right stood Shade with his swords raised while Faye, Elaran, and Faelar brandished drawn bows on my left.

Lords and ladies threw panicked glances around the room and clustered together in groups, leaving the Pernulans stranded on the vast floor like abandoned swimmers between islands.

The Fahr brothers and their pack of treasonous lords backed together while casting uncertain looks between the assassins and the general on the dais. General Marcellus watched the developments with a look of sheer disbelief on his striking face.

"So you see," King Edward said and motioned across the floor, "we are not as helpless as you think."

The shocked general gave his head a firm shake and pulled himself together. He snapped his fingers and all the Pernulans scattered throughout the room drew their swords. "This changes nothing. If these people move on us, we will kill them."

"Yes, and if your people should attack these assassins, they will kill all of you." King Edward tilted his head to the right. "Which means that we are at a standstill. If either side attacks, people will start dying. Are you prepared for that?"

Despite the serious atmosphere, I wanted to chuckle. If this wasn't the biggest and most high-stakes game of chicken I'd even seen, I didn't know what was.

General Marcellus smacked his lips and puffed up his chest. "Regardless of what happens in this room, the rest of your city will still die at the hands of my men."

"Yes, I know you believe that," the king said with a patronizing smile. "But while you have been occupied with this sham reception, the Bashers' Guild, and the rest of the Assassins' Guild not present here at the moment, have relieved your men of their positions throughout the city. Our friends the elves of Tkeideru have also been kind enough to get rid of everyone outside the city walls. So, all your men threatening my people inside and outside the city have now been removed." King Edward made a show of thinking hard by furrowing his brows and tapping his chin. "Oh, and the Thieves' Guild took care of your cannons, so no need to worry about that."

General Marcellus' mouth had dropped open halfway through the king's speech and had yet to return to its original position. He blinked repeatedly as if trying to clear his head of spinning thoughts but no words came out of his mouth. A slow clapping sound echoed through the vast marble hall.

"Well done, well done," the owner of the clapping hands said. Lord William Fahr stepped out from his group and showered King Edward in a smug smile. "You think you have it all figured out, don't you? You who didn't even see the dissatisfaction building among your own lords."

Eric Fahr spat on the floor and picked up where his brother had left off. "You who run with thieves and assassins. You who got my son killed." He sneered at the young man on the platform. "You don't deserve to be king."

The silence that followed was so complete I could almost hear the thousands of candles in the silver chandeliers and candelabras burn throughout the ballroom.

"And you have forgotten one thing," Lord Fahr the elder said and swept his arms to the side. "Us."

The small group of treacherous lords behind him drew themselves up with satisfied looks on their faces as Lord Fahr continued. "We have not been sitting idly by, just waiting for the Pernulans to make us provincial rulers of Keutunan."

So that was what General Marcellus had used to buy their loyalty. For the promise of power and the revenge of a dead son, they had betrayed their city to a foreign power. Damn.

"Knowing about your connections to the Underworld, I had a feeling you might try something like this," Lord William Fahr pressed on, not giving his king a moment to respond. "So I have prepared a surprise for you." He put two fingers to his mouth and blew a shrill whistle.

The gathered lords and ladies drew into even tighter circles as the smattering of running boots resounded from the corridors outside.

Heavy doors banged open and a horde of armed men poured through the openings. Swords, maces, and axes gleamed in the candlelight as they spread out with their weapons raised and encircled the room. These were the men who'd been trying to kill me for weeks.

A cold, heavy weight spread through my stomach as I realized that I'd been wrong before. King Edward hadn't been responsible for everything that had happened with the Pernulans because a lot of this was my fault. If I hadn't decided to kill Rogue then the Fahr brothers wouldn't have had any reason to betray Keutunan and side with the invaders. And if these foreign attackers hadn't had a high-ranking member of the king's inner circle on their side, this hostile takeover might've played out very differently. Damn.

I shoved those inconvenient feelings aside and drew up the stone walls around my heart. Feeling guilty wouldn't make things better.

"Now, *King* Edward," William Fahr said in a mocking tone, "you are severely outnumbered. Would you still like to try and fight?"

General Marcellus had recovered from the shock and gave the treasonous lord an appreciative smile. Weapons and armor clanked all around us as the Pernulans and the mercenaries shifted in an ever tightening circle around us.

The three elves still held their bows drawn but moved them restlessly between different groups of Pernulans. I cast a quick glance at Shade. His eyes were locked on his king.

"You back-stabbing piece of shit," King Edward said and shook his head. A few of the nobles blinked in surprise at hearing their king speak so informally. "You're the one who's been amassing a private army all these weeks. And you've done it with the help of these damn Pernulans. What? They gave you pearls and you bought rogue soldiers with them? You damn traitor."

Lord Fahr the elder smoothened his blond hair. "Throw all the tantrums you like, you child. You have been playing with the big boys and you have been outmaneuvered because you are not even *close* to being in our league. Now it is time to surrender. Or die."

Hatred spilled from King Edward's eyes like water from an icy, black creek. "We shall never surrender."

I shifted the blades in my hands. William Fahr looked to the foreign general on the platform next to Edward. A wide grin spread across General Marcellus' mouth as he nodded back. Letting out a long breath, I rolled my shoulders. This was it.

Lord William Fahr's face transformed into a self-righteous sneer before he raised his voice to a shout that echoed between the marble walls. "Kill them all."

The silence was deafening. No one moved a muscle. All along the edges of the room, the ranks of armed men remained rooted in place.

"What are you waiting for? Attack!" Lord Fahr screamed.

His rogue soldiers paid no heed to the command and simply continued staring at the rows of assassins. King Edward cleared his throat.

"Do you want to know what the problem with mercenaries is?" the king said in a conversational tone. "Loyalty. You see, the thing about mercenaries is that they work for the highest bidder." He gave a nonchalant shrug. "Right now, that's not you."

"You, you..." William stammered and whipped his head between General Marcellus and the unmoving mercenaries.

King Edward drew his arm in a half-circle and snapped his fingers as if he'd just remembered something. "Oh, I knew I forgot something earlier when I explained the deal I'd made with the Underworld guilds." He slapped a light hand to his forehead and twisted his mouth into a fake apologetic smile. "The Pleasure Guild and the Beggars' Guild. Of course, how could I have forgotten? In the time since you delivered your ridiculous ultimatum, they have been bribing your men here. With boatloads of pearls, I believe."

At that, a pair of dark eyes met mine from across the room. Lady Smythe lifted her eyebrows at me. I confirmed her suspicion with a grin and a quick rise and fall of my own dark eyebrows. The talented jewelry forger who'd made the pearls we'd used to bribe the rogue soldiers let out a slight chuckle before once again turning back to her husband.

"So they now work for me," King Edward finished. "I do apologize for not mentioning that before. I can be so forgetful sometimes."

Lord Fahr the elder continued working his mouth up and down without producing any sound while General Marcellus wiped a hand across his forehead.

"I do believe that settles it," the young king said and gave a lazy wave of his hand. "Take them."

Just as the ranks of mercenaries started forward, General Marcellus yelled something in Pernish and leaped from the dais. In the span of a few heartbeats, all the Pernulans had clustered together in some kind of defensive formation.

William Fahr snapped out of his stupor, grabbed his younger brother by the arm, and slunk towards the gathered Pernulans while sticking his other hand inside his vest. We were just about to commence the attack when I saw what he withdrew from his clothes. It was two glass orbs.

"Get down! It's gonna explode!" I bellowed across the room.

The mercenaries hesitated but Shade and the elves didn't doubt my word. I knew what it was because I had used that kind of device myself and Lord Fahr had no doubt picked up a few of his own when he had threatened Apothecary Haber into stopping selling them to me. The assassins, the elves, and I dove for cover right as the treasonous lord lobbed two exploding orbs across the room.

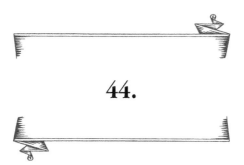

44.

Glass shattered and two deafening explosions roared throughout the room. The vaulted ceiling expanded the rumble at the same time as waves of heat rolled over my body. Fortunately for me, it had been air and not fire.

When I lifted my head from the cool marble floor, I saw my elven friends climb to their feet a few strides away while Shade was already up, dashing across the room towards his king. They, as well as the rest of the assassins, looked unharmed. The mercenaries on the other hand, not so much.

The exploding orbs had blown two large holes through the ring of rogue soldiers. Dead bodies littered the floor around the entrance to the ballroom. Over the high-pitched ringing in my ears, I could hear the survivors scream as they ran around trying to put out the fire caught in their clothes. As my eyes came into focus, I just managed to catch sight of the Pernulans, along with the brothers Fahr and their supporters, disappearing through the doors in a swishing of colorful clothes. I shook my head to clear it and jumped to my feet.

Shade and King Edward were engaged in a rapid conversation up on the dais while the rest of the Assassins' Guild got to their feet and closed in on the platform. I turned my head to the three elves.

"You alright?" I called.

The ringing in my ears made it impossible to know how loudly I was speaking but they seemed to have heard me because Faye gave me a thumbs up while the other two nodded.

"What in Nature's grace was that?" Faye said while she bent to gather a few arrows that had escaped her quiver when she dove.

I was about to inform her that nature probably had nothing to do with Apothecary Haber's chemical creativity when an authoritative voice cut through the room.

"The Pernulans will be heading for their ships," King Edward called. "Make sure they are either dead or out of the harbor by sunrise. Preferably dead. But do not take unnecessary risks. If most of our city's fighting forces die trying to kill these people, Keutunan will be vulnerable in the long run and that, I will not accept." The king drew himself up to his full height. "Make sure they are dead or leaving but do not get yourselves killed. Understood?"

Shade's assassins and the surviving mercenaries nodded and when the dark-haired king flicked his wrist, they took off after the escaping Pernulans. When the Master Assassin leaped from the platform, I raised an eyebrow at the three elves. They confirmed my unspoken question with a nod and the four of us joined the assassin in his pursuit. I was so deeply entangled in this mess that I might as well see it through to the end. And besides, the Fahr brothers and I had some unfinished business.

Outside the Silver Keep, chaos reigned. Men screamed, and explosions and gunshots echoed from every direction. Flames licked trees and bushes up and down the wide streets of the Marble Ring and the smell of black powder hung in the air. A pair of bashers stampeded past us with their bats raised. The closer we got to the Harbor District, the more people we ran into. Bashers, assassins, mercenaries, and Pernulans dashed in and out of every street in a mad scramble for victory and survival.

Air rushed from my lungs as a heavy body slammed into my chest. Dark eyes that mirrored my own surprise stared at me as the Pernulan who'd run straight into me from a side street and I toppled to the ground. Shouts rang out around us as the rest of his group collided with my four companions. I hit the stone street hard, one second before the man's weight crashed down on top of me. Fumbling with my hands to push him off, I tried to refill my oxygen-starved lungs while also making sure he didn't stab something at me from above. He rolled slightly to the side to get his sword into a better position but the small gap was all I needed to slink out from underneath him.

Blades whooshed through the air and the twang of bowstrings filled the street behind me but I had no time to look at the battle Shade and the elves were no doubt engaged in because my attacker had finally gotten his sword into position. Both he and I had only managed to get to our knees but he swung his curved sword at me anyway. I yanked up the knife from my boot to deflect the strike. It spared me from having my arm cut off but the small knife flew from my hand and clattered to the stones somewhere up the street.

Without missing a beat, the Pernulan flicked his sword back at me from the other direction. I tried calling up the darkness but it didn't respond. Shit. While we were still on our knees, the sharp edge of his sword sped towards my ribs forcing me to throw myself back down to avoid it. It zipped over my face in a rush of air. I drove my leg up hard. My boot connected with his groin. The impact made him draw a sharp gasp and stagger to the side. I used those precious seconds to roll to the side and up to my knees again. Steel whizzed in the air as I drew a hunting knife through his right hamstring.

A cry of raw pain vibrated in the air. The curved sword clattered to the stones shortly before my attacker crumpled down next to it. His screams threatened to shatter my eardrums so I put a hand on the back of his shirt collar and yanked him towards me. The swift stroke of a sharp blade cut the ear-splitting cries short and he fell forward, blood dripping from his throat. I shot to my feet and whipped around.

A bowstring twanged and a well-aimed arrow to the heart from only a short distance away sent a Pernulan flying into the wall while Shade withdrew a sword coated in blood from the body of the last attacker standing. I sucked in a deep breath of relief to see them all unharmed. After collecting my missing boot knife, I joined my four companions as we took off towards the harbor again.

Madness covered the waterfront. Fleeing Pernulans poured in from every side street with pursuing assassins, bashers, and mercenaries snapping at their heels. Swords clashed on the pier while an army of rowboats raced across the bay and towards the anchored ships. You had to appreciate the irony of the fact that the Pernulans were fleeing in the same rowboats we had used to sneak aboard their ships earlier tonight. However, before I could dwell on it too much, we were pulled into the fighting as well.

I moved along the pier in a dance of death until there were no more enemies close enough to kill. Scattered fighting took place around me but the battle frenzy had died down as most

Pernulans were either dead or already in the rowboats speeding away.

"We are not done!" a man's voice boomed across the dark water.

By now, I recognized it very well. It was Eric Fahr's voice and if I squinted, I swore I could see him standing up in one of the rowboats far out in the bay.

"We will not rest until we have brought this city to its knees," the younger Lord Fahr continued shouting. "You tell King Edward and the Oncoming Storm that just as they have taken everything from me, I will take everything they hold dear. I *will* have my vengeance!"

An arrow zipped past me and sped into the bay. The boat I suspected the Fahr brothers to be on rocked as Eric dove for cover. I whipped my head around.

"A bit longwinded, that one, isn't he?" Haela said with shrug.

She flicked her raven hair over her shoulder as she strode towards me. Right behind her, another black-haired elf approached with a human in tow. A human I knew very well. Liam rushed forward and pulled me into a quick hug.

"You're alright!" he stated.

"Yeah," I answered and bumped his shoulder with mine once he'd taken up position next to me. "And so are you. I'm glad you stayed out of the fighting."

While we watched the rowboats escape across the bay, three more elves and an assassin joined the line we'd formed at the edge of the pier until it comprised of five elves on the right and three humans on the left.

"How's everything outside the city?" Faye asked.

"It's all clear," Haemir answered. "In here?"

"Same," Elaran said before turning to the black-haired twin. "Any casualties?"

Haemir looked to his sister who shook her head. "A couple of injuries but nothing too serious."

"Good."

For a moment, the eight of us just stood there listening to the waves break against the pier. I could barely believe it. We had actually pulled it off. Their cannons had been sabotaged, their people across the city had either been killed or chased out, and by using all the fake pearls we hadn't had time to distribute, the Beggars' and Pleasure Guild had managed to buy back the rogue soldiers. The men who'd been trying to kill me for months were gone, King Edward was still in power, the Underworld was safe, and the Pernulans were leaving our shores. I released an astonished chuckle. Our crazy plan had actually worked.

More than that, though, the people I cared about were okay. Relief had flooded my heart when I'd learned that none of the elves had been killed. Liam was alright and the rest of our guild had stayed inside during the fighting so they would be unharmed as well. I hated caring about people. It was so stressful. Sometimes I was afraid that my heart wouldn't be able to bear the strain but there was no way back now. I cared about the elves, about Liam, Bones, and the rest of my guild. Even about King Edward. I flicked a quick glance at the assassin next to me. Yeah, him too. In a strange sort of way.

"General Marcellus got away," Shade announced when he noticed my gaze.

"Lord Fahr and his brother too," I said.

"Let's at least give them a good send-off then," Faye said at the furthest end of the line.

Haela let out a low chuckle. "Yeah, let's show them what's waiting for them if they ever dare come back."

String and wood creaked softly as all five elves nocked an arrow and drew back. Their beautiful bows curved in graceful arcs. Five twangs rang out. The arrows whizzed through the air and sailed towards the closest rowboats. Shrieks of pain and surprise rose as the projectiles connected with their targets.

The elves drew their bows again. And again. When their quivers were empty, they all hooked their weapons behind their backs again.

Out in the bay, sails were hoisted and anchors pulled from the deep while the last remaining Pernulans scrambled up the side of the ships and left the rowboats floating in the dark water. There weren't enough of them left to operate all three ships, especially not when the skeleton crew was dead on two out of the three ships, so they'd reorganized in a panicked frenzy and clumped together on two ships instead. They abandoned the third one, leaving it floating in the harbor like a ghost ship, while the other two caught the strong morning wind and glided out of the bay.

"Can the screaming and the bloodshed finally stop now?" Liam asked next to me.

Twisting my head slightly, I studied his face. That look of defeated exhaustion, the look that screamed of desperately wanting a different life, was back in his eyes. Sadness dripped into my heart, mixing with the relief previously fluttering in there.

"Let's hope so," I said and gave my friend an encouraging smile.

On my other side, I could feel the Master Assassin watching me from the corner of his eye. He and I both knew that the real answer to Liam's question was a resounding *no*. The battle was won but not the war. If left unchecked, these people would come back with bigger guns and a massive army and wipe us out.

A new dawn was breaking. The red sun rising in the east cast its rays over the water. As I watched their ships sail across the red-streaked sea and towards the mysteries that lay in the land beyond the horizon, I knew what I had to do. I had to follow them.

Acknowledgements

This book exists because of you. When I wrote the first book, *A Storm of Silver and Ash*, I planned for it to be the first in a series but around the time of publication, my confidence was wavering. Some things occurred around that time that made me think no one would like the book and that I should just give up and move on to other writing projects instead. But then something extraordinary happened. You. All of you amazing readers who bought the book, read it, and then wrote reviews or social media posts telling me that you loved it. Some of you even contacted me directly, asking when the second book would be out. I was completely floored. And *that* is the reason I decided to continue Storm's adventures. This book would not exist without you. From the bottom of my heart, thank you for taking the time to share your thoughts and feelings with me. Your kind words made all the difference.

I would also like to say a huge thank you to my family and loved ones. Mom, Dad, Mark, thank you for the enthusiasm, love, and encouragement – I truly couldn't do this without you. Lasse, Ann, Karolina, Axel, Martina, thank you for taking such an interest in my books. It means so much to me. Yujin, thank you for your endless support, and also, I'm sorry for spending so much time behind the computer. It will get better. At some point. I hope.

Another group of people I would like to express my gratitude to is my wonderful team of beta readers: Deshaun Hershel, Jennifer Bourgeois, Jennifer Nicholls, Kaitlyn Jensen, and Luna Lucia Lawson. Thank you for the time and effort you have put into reading the book and providing helpful suggestions, comments, and encouragement. Your feedback helped me a lot.

To my amazing copy editor and proofreader Julia Gibbs, thank you for all the hard work you put into making my book shine. Your language expertise and attention to detail is fantastic and makes me feel confident that I'm publishing the very best version of my book.

Dane Low is another person I'm very fortunate to have found. He is the extraordinary designer from ebooklaunch.com who made the stunning cover for this book. Dane, thank you for the effort you put into making yet another gorgeous cover for me. You really knocked it out of the park with this one.

I am also very fortunate to have friends both close by and from all around the world. My friends, thank you for everything you've shared with me. Thank you for the laughs, the tears, the deep discussions, and the unforgettable memories. My life is a lot richer with you in it.

Before I go back to writing the next book, I would like to once again say thank you to you, the reader. Thank you for being so invested in the world of the Oncoming Storm that you picked up the second book as well. It's because of you this book exists. If you have any questions or comments about the book, I would love to hear from you. You can find all the different ways of contacting me on my website, www.marionblackwood.com. There you can also sign up for my newsletter to receive updates about coming novels. Lastly, if you liked this book and want to help me out so that I can continue writing books, please consider leaving a review. It really does help tremendously. I hope you enjoyed the adventure!